Gretchen and the Bear

Gretchen
and the
Bear

CARRIE ANNE NOBLE

WordCrafts Press

ISBN: 978-1-952474-07-1

Gretchen and the Bear

Cover art by M.S. Corley

Published by WordCrafts Press
Cody, Wyoming 82414
www.wordcrafts.net

To John

Chapter One

21 June, 170 N.E.

Every color Gretchen had ever seen was a lie—or at least a serious understatement.

Four months ago, when she'd first set foot on New Earth after spending every day of her sixteen years on an orbiting refugee station, she'd been stunned. It was like she'd only seen the ghosts of colors until then, pale specters playing at being red and gold and blue. Viewed in person, nature's hues were far from ghastly: the glowing green of the leaves and grasses, the piercing blue of the sky arching above her, the potent yellow of the little flowers bobbing around her ankles… These colors had hurt her eyes—in a most beguiling and wonderful way.

The mountains and meadows outside North American Colony Two were definitely the greatest spectacles in the universe.

Or so she'd thought. Now, seconds after the cockpit dome of her V-17 Airskipper slid open to reveal the forbidden hills and forests of Britannia, nature gobsmacked her again. If the other wonders of the regenerated planet had been a feast for the eyes, these were a gluttony of glory. She stood and turned slowly, awed by the soaring trees dripping with ripe, round fruit, the nodding blossoms, the clear-as-glass water rushing between pebbled banks. This was all too, too much.

She stared. She couldn't help it.

Danger, her brain reminded her. *This place is dangerous, full of faerie tricks meant to entice you to stay forever. The sooner you get out of here, the better.*

The sickly sweet scent of nearby fruit made her stomach rumble. She put her hands in her pockets and fingered the salt crystals she'd hidden there as protection. Her skin prickled anyway, as if any magic present saw no threat in old-fashioned charms meant to thwart it.

Gretchen grabbed her knapsack and slung it over her shoulder before jumping out of the airskipper. The spongy ground belched as her boots sank into it. She thought she might be sick all over the pretty grass—because her mission wasn't just foolish, it was probably impossible. Why had she let Stepmother talk her into it? After all the years of bitter words and cruel treatment, why did she still crave that woman's approval?

There wasn't time to dwell on questions. If night fell, she'd be in ten times the danger she was in already. But back to the task at hand. All Gretchen had to do was avoid inhospitable faeries, locate a runaway eighteen-year-old, and get the girl safely off a magic-infested island.

Simple.

Simple—if she could find the girl.

The trouble was she was pretty sure Ruby didn't want to be found.

The message arrived on the warm breath of afternoon, a

wordless whisper slipping into the minds of every wild creature on the island, including Arthur's. *The time is coming to greet the summer solstice*, it said, and in reply, every leaf and limb quivered with expectation. Things seen and unseen stirred, stretching arms, legs, wings.

In homes hidden within trees or under the mossy ground, some faerie folk began to don their finery, making ready to celebrate with dancing, feasting, and mischief. Other faerie tribes anticipated shifting from one shape to another; some of wilder blood prepared to wage battles for territory or mates. As it had been in the days of old, so it was in this Britannia. With the humans gone and the forests restored by the Great Regeneration, nothing and no one could interfere with the various tribes' rites and traditions.

The summer solstice magic demanded obedience, and obedience it would have.

In the form of a young man, Arthur paced within the thick stone walls of his cottage home. Too restless to draw, he still kept his pencil in his right hand, twirling it between his fingers. The seventeen years he'd lived seemed shorter than these hours between noon and twilight. These hours of waiting and waiting.

Change called to Arthur: it was a gentle ache in his bones, a fluttering in his stomach, a tuneless song tugging at the edges of his soul. He wanted it as much as he wanted his next breath. How could he not? It was the sacred birthright of his kind, a tradition both powerful and ageless.

With trembling hands (for it was a fearsome thing no matter how many times he'd done it), Arthur lifted the lid of the wooden chest at the end of his bed. Reverently, he drew forth a heavy mass of black fur. The pelt had grown since he'd last worn it in early spring, but then so had he. His trousers ended inches above his ankles now, a telltale sign that he had not yet reached his full height.

In his grasp, the fur warmed, a living thing, its enchantment responding to his touch. It knew him, as well it should, for it was a part of him as much as he was a part of it.

Soon, the pelt's magic whispered.

And he answered, *Yes*.

Chapter Two

Stupid Ruby.

As Gretchen adjusted the settings on her life-form detector to "human female," she thought of a few other, far less complimentary things she planned to call her stepsister once she found her. The device had better work well and quickly. By her estimation, there were few hours of daylight left. Being stuck in Faerie Land once twilight fell could mean being stuck there forever, if what she'd been taught was true.

Dancing herself to death or being forced to bear some weird faerie man's children did not appeal to Gretchen as it must have to Ruby.

The life-form detector beeped faintly, urging Gretchen to travel northward—right into a dense, sinister-looking forest. As much as she loved studying unusual plant life, this place gave her the shivers. The trees, thick-trunked and dark-leaved, loomed over her like ill-tempered guards. Ferns stabbed out of the ground among their roots, their silver-tipped fronds adorned with knifelike serrations. A little breeze swept through the valley, causing the leaves above her head to clink against one another like thin slices of glass.

Gretchen looked down at her dark brown boots, as if by doing so, she could convince her feet to move. "I'm going to wring your neck, Ruby," she said as she took a few stiff steps into the shadowy woodland.

The detector's insistent beeping spurred her onward. Maybe this wouldn't take long at all. Maybe she'd be home in plenty of time to read a few chapters of the horticulture manual she'd just bought—while tucked safe and sound into her own comfy bed. She walked faster.

Funny how, as a child, she'd found the stories of this place quaint, categorizing them in her mind alongside legends of Santa Claus or King Arthur—stories that might have had roots in truth but had blossomed into wild volumes of fiction as time passed. Here and now, with the evidence of faerie magic revealed in every branch and puddle, the frequent classroom warnings against visiting what had once been Britain suddenly made perfect sense.

Memories of Professor Reynaud's lessons returned to her with blazing clarity, narrated in his doleful tone. "History has taught humanity that science can never tell magic what to do. For while Earth's flora and fauna regenerated nicely in most places after the Final War (thanks to the work of a few brilliant scientists), strange things happened in former Britain's forests and fields. There, faeriekind did not perish when all other life succumbed to the poisons of man's weapons. Instead, they flourished. Explorers sent from the orbiters in 150 N.E. reported that faerie magic had affected both plants and animals. Faerie tribes ruled as they had not ruled since humans had first invaded the island and driven the faeries into hidden glens and underground realms.

"The power-drunken faeries slaughtered our expedition

teams. Afterward, the fae leader sent word that they would not be subjugated by a few hundred dim-witted humans who'd abandoned the planet after destroying it. He offered our people these choices: remain in the sky-bound metal boxes we'd called home for a century and a half, choose to abide on the other side of the New Earth, or face the wrath of faerie tribes armed with magic as old as time."

Even in her imagination, Professor Reynaud was a pompous windbag. The fact that he'd been telling the truth didn't help her like him more.

The high collar of her standard-issue outdoor coveralls dug into the skin of her neck and threatened to choke her, so she yanked at it until she heard the seams start to pop. Ruby would have been horrified. The pale green and tan jumpsuits were Ruby's first project as a member of the government's Department of Garments, and she was proud of every meticulously placed stitch. Gretchen found the darn things too tight and a little itchy, but since Ruby was an indoors kind of girl, she'd probably never wear them. One thing was certain: Ruby wouldn't have worn such an outfit to run away with her faerie boyfriend. The girl was probably flitting about the forest in some silky evening dress and a pair of impractical, glitter-encrusted shoes.

Strange birds trilled high above Gretchen's head. One of them copied the sound of the detector, echoing its beeping through the treetops. At least Gretchen hoped it was a bird and not some faerie creature with a fondness for munching on human bones.

Weird how it wasn't completely dark under the canopy of leaves. Not that it was sunny, either. *Eternal twilight*, she thought. The phrase had either come from a poem or one of Professor Reynaud's infernal lectures.

The detector stopped beeping. With a crackle and hiss, its screen went dark. Gretchen shook it, tapped the screen with her fingernail, and tried the on-off switch a few times, but it was hopeless. The thing was dead.

"Great," she said, shoving it into the pocket at her left hip. Her right hand checked the holster on her right hip. Touching the weapon bolstered her confidence a little.

"Now what?" She halted, hand still poised on her laser blaster, and considered the situation.

Without the detector, it was highly improbable that she'd find Ruby in the tangled, endless forest. She'd have to go home and get another device before continuing her search. By that time, it might be too late for Ruby. Heck, it might already be too late. She hadn't had a chance to think through the rescue very thoroughly. Had she imagined the faerie boyfriend would just let Ruby go? Would her human weapons, the salt in her pocket, or any other charm she'd brought truly help her if it came to a fight against a bunch of faerie folk?

"Home it is," she said. She turned around and took a few steps. Wait, was that the way she'd come? The trees looked different; she definitely would have remembered that patch of yellow mushrooms.

Trying to remain optimistic, she pulled her sleeve up a little to expose the communicator she wore on her wrist. Its guidance function would lead her back to her airskipper by the shortest route possible.

Unfortunately, it, too, had lost power.

Panic kicked her heart into a gallop. She took a few deep breaths and tried to think happy thoughts, but the happiest outcome she could imagine was a quick death rather than a slow and painful one. The sudden stillness of the forest only made her feel worse. She knew she was being watched by beings older and cleverer than she, beings skilled in the arts of illusion and magic. Had they been visible, few in number, and small in stature, she might have stood a tiny chance against them.

Or not.

"Relax. Breathe deeply. Practice gratitude," the health monitor built into her jumpsuit said in an ethereal female voice. Which made her hate the blasted suit even more. Of all the gadgets, why did the least helpful one have to keep functioning?

For the first time ever, she regretted spending survival class sketching designs for her someday-gardens. What was the thing you were supposed to do when you were lost? Stand still and await rescue? That wouldn't help here. Send out a message requesting support? Another useless idea since her wrist comm was dead. Even if a signal could have gotten through to the colony, it would have taken hours and hours for anyone to reach her. By then…

She turned slowly, scanning the woods for the brightest part. If she followed the light, maybe she'd find the way out before nightfall. Outside the forest seemed preferable to inside, even if it wasn't any less likely to be populated by dangerous creatures.

There. It was definitely lighter past that pair of pines. She hurried forward, keeping her eyes fixed on the faint glow ahead. On and on she walked, shoulders tensed, keenly aware of unseen observers. Where were their traps? Every footstep was risky, every second an opportunity for disaster.

Disaster. She'd had enough of that in her life. A station repair accident had taken her mother when Gretchen was only four years old. She still had nightmares about the incident, too-real dreams fraught with imagined scenes of her mother's tether line snapping, sending her flailing form floating away into frigid, empty space. Another disaster ensued soon after: her father's remarriage to a haughty politician with a spoiled daughter. Ruby wasn't so bad, sometimes, but Stepmother Ivory… The woman was a walking nightmare, shrewd as any storybook witch.

And the only mother Gretchen had known for twelve long years.

Something fluttered across Gretchen's path, its wings whirring. Seconds later, it returned to hover before her at eye level, staring at her with tiny black eyes. Its bullet-shaped body was covered with pale green and white fur and ended in a flourish of short black and red plumes. Two bobbing black antennae stuck out of its forehead.

Some sort of birdlike moth. Or some sort of cleverly disguised faerie. If it was a moth, it was adorable. If it was a faerie creature, she preferred to send it on its way before it caused her any problems.

She waved a hand dismissively. "Shoo. Go home, whatever you are."

In reply, the moth zipped upwards and out of reach.

"You might as well leave. It's not like I'm going to follow you anywhere."

The moth flew in a quick circle above her.

"Fine. Don't go home. Just keep your distance."

The moth dipped down and gave her a look of indignation. Heavens, she was tired. To be interpreting the expressions of an insect while lost in an enchanted forest was nothing short of madness. When she found Ruby, that girl was going to face a veritable tornado of wrath.

Gretchen trudged onward, gaze once again fixed on the faint glow in the distance. Irresistible weariness washed over her from head to toe. She yawned and stumbled over a tree root.

Glancing up at the moth, she asked, "You haven't seen my stepsister Ruby, have you? Hair the color of a crow's wings, skin pale as milk? Probably wearing a flowy pink dress?"

The moth gave no discernible answer.

"Didn't think so," Gretchen said, fidgeting with the scratchy collar again.

Hunger had finally outwrestled fear inside her belly, but she wasn't about to take her attention off her surroundings to dig food out of her pack. She had to concentrate on returning to her airskipper—and concentrating was becoming a challenge. A strange calmness seemed to be taking hold of her, a desire to lie down and rest a while on the pine-needled ground. She understood now how people gave in to hypothermia and perished. It would be so easy…

The later it got, the more strange hums, chatters, and whistles seeped out of the underbrush and treetops. Mist swirled just above the ground, fragrant with pine and unseen flowers. The trees creaked and cracked although not the slightest breeze prodded their branches.

Ahead, miraculously, a pretty cottage made of gray stone came into view. Golden light spilled from one of the arched windows flanking the door of wide oak planks. The slate shingles of the cottage roof lay in neat scallops, and a tendril of white smoke wandered out of the chimney as if in no hurry at all. The moth hovered above the doorstep, wings whirring.

Something howled nearby and was answered in kind from across the forest. Goosebumps rose on Gretchen's arms.

This was all stupid. The entirety of the last two days of her life had been pure folly. Following Ruby, flying to Britannia, getting lost, conversing with a moth… Now she was about to do something just as dumb as all those things, possibly dumber. But her legs felt like rubber and her thoughts were getting fuzzier by the second. Seeking shelter seemed like the best option on her mental list of dreadful options.

Trying not to envision what might answer the door, she gripped the handle of her holstered weapon. With her other trembling hand, she lifted the brass knocker and rapped it hard against the wood.

Chapter Three

The door swung open slowly, set into motion by the urgency of Gretchen's knocking. The moth slipped inside without hesitation, but Gretchen wasn't as keen to enter a stranger's home uninvited.

"Hello?" she called, leaning into the dimly lit room. A pleasant draft of warm, cinnamon-scented air greeted her as she waited on the doorstep with her hand still poised beside her weapon. Peering into the cottage was like looking into a storybook. Orange flames danced and crackled in the hearth, glass jars and colorful dishes adorned the shelves. Someone had set the round table with a blue and white tea set, a half-loaf of crusty brown bread, a pot of berry jam, and three steaming bowls of creamy-white custard. The scent of the meal drove her stomach into a frenzy of growling and gurgling.

If her love of food got her into trouble, it wouldn't be the first time. Food was her second favorite thing—a close second to plant life. But no. Professor Reynaud's warnings against eating faerie food echoed gravely in her mind. "Tantamount to surrender and close cousin to suicide," he decreed. As tasty as the pudding appeared, it wasn't worth the risk. She stood her ground and tried not to drool as she awaited a reply from the tenants.

"For the love of heaven, let them be human," she whispered.

There was a chance they would be, right? Everything she could see indicated a normal—albeit old-fashioned—human household. Maybe the cottagers were survivors from one of the humans' expeditions. If so, they'd know their way around the countryside. They'd be able to help her find Ruby—and in return, she could reconnect them to human society. She'd be a hero twice over if that was the case, the savior of her stepsister and long-lost, stranded explorers. Stepmother would have to be proud of her. Heck, Stepmother might even give her a medal.

"Hello?" Gretchen repeated in a louder voice. "Is anyone home?" Keeping her eyes open was becoming difficult. *So sleepy.*

The moth zipped to and fro as if beckoning her inside. "Oh, all right," Gretchen said with frustration. Yawning, she took a couple of cautious steps into the room, closed the door behind her, and then hurried past the tempting table.

Onward the moth led her, through an arched doorway and into a little sitting room. How quaintly furnished it was, with its three mismatched chairs, a side table set with a flickering lamp, and a waist-high wooden cabinet. Neatly arranged on the cabinet's shelves were a stack of hand-stitched journals, a few shiny rocks, and a knitting basket.

"Hello?" she said again, sending her voice up a set of steep stairs that began near the smallest chair. When no one answered, she fished a nourishment bar out of her bag. Maybe eating something would perk her up. Sitting cross-legged on the floor, she ate every disappointing crumb of the bland but filling rectangle.

She surveyed the room from where she sat. It was definitely more charming than the common rooms aboard the orbiter. Someone had pinned drawings to the walls, charcoal sketches of trees and flowers flanking portraits of a bearded gentleman and a somber-faced woman. The moth landed on a shelf above the door and made itself at home between two roughly sculpted clay figurines of bears.

Wind gusted, rattling the sitting room window. Tree branches scraped the roof as if desperate to break through. Not far away in the forest, something shrieked. As night shoved day aside, the wild elements of the wood—including the fae—were venturing forth to hunt or indulge their sordid natures.

She was grateful for the strong walls surrounding her.

Grateful but still apprehensive. For how could she be sure the cottage wasn't some clever faerie trap?

She stood and forced herself to pace the length of the sitting room in an effort to conquer her drowsiness. All too quickly, she worked up a sweat—in spite of Ruby's specially woven "all-climate fabric." She unfastened the choking collar of her jumpsuit to an inch below her collarbone and swiped moisture from her brow. Her thoughts drifted from survival to other matters. One: her growing anger with Ruby, and two: her stepmother's selfish audacity. She climbed into the smallest of the three chairs, arranged the brightly colored cushions around her, and let her dark feelings simmer.

Ruby's running away hadn't come as a big surprise to Gretchen, although how the girl had met a faerie boy perplexed her. There weren't supposed to be any faeries in North America, and as far as she knew, the fae hadn't communicated with the colonists even once since they'd begun the colonization project two years ago. The big shock had been Stepmother's reaction to Ruby's leave-taking. Immediately, the woman had demanded that Gretchen bring her Ruby home as proof of Gretchen's family loyalty—as if Gretchen had ever done anything to make her doubt it. No one was more loyal to the Werner family than Gretchen. No one had done more to quiet rumors about Stepmother's little crimes and Ruby's dalliances with Stepmother's fellow parliament members. Not long ago, Gretchen had spent weeks coaching Ruby so she'd be able to ace her interview for the prestigious uniform-designing job—never once complaining that the summer job *she'd* been assigned ("personal aide" to her stepmother) was basically household drudgery.

And, unbeknownst to Stepmother, Gretchen had been solely responsible for keeping Father's ever-increasing flightiness from ruining the family finances multiple times. It would serve Stepmother right if he lost everything betting on illegal airskipper races while she was traipsing after Ruby.

Unbidden, a name came to mind: Barrett. She'd seen it written on Ruby's arm with pink ink not long ago. At the time, Gretchen had assumed it was the name of someone Ruby fancied at work. She knew better than to get into a silly conversation with her stepsister about boys. Ruby could go on for hours about their glorious hair, their sculpted muscles, and their twinkling eyes. Bleh.

Odds were Barrett was the faerie boyfriend's name.

Gretchen's head bobbed. She hadn't realized she was falling asleep. She shook herself hard, stood, and resumed pacing. She checked her wrist comm as she wandered back into the kitchen. A faint green glow emanated from its screen. "Come on," she said, tapping it. "Wake up."

"One message," the comm replied faintly.

"Read message," Gretchen said, stopping next to the fireplace.

"Message from Ivory Werner: Do not come home without Ruby, or your father will pay the price with his life. End of message."

The screen darkened as the comm lost all power again. Gretchen took a few slow, shaky steps and slumped into one of the chairs at the table.

Stepmother's words were a knife twisting in her heart.

How dare that woman threaten Father's life? Without his social standing and guidance, Ivory Werner never would have risen so far in politics. She'd probably still be keeping records for the environmental services department. Even if she didn't love Father at all—she *owed* him.

It was dawning on her that she might as well expect to squeeze blood out of a rock as expect tenderness or gratitude from Ivory Werner.

Gretchen rested her forearm on the table and laid her head in the crook of her elbow. She closed her eyes and wished she'd never left the colony. As if she'd had a choice. Stepmother was practically queen of Colony Two. No one said no to her, not even the prime minister.

The homely aromas of nearby bread and jam were comforting, but not enough to hinder her from shedding a few tears of frustration onto her sleeve. Seldom did she let herself cry. It simply wasn't "done" in Stepmother's household.

If only she'd grown up in a place of affection and safety, perhaps in a snug cottage like this one, alone with her kind-hearted father. If only…

The sound of the raging wind and wild things roaming outside the cottage walls faded as she fell, unintentionally, into a deep sleep.

As the gray haze of twilight settled on the forest, Arthur found the urge to Change as difficult to ignore as an unreachable mosquito bite. He wished he'd had the foresight to refuse to accompany his parents on their pre-supper walk. Mama's gait was slow on a regular day; today, with the solstice obligations looming, she seemed to be making the short journey between the brook and the cottage take an eternity.

Perhaps the imperative to shift forms didn't affect older

Bearfolk as much as it affected the young. More likely, stubbornness was what kept her from rushing to obey the magic's call.

"I'm going on ahead," Arthur said as he lengthened his stride. He felt like he might pass out if he didn't shift soon. His heart beat all wrong, every muscle burned, and he couldn't catch his breath.

"Don't Change without eating first," Mama shouted after him. "It isn't good for you."

"I'm not hungry," Arthur said without stopping. "I'll eat later, at the gathering."

"Arthur!" she scolded. "Obeying your elders is Bearfolk law, and—"

"Let him be, Lusela," his father said. "He's anxious to shift, which is right and proper for a lad his age. He'll be fine."

Arthur took off running.

He pictured what would come soon and not soon enough: undressing quickly, kneeling and draping himself with the sacred pelt, closing his eyes, being overcome by the sweet and terrible pain of transforming from human shape to bear shape. The unspeakable joy of being swathed in enchantment, immersed in magic, full of wild blood, one with nature and faeriekind.

The cottage came into view. It would only be minutes now. His whole body shook with longing. There was the front door, steps away. He was so, so close…

He stopped.

The door was ajar, in spite of the fact that he'd closed it firmly when he'd followed his parents outside. He remembered feeling it thud shut.

On the doorstep was a single boot print etched faintly in mud and pine needles.

An unfamiliar scent lingered in the air, sweet and strange.

Someone was inside their cottage.

Someone not of the Bearfolk.

Chapter Four

It was a girl.

Or rather, *she* was.

A human girl, as far as Arthur could tell, having never met one before.

There, at his family's kitchen table, she slept with her head resting on her forearm, breathing deeply. Arthur approached her slowly, loath to startle her awake before he figured out a plan.

When he was close enough to reach out and touch her (which he wasn't about to do, for only Ursa the Great She-Bear of the Sky knew if she was diseased), he examined her profile. Her nose was smaller than the usual Bearfolk woman's, her skin a little paler. Her eyelashes looked damp, as if she'd fallen asleep while crying. But the most startling thing about her was her hair.

No Bearfolk female had hair that color, somewhere between honey-gold and marigold yellow. Nor had he ever seen a member of his tribe with an inch-wide streak of silver running through his or her locks.

She wasn't at all what he'd expected a human to be. He'd

been taught they were ferocious and reckless, but this girl looked vulnerable and small. Worn out. Instead of feeling threatened, he felt concerned.

For if Mama found her in their house, in *her* chair, she'd surely kill the girl.

In spite of all he'd been taught about the evils of human-kind, he rankled at the thought of the girl being put to death without finding out why she'd come. Maybe it had been a mistake, an accident. Ursa above knew he'd done his share of trespassing as a child. She didn't deserve to die for that.

He didn't have time to concoct a grand scheme. His parents would be home any minute, and he needed to Change, desperately. He scooped her out of the chair and slung her over his shoulder like a sack of grain. Before he made it out of the kitchen, she stiffened and gasped.

"If I were you, I'd keep quiet," he said, tightening his grip around her waist as she struggled to get free. She kicked his gut hard and clawed at his back.

He'd definitely underestimated her strength. But with magic beckoning and his Bearfolk blood stirred, he kept a firm hold of her as he scaled the steps to his room. A colorful faerie moth zipped ahead of him and settled on his bedpost. His mother would have had two fits if she'd observed the scene: one for the girl he lugged, and another for the insect-like creature making itself at home in her cottage.

He used his foot to shove the door shut behind him, nearly losing his balance as the girl continued to squirm and kick. Her foot jabbed out at the oil lamp on his bedside table, almost toppling it.

"Put me down," she demanded.

"Not until you promise to be still and quiet. You don't know how much danger you're in here. I'm just trying to help."

"Help? Since when is manhandling a sleeping girl helpful?"

Her words slurred, evidence that she was under the influence of the solstice magic. It was surprising she was conscious at all, since the day's strong magic usually made quick work of putting anything not faerie-blooded into a state of deep slumber.

"Promise you'll behave and I'll put you down," he said as calmly as he could. The musky scent of his pelt beckoned him from across the room, even though it was shut inside the wooden chest. He *had to* put her down. He couldn't wait any longer to Change.

"Oh, fine," she replied peevishly.

He set her on her feet and backed away from her, hands raised. "I don't have time to explain," he said. "But you must do as I ask or you'll not likely make it through the night alive."

In the space of a heartbeat, she reached for the weapon at her hip, drew it, and pointed it at his head. "Step aside and let me go," she said. "Now."

"If you leave this room, you'll be in more danger than you can possibly imagine. I swear it."

"Why should I believe you?"

Downstairs, the door slammed. His already tense nerves tautened further.

"My parents are home. You have to hide. Get into the wardrobe and stay there until I let you out. It's the solstice, and the fae are already running wild outside, so jumping out the window would be unwise. If they didn't kill you for sport, you'd either be enslaved or forced into an inescapable marriage."

Her expression shifted from angry to baffled. "How have you survived here, then? What's stopping them from barging into your quaint little home?"

"I'll explain in the morning. Get into the wardrobe. Now." He gritted his teeth in frustration.

"Arthur?" Mama called from below. "Are you still here?"

"I'm fine," he replied. "Just getting ready to Change."

"Seriously?" the girl said through a huge yawn. "The faeries are coming to kill us and you're concerned about what you're wearing?"

He considered picking her up and stuffing her into the wardrobe. By all that was holy, he couldn't wait another sixty seconds. He felt like he might die. He gestured toward the wardrobe. "Please," he begged.

She lowered her weapon with a huff, her hand trembling as she did so. He could smell the solstice magic on her; he could see it in the glazed eyes she struggled to keep open. Her shoulders slumped as she said in a slurred voice, "Oh, all right. But only because you look like you're about to faint or throw up. You're going to owe me big in the morning, though."

"Anything. I'll do anything you ask then." He opened the wardrobe door and held it as she climbed inside and plopped down among his neatly folded shirts. He closed the door and turned the key in the lock.

"Hey! You didn't have to lock it!" the girl said. He didn't waste time replying.

Finally, he thought. He extinguished the lamp—just in case she was able to see through some crack in the wardrobe.

In complete darkness, with solemn steps, he approached the wooden chest where his pelt lay in waiting.

When he was younger, Papa had stayed with him during the Change. With pride and tenderness, he'd helped Arthur wrap the heavy hide around his body. He'd spoken calming words to his son to reassure him that the pain would be fleeting and the joy to come would be worth it. Now that Arthur was a young man, he faced the Change alone. This was the way of the Bearfolk. The shifting was a sacred thing, an intimate time of unbecoming and becoming again best spent in one's own quiet company.

He all but tore off his shirt and trousers and then shed his undergarments, letting all his clothes fall where they might. He hadn't the time to be tidy. He reached through the blackness to touch the wooden chest. Finally, eyes misted with tears of longing, he opened the lid, lifted the bearskin out, and wrapped it around his naked body. It clung to him, bonded to him, became one with him. His bones cracked and rearranged. The shape of him shifted slowly, painfully. And within minutes it was done.

Simple joy shoved all his cares to the back of his mind, quieted all his worries about the girl hidden in his wardrobe.

From outside Arthur's room came Papa's low growl and Mama's answering grunt. He pried open the door with his paw and met his Bear-parents on the landing. One after the other, they shambled down the steps, through the parlor and kitchen, out the door, and into the night.

Together they ran on all fours over roots and rocks, uphill and down, hurrying toward the Bearfolk's traditional meeting place, a consecrated glade a few miles from their cottage. They paid no mind to passing pixies and parading woodlings. Nor did they pause to listen to the strange songs or shrill cries echoing through the treetops and acres of ferns. The nighttime hours were few, and to waste them among creatures lacking Bearfolk blood would be ludicrous.

Arthur relished the strength of his bear muscles as they carried him through the woods. His perked ears caught the sound of paws pounding drums in the distance, and the faint echo of ancient solstice songs performed in grunts and snuffles. His sensitive nose picked up their scent: a deep, musky aroma laced with hints of pine sap and honeycomb.

His pulse quickened, spurred on by the magic of the night and the thought of feasting and frolicking.

With a few easy bounds, Arthur sprinted past his parents and through the thick brush that formed the walls of the glade. There, in the light of the bonfires, his fur-clad kinfolk danced on hind legs, leaping and twirling, sharp teeth glinting in bear smiles. Log tables were piled high with fresh berries and leaves, squirming grubs, silvery-scaled fish. Offerings of bright flowers blanketed the altar stone. The drumbeat reverberated within his ribcage like a second heart.

Bliss overcame him, drowning every one of his worries.

This was his tribe. This was what it meant to be Bearfolk. No human would ever know this perfect, untamed, primal delight.

With a glad growl, Arthur rose up on his hind legs to greet his kind.

A piercing, hawk-like shriek from over her head shocked Gretchen awake like a bucket of cold water splashed into her face. She'd fallen asleep again, blast it, if only for a few seconds. Surely the island's magic was to blame for her fatigue. The source of her drowsiness didn't matter much as long as she could force herself to resist giving in to it. She shook out her arms and took deep breaths.

It was darker than midnight inside the wardrobe, and a little stuffy, but at least she was safe from whatever faerie bird of prey was hanging out on the rooftop. The clothes piled under her gave off a faint odor, something herbal mixed with boy-scent, unfamiliar yet not unpleasant. It might have been a cozy refuge had she been playing hide and seek, but being held hostage there greatly reduced its appeal.

Trying not to panic, she pressed her ear to the crack between the doors. She listened to the boy's footsteps, the sound of something soft hitting the floor (For heaven's sake, was he really changing his clothes?), the creak of hinges, a low moan of deep pain that made her breath catch.

"Are you all right?" she whispered, hoping not to alert the boy's parents of her presence.

He did not answer.

A minute or two passed, and then she heard something growl low, probably a wild animal just outside the cottage—or something faerie-blooded and far worse. The creak of the bedroom door followed, and then the thumping of clumsy footsteps descending the stairs. For three people, the boy's family certainly made a lot of noise.

She closed her eyes. There was, after all, nothing to see but blackness.

The wardrobe shook a little, rattled by a door being slammed hard downstairs. Had they left the cottage, the boy and his greatly-to-be-feared parents? If so… She fingered her holstered blaster. A couple of thin wooden doors wouldn't stand a chance against the weapon. She'd be free and gone within two minutes.

She paused to think, hand still planted on the blaster, aware that waiting too long might mean another accidental nap. She couldn't afford to make a mistake, and the boy had said that leaving his room would lead to death or enslavement. He'd seemed sincere—and possibly more distressed by the situation than she was.

Maybe he was trustworthy.

She took her hand off her weapon and rested her head against the inside wall of the wardrobe. In her increasingly groggy mind, she considered the boy further. He had an honest face. Kind, deep-brown eyes. A lot of messy dark hair. He was rather tall, too, and looked uncomfortable being so. In an almost charming sort of way.

Maybe he wasn't used to being around girls their age. Maybe he was stuck in the woods with no one to talk to but his parents. Maybe he was lonely.

Heavens, she was tired. She wasn't one to think much about boys. She wasn't *Ruby*.

Was he even human? He'd seemed human to her. What else could he be?

And she was falling asleep again.

This time, she couldn't stop herself.

CHAPTER FIVE

22 June, 170 N.E.

Arthur crept into his bedroom an hour after dawn. The pads of his bear feet ached from all the dancing he'd done in the glade with his kinfolk. His stomach was rounded and taut, stuffed full of berries, fish, and tender greens. He'd spent the night well, indulging his Bearfolk nature and observing their traditions. He was happy.

And he was tired. The pelt hung heavy on his frame, and an ever-increasing itching sensation goaded him to remove it and put it away. When the equinox came, he would wear it again. Until then, he'd live life in the form of a young man.

If his mother didn't find out about the girl he'd hidden last night. If that happened, Mama might murder them both. Well, he doubted she'd actually kill her only son. But she was more than capable of making his life miserable enough that he'd *wish* he was dead.

He lay down on the floor and shut his eyes. Changing back into human form took longer and hurt more than becoming a bear. It was a matter of surrendering to the magic and waiting for it to work, waiting for the bearskin to loosen its grip on his body and then enduring the slow shifting of skin and bones and organs.

Now, he thought. With all his will, he invited the Change to come, and to be as quick as possible.

The pain started at his snout, a little flame of suffering, and as it worked its way back along his spine and spread to encompass his belly and legs, the sensation became a fierce fire of agony. With his bear voice, he moaned. When his human form overtook him, he sobbed aloud.

"All good things come at a cost," Papa had told him when, as a small child, he'd asked why the Change caused such agony. Papa had patted his head and added, "If we did not suffer, we would not recognize joy."

And then the fire ceased, snuffed out all at once, and his body felt new and clean and good.

Human and naked, he rested on the carpet beside his pelt, trying to catch his breath.

"Hey," the girl called softly from within the wardrobe. "Are you all right? Are you hurt?"

"I'm fine," he answered, voice cracking. He wasn't ready to deal with the girl. He wanted to stare at the ceiling in silence for a while, to relish his memories of his night with the Bearfolk. The feast had been glorious, and he'd danced with a Bear-girl his age. Birna. He'd known her since they were cubs, and he liked her well enough not to object to the idea that they might be betrothed at the fall equinox, paired up by the elders in the traditional way.

"Good," the girl in the wardrobe said. "Let me out of here, then."

With a groan, he sat up and reached for the pile of clothes he'd shed the night before. "Give me a minute to…uh…"

"Let me guess. Another wardrobe change? You're worse than my stepsister with all your fussing with clothes."

"It isn't the same, believe me." He shimmied into his undergarments and then pulled on his trousers and shirt. He buttoned the shirt more slowly than usual, taking time to consider what to do about the girl. After placing his pelt in its chest, he approached the wardrobe. "Promise you won't run when I open the door," he said.

"Sure," she said, unconvincingly.

"If my parents find you—"

"Yes, I remember. They'll eat me alive or something. Please, just let me out. I could really use some fresh air."

He turned the key and opened the door.

She sprang out like a wildcat, weapon pointed at his head. He gasped and stepped backward.

"Hey," she said. "It's time we had a little chat."

The boy stumbled backward and ended up perched precariously on the edge of his bed. To Gretchen, he looked even more unwell than he had before he'd locked her up. Maybe it was just his "scared" look.

She kept the blaster aimed at him. "Who are you?"

"I'm Arthur," he said. "Would you put that away? I'm not going to hurt you."

"Forgive me if I don't trust the person who held me hostage all night." She adjusted her grip on the blaster. "So, Arthur, what are you doing living here in Faerie Britannia?"

"I was born here."

"And you're human?"

A little color rose on his cheeks. "You shouldn't waste time asking questions. It isn't safe for you to be anywhere on this island. I—"

"I know that. I'm only here to find my stepsister. Once I do, we'll leave." Out of the corner of her eye, she noticed the weird moth from the night before, perched on the windowsill. Was it stalking her? Like she needed that!

"If you stay here much longer, if you go out wandering in the forest, neither you nor your sister will ever leave. It's a wonder you weren't already snatched up by one of the woodland fae princes. It's been well over a century since they had easy access to young girls, and their appetite for human brides is legendary, to put it mildly."

Her stomach sank. She asked, "Is there a prince called Barrett?"

"Barrett Turnleaf. He's the faerie high king's sixth son. Wild even by fae standards."

She swallowed her disappointment and straightened her backbone. "I need you to take me to wherever he keeps his… Wherever he'd hide a girl."

He shook his head. "If he has your sister, you might as well go home immediately. There's nothing you can do."

"Doing nothing isn't an option." Her arm was starting to cramp from holding the blaster on him for so long.

Heavy footsteps clomped on the steps leading up to Arthur's room.

"That's my mother," Arthur said, eyes widening with panic. He gestured toward the wardrobe.

Gretchen put her free hand on her hip. "No way am I getting in there again. Tell her to go away."

"Arthur? What's that strange smell?" Arthur's mother called from the other side of the door.

"Um, I'll be out in a few minutes," Arthur replied in a shaky voice. "Just got dressed."

The door burst open. Gretchen spun on her heel and aimed her weapon at a broad-shouldered woman clad in a high-collared, floor-length, green dress.

"I knew I smelled something odd," the towering woman said, peering down at Gretchen like she was a filthy toad. "You'd best put the gun down, child. Won't work anyway, I reckon."

"Oh really?" Gretchen shifted her aim toward a bed pillow and pulled the trigger.

Nothing happened.

Fear squeezed Gretchen's heart with icy fingers.

"Like I said, that thing's useless here." Arthur's mother grinned smugly and pointed to the bed like a fearsome empress commanding a subject. "Now, sit yourself down and explain how you came to be in my son's bedroom."

Chapter Six

"What have we here?" Papa said from the doorway, startling Arthur. He was dressed for the day in a white shirt, checked waistcoat, and gray trousers. His thick black and silver hair was brushed back from his forehead in a wide wave, and his beard looked newly trimmed. When he saw the girl sitting on Arthur's quilt, an impish little smile turned up the corners of his mouth. "Arthur, lad. Up to mischief?"

Arthur's face went hot. He opened his mouth to object, but Mama interrupted.

"This isn't funny, husband," she said.

"Of course not, my love." His smile disappeared, mostly.

"Just let me go," Gretchen said. "Please. I'll never bother you again."

"Look at her," Papa said. "Pale as milk and scared half to death. Your hospitality could make a dragon turn tail and run, woman."

"I'm sure she came here by mistake," Arthur said. "I think we should let her go."

"Nonsense," his mother said.

"'Breakfast before big decisions,' as my father used to say," Papa said, scratching his black and silver beard. "Come down to our table, miss. I've made porridge with berries, and a stack of toast spread thick with honey."

She surprised Arthur by looking his way as if for approval. He nodded. It was a good thing Papa had come in when he did. Papa kept Mama reasonable—sometimes.

Once in the kitchen, Papa offered the girl his chair and poured mint-scented tea into the cup in front of her. "You look like you could use a hearty meal, lass."

Her stomach growled. "I'm not very hungry, really," she said.

Mama mumbled something and grabbed a slice of toast from the platter. She made no effort to offer the dish to their guest, who was staring at her own plate and frowning.

The colorful moth darted into the room and landed on the girl's shoulder. She gasped with surprise.

"A friend of yours, lass?" Papa asked.

"I'm not sure," the girl said.

"It's always best not to trust flying things," Mama said briskly. "Or uninvited guests."

"Mama," Arthur chided. "Manners."

"That's the truth, and I stand by it," Mama said. "There's no law that says I owe trespassers refuge. Or breakfast."

Papa dragged a stool over from the fireside and sat upon it beside the girl. "So, tell us your name and what brought you to our door, if you please."

Again, she looked to Arthur for an indication of approval. Strange how she seemed to trust him now. He nodded, and then she said, "My name is Gretchen, and I'm here to find my stepsister."

"Prince Barrett likely has her," Arthur said. He grabbed the platter of toast and passed it to Gretchen.

"Ah," said Papa. "A worthy quest."

"But one doomed to fail in a dozen ways," Mama said. "A slip of a girl like her, a human wandering around on fae lands!" She shook her head with disbelief. "And to even consider going up against one of the royal families! It's madness."

"We should help her." The words spilled from Arthur's mouth before he had time to consider them. "It's the honorable thing to do."

Gretchen met his gaze across the table. She looked different, all of a sudden. A little relieved, he thought, and perhaps even grateful.

Mama frowned. "No. The elders would not approve. And with the betrothals so close… I must forbid it."

"The elders need not hear of it," Papa said. "And while I would not consent to letting the boy venture out with her alone, I see nothing improper in us helping her, as a family."

"Oh, no," Mama said, standing and bunching her fists at her sides. "I will not risk my standing among our kind—and my very life—for the likes of her."

Papa leveled his gaze at Mama. "Well, then, Arthur and I will accompany her without you."

Mama stormed out of the room.

"Don't worry. She'll come around." Papa reached for the jam. "Like a passing thundercloud, she is. A lot of noise and threats but rarely a lasting downpour. Finish up, the two of you. We'll leave after breakfast."

Gretchen clutched the mug and pretended to drink. She tried her best to ignore the scent of the buttery, honey-slathered toast on her plate. The family might be human, but the food was grown in faerie soil. She wasn't about to consume it and wind up stuck in Britannia. She wondered if Ruby had remembered to abstain. Probably not. Ruby had a weakness for sweets, and if her prince had offered her a tray of dainty cakes or chocolates, no doubt she'd ravaged them like a starving wolverine.

Regardless, she'd do her best to get her sister away from her faerie boyfriend and home to the colony. Curing Ruby of any ongoing cravings for faerie food would be Stepmother's problem.

The boy was staring at her as he ate his porridge. His father, who she'd just learned was called Thorburn, had finished his meal and gone to gather a few things "for their outing." He'd made it sound more like a picnic than a dangerous search and rescue mission.

Arthur pointed his spoon toward her dish. "You're not eating," he said.

"I'm not stupid," she replied. "I know humans can't eat faerie food without consequences. Maybe you chose to eat it and stay here forever, but personally, I'd prefer not to give up my right to go home for the sake of a slice of toast."

"On that subject," Arthur said in a low voice. "I think you should know—"

Arthur's mother strode into the room, a black look still on her face. She dropped Gretchen's pack at her feet with a grunt. "Found this cluttering up my parlor."

"Thank you," Gretchen said. The thought of digging a nourishment bar out of the bag made her mouth water. She was almost hungry enough to eat her own boot.

The big woman leaned closer, inspecting Gretchen's hair. "Well, I'll be," she said, reaching out to touch the streak of silver near Gretchen's left ear. "The Silverhair has come, and to my own front door."

Gretchen cringed a little at the unexpected touch. "It's an inherited thing," she said. "All the women in my mother's family have had it."

"Of course they have." The woman's demeanor brightened.

Apparently Thorburn had told the truth about her passing-storm-cloud temperament.

Arthur looked at his mother with astonishment. "Mama, you don't really think that—"

She grunted and waved a hand. "Hush, lad. You know I'm not one for silly old tales. Now, fetch your shoes and father and let's be off. The day's a-wasting."

Chapter Seven

"When one sets out on a journey, it's always good to know one's approximate destination," Thorburn said as he led Gretchen, Arthur, and Arthur's mother, Lusela, down the pebbled path winding away from the cottage. "Although this is our only safe route to the Fernaglen Crossroads."

The lush foliage and thick branches overhead made midmorning as shadowy as dusk. Miniature prisms of dew caught the scant light and cast tiny rainbows onto the forest floor and Arthur's cheek. Gretchen inhaled air so crisp and sweet that it made her wish for apples.

Heavens, she was hungry.

The hummingbird-like moth buzzed above Gretchen's left shoulder. She tried to shoo it away for the umpteenth time, but it refused to leave her.

"Gretchen thinks Prince Barrett Turnleaf has her stepsister," Arthur volunteered as the path beneath their feet became less gravel and more pine needles and dead leaves.

"So your father told me. Woodland fae royals fancy spending the solstice month up north," Lusela said. "Near the Myriad Lakes."

"Too far to walk," Thorburn said. "Reckon we'll have to borrow Elder Orson's cart and horse."

The buzzing near her ear was really getting annoying—as if her nerves weren't frayed enough from hunger. She swatted at the moth, and it darted up to linger above her head.

"I wouldn't do that, lass," Thorburn said. "She'll do you no harm. Indeed, she might do you a good turn. To be chosen by a faerie flutterwing is rare and auspicious. Leastwise, that's what my dear old mother always said."

"Yeah? I could use some luck," Gretchen said. "Fine," she told the moth. "If you could try to stay two feet away, we might get along better."

The moth flew in a celebratory circle and then took her place hovering an arm's length away.

"We'll all need luck, going to see royals without an invitation. Wars have been started for lesser reasons," Lusela said. "Don't frown at me, Thorburn. You know it's true."

Thorburn scratched his beard. "Sorry to agree with you, wife. But the truth of the matter is, Gretchen, the faerie folk tend to be passionate, and those ruled by their passions often end up in a tussle of one sort or another. Some of the Bearfolk, for example, have been skirmishing with their foes these last seventy-nine springs over a disagreement about one holy well."

Gretchen ducked under a low-hanging branch that smelled like licorice. "Bearfolk?"

"A noble and righteous race," Lusela said—a little too loudly. "Well, look there! A wee dragonfaerie." She pointed to a little green and orange winged lizard clinging to a knot on a tree trunk. Tiny blue flames shot from its nostrils each time it exhaled.

Gretchen stopped to admire the creature. Longing to stroke its scaled back but afraid of startling it, she lifted a cautious hand in its direction.

Lusela grabbed her wrist. Gretchen gasped.

"Look with your eyes and not your hands," Lusela scolded. "Their skin is coated with poison when they're young, strong enough to bring down a full-grown troll for a week. You'd need at least a month of nursing if you laid a finger on one."

Heart pounding, Gretchen jammed her hands into her jumpsuit pockets. Better not to touch anything at all while in the faeries' forest. "Thanks for the warning," she said sheepishly.

The path narrowed after they passed through a gap in a waist-high stone fence. What the fence was for, Gretchen couldn't begin to guess. But it seemed a waste of time to speculate about why faerie folk did anything. They weren't human, and therefore couldn't be expected to behave in a manner she'd find rational.

Arthur matched his stride to hers. They fell a little behind his parents, who had started a hushed conversation of their own. "How did your sister become involved with the prince?" he asked.

"I have no idea. But Ruby has always been fond of breaking rules and tempting fate," Gretchen said. She slipped her pack off her shoulder and extracted a nourishment bar. Never had she been so thrilled at the prospect of eating gritty, ground-up stuff coated in vitamin powder. She tore open the wrapper and bit into it with a moan of pleasure.

Arthur grinned at her, no doubt amused by her voracious attack on the bar. "You must be a rule breaker as well, or you wouldn't be here."

She swallowed the last bite and stuffed the wrapper into her pocket before answering. "Nothing more serious than sneaking out of the colony at night to watch fireflies, or playing games on my wrist comm during class. My stepmother's a high-ranking politician. I can't risk making her look bad by behaving poorly. You?"

"I like rules. They keep us safe in this wild place. Without our own rules and traditions, we'd be just as uncivilized as the—" He stopped short, cheeks reddening. "Anyway, I'd rather climb trees and draw than make trouble." He gestured toward a jagged set of naturally formed rock stairs his parents had already begun to climb—stairs only wide enough to allow for one traveler at a time. "After you."

"Thanks. So, you're the one who did the drawings in the sitting room?" Gretchen looked for the least pointy places to set her feet as she climbed. Some of the rocks looked razor sharp, and she couldn't afford to ruin her boots—or her feet.

"It's just a pastime," Arthur said behind her. "Nothing special."

"Are you kidding? You would have been put into advanced fine arts courses back on the orbiter stations. Hey, if you come home with me to the colony, I can make sure you get into a good class. I might as well use Stepmother's connections for something good, right?"

They reached the top of the steps, where Lusela and Thorburn waited. The peeved look had returned to Lusela's face.

"Hush," Lusela said in a loud whisper. "There are *things* about. Best be quiet until we reach Elder Orson's place."

Gretchen bit her lip, knowing the grumpy woman was right. She *was* being too chatty with the strangers, probably out of sheer nervousness (although she couldn't rule out the influence of forest magic after experiencing its irresistible effects the night before). Besides, she couldn't be one hundred percent certain these people were trustworthy—no matter how nice the boy and his father seemed. She'd only let them lead her out of desperation. Without her devices, she was more helpless than a blind kitten wandering around in a crocodile's nest.

Just ahead of her, the moth bobbed up and down on a current of air, wings humming cheerfully. At least someone wasn't worried about the perils of the woods or the risks involved in trying to steal Ruby away from a faerie prince.

The nourishment bar sat in her stomach like a boulder.

In the wooden bed of Elder Orson's wagon, Arthur was jolted and rattled until he thought he'd end up more bruise than flesh. Unbothered by the rough ride, Mama dozed beside him, her chin bobbing against her chest. Gretchen sat on the bench beside Papa as he drove.

Elder Orson had not been pleased to lend his horse and wagon to them, at least not at first. He'd grumbled and scowled until Mama took him aside and spoke to him for a few minutes. He'd returned from their discussion with an odd look on his face and a more generous attitude. By the sky's Great She-Bear Ursa, Arthur hoped Mama hadn't brought up the Silverhair legend. It was nothing more than a silly bedtime tale for Bearfolk children. Gretchen was no warrior maiden sent by the gods to end a war. From what he'd seen, she barely knew how to keep herself alive in unfamiliar territory.

The exact words of both the short prophetic poem and the more detailed Silverhair stories escaped his memory, but he remembered the images they'd brought to his mind when he was a cub: a human girl racing into the heat of battle mounted on a fine steed, gripping a gilded pole from which a royal pennant flew. The stories said the Bearfolk's foes would fall at her feet and Silverhair's blood-kin betrayer would be brought down by a blade of purest silver. Her praises would ring throughout the valley, and victorious, she'd ride away from the bloodstained field upon the back of one of the Bearfolk.

Arthur loved tradition even more than most of his tribe, but some stories were just stories.

Mama snored mightily. He looked forward to sleeping

in his own bed when they returned from delivering Gretchen to her stepsister. The sooner this excursion was over, the better. Then he could continue his life as he'd planned it, a simple life with a proper Bearfolk wife and a few cubs, holidays rejoicing in the glade, perhaps becoming a respected elder in his second century of life. And at the end, he'd slip from sleep into a peaceful paradise where he'd live forevermore as a majestic bear.

He glanced at the girl and then wished he hadn't. She'd disturbed something in him. He felt unsettled—like he never had in his life. As if she'd drawn a question mark at the end of what he'd considered a solid statement.

Perhaps he'd been a little lonely and hadn't realized it until now. Bearfolk weren't much for visiting one another, so apart from holidays and a few picnics, he'd rarely seen anyone but his parents—day in and day out, week after week.

Perhaps, although he didn't want to admit it, he liked the surprise of her. The spark her sudden appearance had added to his comfortable, predictable life.

He knew, without a doubt, that she'd only just begun to cause him trouble.

Papa chuckled at something she'd said, and Arthur shivered. He closed his eyes and tried to force his thoughts to realign with righteous standards by mentally reciting the Twelve Great Laws of the Bearfolk.

Chapter Eight

Every time Gretchen thought she'd seen the most amazing thing possible, something proved her wrong within the hour.

Riding beside Thorburn on the wagon seat, she'd passed through meadows of swaying silver grass that chimed at the touch of the wind. She'd witnessed a cloud of jewel-toned dragonflies, saddled and bridled and ridden by tiny, blue, gossamer-winged boys and girls. She'd seen—and she still could hardly believe it—a stately unicorn with a sparkling mane and a horn whiter than new-fallen snow. When it nodded at her in salute, she'd forgotten how to breathe until Thorburn pounded her on the back.

The light was shifting now. Surely darkness would overtake the forest soon. Her throat tightened with worry. Another day gone. Another day in which she hadn't found Ruby. She tried not to imagine her stepsister hurt or frightened—or chained up in some faerie harem.

She tried not to imagine what small tortures Stepmother might be doling out to Father as punishments for her delay.

Thinking about herself didn't make her feel better, either.

When darkness fell, would nocturnal beasts creep out of their lairs and attack? Would wicked fae seize the opportunity to ambush them and take them captive? She was afraid to ask aloud.

And then, the path turned, and the wagon rolled through a wall of ivy tendrils. Beyond the green curtain of leaves was a well-tended flower garden hung with golden lanterns, and in the center of the garden stood a house built entirely of sea shells. In the arched doorway stood a woman so beautiful that Gretchen sobbed at the sight of her. Her hair was like flowing molten copper, her skin like polished bronze. Her eyes were sapphire blue. She wore a shimmering, pale gold gown and a crown of silver branches embedded with rubies and pearls. A pair of delicate, translucent wings protruded from her shoulder blades.

The moth settled on Gretchen's shoulder and stilled its whirring wings.

"Welcome, Thorburn. I have been expecting you and yours," the faerie woman said, her voice light as birdsong. "Your beds have been prepared, and you shall sleep here in peace."

"We thank you, fair Grilsa," Thorburn said, bowing his head low. The horse knelt down and whinnied softly, worshipfully.

Although Gretchen tried hard to regain her composure, tears leaked from her eyes in two steady streams. Thorburn patted her arm. "There, there, lass. You'll get used to Grilsa once the shock dies down a wee bit. She is lovely, though."

"Enough swooning," Lusela said from behind them. "Hurry and help me out of this blasted wagon, husband. My legs feel like jelly from sitting so long."

Gretchen stood beside the wagon while Lusela clambered down with Thorburn's aid. Arthur hopped to the ground, his expression strange and serious.

"How much farther is it to the prince's place?" Gretchen asked.

"I've never been this far from home," Arthur replied

without meeting her eye. "You'll have to ask Papa." He headed toward the house.

Had she angered him? Perhaps he was just tired. Or hungry. She certainly was.

She'd eaten another nourishment bar less than an hour ago, but her stomach craved something more. Unfortunately, she only had four bars left. She'd have to ration them carefully if they were to last until she got back to the airskipper. And if she had to share them with Ruby…

"Come, weary travelers," Grilsa said. "My table and hearth are yours."

Gretchen's stomach growled like a wild beast at the mere idea of a well-stocked table. Crusty bread and silky butter. Ripe fruits. Cheese!

She wished she'd had a chance to ask Arthur how he got away with eating faerie food. Maybe it *was* safe for humans. Or maybe he and his parents were stuck on the island forever because they partook of it.

She glanced at Grilsa and decided against bringing up the subject. How did one ask a goddess-like being if the food she served was safe?

Abstaining from dinner was going to be pure torture.

"The thing about some of these faerie roads," Thorburn said as he slathered pale yellow butter on a steaming roll, "is that they can change three or four times in a day. Once, I was headed to the market in Badgerfells and ended up at the seaside. A pity, that was, as the sea pixies didn't have a taste for the apples I'd brought to trade."

Arthur tried not to watch Gretchen not eating. Seated across from him at Grilsa's table, she shoved things around on a large clamshell dish with her gold fork but never took one bite.

By Ursa, she looked hungry, though. Hungry as a Bearfolk child headed to the winter's end feast after months of near-fasting.

"Sea pixies are nasty little things," Lusela said. She spooned a huge portion of fish pie onto her dish, grinning like she'd found herself seated at heaven's banquet. "Got bit by one of them once, and my arm itched like the devil for a month."

"Most creatures only bite when threatened," Grilsa said. "Perhaps they were afraid of someone of your height. But let us not speak of unpleasant matters. I, for one, am grateful that the road turned to bring you to my door. Rarely do I entertain guests these days."

Arthur blushed under her steady gaze. Her deep blue eyes made him feel small and scrutinized, yet cherished. It was the strangest sensation.

"You have your father's good heart, Arthur Woodley," Grilsa said. "That much I fathom."

"If you're telling fortunes, do tell us who his bride will be," Lusela said around a mouth full of pie. "His betrothal day's coming soon, and you know a mother's heart. Always hoping for the best for her cub."

Arthur cringed at the word "cub." He hoped Gretchen hadn't noticed, or if she had, that she'd think it a colloquialism.

Grilsa stood. "You mistake my gifts, Lusela Woodley. I see character and potential, not future events. Now, the hour is late, and poor Gretchen is wilting. In the morning, I'll have a word with the road and set you on the proper path to find the ones you seek. But now, to our beds we must go."

A pair of brownies, knee high to Arthur, scampered into the dining room. Wizened, bony, and pointy-nosed, dressed in red caps and shabby green tunics, they exuded the aroma of strong soap. They started to clear the table with methodical efficiency as another brownie appeared at Lusela's side and tugged her skirt.

"Mrs. Lumple will show you three to your room," Grilsa said. "And I will take Gretchen to hers. Do not furrow your brow, Arthur. No harm will befall her beneath my roof."

His face burned and he turned to follow Mama and the brownie. Did Grilsa think he fancied the human girl? The idea was such an affront to his Bearfolk morals that he couldn't speak to reply. A Bearfolk man would as soon burn his own sacred pelt as he would court a human—or anyone other than a Bearfolk female. To break such a rule would mean he'd be shunned by his kind forever. No, no human would be worth such a sacrifice.

Not even Gretchen.

Chapter Nine

"After you," Grilsa said. Gretchen stepped into a square room with walls decorated with row upon row of tiny scallop shells. Short, chunky candles burned in seashell candleholders on the room's many shelves and on the bedside tables. The bed in the center of the chamber was thick-mattressed and covered with snow white blankets. Gretchen wanted to dive in and sleep for days.

Heavens, she hoped that wouldn't happen. She couldn't afford such a luxury, not at the cost of Ruby's and Father's lives.

She set her pack on the floor. The moth buzzed across the room and perched on a small table beside a mother-of-pearl-handled hairbrush.

Grilsa took hold of Gretchen's upper arm and gently turned her so they stood face to face. "You must eat, my darling," she said in a tender, motherly tone. "Or you'll not have enough strength for your journey."

Gretchen picked at her cuff and tried not to look guilty. "I…"

Grilsa smiled and continued, "You have been wise not to

rush to eat faerie food, but not all of it would harm you. Any-thing not purposefully blessed or cursed by faerie hands will do no ill to humans. You might pick the fruit of the forest or gather nuts and mushrooms and safely eat your fill—whereas feasting at a stranger's banquet table would be folly indeed."

"I still think I should stick with what I brought. No offense," Gretchen said timidly. She didn't want to provoke the anger of the powerful faerie woman.

"I thought you would say as much." With long, elegant fingers, Grilsa reached into a pouch that hung from the braided golden belt girding her hips. She withdrew a blood red marble the size of Gretchen's pinky fingernail. "If you swallow this, it will abide in your stomach and break any magic you might ingest. It also nullifies poison, should any pass your lips."

Gretchen took the cold sphere from Grilsa's hand. "Thank you."

"There is doubt in your eyes. Let me assure you, it is not possible for my kind to utter any falsehood. My words are trustworthy, always."

"I believe you," Gretchen said, because she did. She put the marble in her mouth and swallowed it. It trailed cold from her tongue to her belly as if she'd gulped down an ice cube.

Smiling, Grilsa pointed to a covered tray on a stand near the door. "I shall leave you to enjoy your supper and a good night's rest, then."

As soon as Grilsa shut the door behind her, Gretchen attacked the tray of food like a wild animal. Stepmother would have passed out had she seen her using both hands to stuff her face—but manners be blasted, she was starving.

Later, after changing into a nightdress soft as rose petals, she lay sated among plump pillows and silky blankets. She could hardly remember what foods had been on the tray. Her mouth had taken priority over her eyes. But, heavens above!

Never had anything tasted so good! The flavors—so strong and pure, yet delicate. The spiced, grapey drink she'd sipped from the goblet had left her warm and tingly and totally relaxed.

The food might not have sentenced her to live forever in Britannia, but it had certainly ruined her appreciation for the colony's food services.

With her gut full and her trust in Grilsa's promise of safety, she settled in for a night of deep, restorative sleep.

Arthur pretended to be asleep.

He *wished* he could sleep. Drawing would probably have helped him relax, but he had neither pencil nor paper. He had no choice but to eavesdrop on his parents as they whispered in their shared bed across the room.

"The silly girl thinks we're humans," Mama said.

"Why wouldn't she?" Papa replied. "We look human. We act human."

"As long as she doesn't get any ideas about Arthur. Sometimes I wonder if being handsome causes more trouble than being ugly."

"Now you're being ridiculous, wife. She's here to find her stepsister, not to steal your son."

"She's here for more, mark my words. Surely you've noticed the silver in her hair."

"Ursa above," Papa swore. "You and your flights of fancy."

"The poem's come back to me now, clear as anything, like Ursa herself meant for me to remember it. Listen, husband:

> *When war upon our sacred field is fought*
> *And Bearfolk fall before the axe and bow*
> *Then shall the human Silverhair arise*
> *And rally us to crush our many foes.*

She'll ride upon a charger black and white;
Aloft she'll hold the standard of the brave.
Her enemies shall tremble at the sight,
Then yield to us or go down to their graves."

Mama paused, and then added, "You must admit it's more than possible. The war's lasted far too long. I reckon even Fate's ready to see it ended."

"What I reckon is that you need to set your mind on things that are your business instead of a far-off war. Your son's marriage, perhaps? Would it help you set your fantasies about the human aside if I told you there's been talk of Elder Bern's niece Birna being matched up with Arthur at the fall equinox?"

"Birna Cloverfield?" Excitement raised Mama's voice by an octave. "Oh, Thorburn!"

Arthur smiled into his pillow. He couldn't recall the last time Mama had sounded giddy. And he did like Birna. She was clever and strong, and had been raised to honor the old Bearfolk ways.

Papa chuckled, then said, "Yes. One of the finest families—as you're always saying."

Mama sighed with contentment. "We couldn't hope for a better match."

"Aye. And I saw them at the solstice, dancing together. I think Arthur will be happy with her, and she with him. Now, go to sleep, wife. And I beg you, no more of this Silverhair nonsense, please."

"Fine, fine. Good night, husband dear." The smack of their goodnight kiss punctuated the end of the discussion.

More awake than ever, Arthur rolled over and pulled the blanket up to his forehead. He tried to picture Birna Cloverfield standing beside him in bridal finery—and couldn't fathom why it now seemed as ridiculous as Gretchen being the Silverhair.

He watched shadows shift on the wall until morning.

CHAPTER TEN

23 June, 170 N.E.

When she awoke, Gretchen found a deep blue linen tunic and a pair of wheat-brown leggings draped over a chair. A pair of lovely tan boots stood nearby. Her itchy jumpsuit and clunky uniform boots were gone, and she wouldn't miss them one bit. Heck, she wouldn't even ask to have them back. The brownies or other servants had probably used them to size the clothes they'd left for her—and they were welcome to them.

She washed up using the basin of water and lavender soap (also left in the night by the sneaky servants), slipped on the perfectly tailored clothes, brushed her hair, and then braided it into two shoulder-skimming plaits. Being clean and not half-starved certainly made a person feel better.

And hopeful.

Today could be the day she'd find Ruby. By tomorrow or the next day, they might be home in the colony. Her father would be safe, her stepmother appeased.

Out of habit, she fastened her still unresponsive comm

onto her wrist. The moth zipped in a quick circle around her head as if to say good morning.

"Hey, Millicent," Gretchen said. She was getting used to the little thing, maybe even starting to like her. "Since you insist on following me everywhere, I claim the right to name you. So, from now on, you're Millicent."

Millicent did a little dip in the air, a kind of moth salute. Gretchen smiled. "I guess you don't mind the name, then?"

A light knock on the door preceded its opening. A brownie woman popped her kerchief-covered head in and said in a gruff voice, "Breakfast. Now."

Gretchen's stomach gurgled in approval. The scents of pastries, warm fruit jams, and pan-fried sausages beckoned her to the table. She grabbed her pack and tried not to run to the dining room—but memories of the previous night's scrumptious bedside feast made walking in a slow, dignified manner nearly impossible.

Yes, it was going to be a very good day.

Yawning, Arthur took a seat at the breakfast table across from his parents. They greeted him as if it was any other morning, and for that, he was grateful. He was too tired to face discussions of impending marriage or absurd ancient prophecies. Papa passed him a platter of pale golden griddle cakes, and he shoved a few onto his plate.

When the girl entered the dining room, all clean and grinning, Arthur dredged up a small, polite smile and then promised himself he wouldn't look at her again for the rest of the meal. She was *too much* before, with her quest and her questions and her un-Bearfolk ideas. Now, all shined up like one of Papa's prize apples and beaming as if all her wishes had been granted overnight, she was even more *too much*.

Too much to try to comprehend.

Too much to ignore.

He sliced and shredded his griddle cakes into bites small enough to feed a baby pixie while he forced himself to think of Birna, his alleged future wife. He'd met her a number of times over the years, at holiday gatherings and youth picnics. She was modest and traditional. *She* never would have eaten three helpings of sausage and four griddle cakes in under five minutes—unlike Gretchen.

"You have quite an appetite this morning," Thorburn said as he poured water into the girl's goblet. "Glad to see it, lass. One needs to keep one's strength up when traveling."

"I feel better today," Gretchen said. "Much better."

"You won't feel better for long if you keep stuffing your gullet like a bog troll in a sheep pen," Lusela said with a wry chuckle. "You'll have to be rolled along the path like an oak barrel, bemoaning your gluttony all the while."

Grilsa swept into the room, bringing with her the perfume of roses and sage. "My servants tell me that the preparations for your journey are complete. Your horse is ready, and your wagon is stocked with provisions. The north road will lead you straight and true toward Midloth Castle, if you follow it without wavering. If all goes well in Haversbiddle Forest, you should reach the lake district within two days."

"We thank you, fair lady," Thorburn said. "We'll not forget your kindnesses. Should you ever need aid from the Bearfolk…"

"Your heartfelt words are payment enough, Thorburn Woodley," Grilsa said. "After you finish your meal, you may resume your journey at the hour of your choosing. Although I would like a word with Gretchen first, if I may."

"Of course you may," Thorburn said. "Isn't that right, Gretchen lass?"

Out of the corner of his eye, Arthur saw the girl nod

while simultaneously chewing and smiling. He wanted to be appalled by her. He wanted to despise her and her differentness. He wanted to be unappreciative of the way the blue tunic complemented her rosy cheeks, to be unamused by the blob of jelly on her chin.

He wanted not to think he might miss her once she'd left Britannia.

What in the world had come over him?

He felt Mama's pointed stare before he met her eye. She shook her head and crossed her arms over her wide chest. *You know better*, her narrowed eyes scolded. *Mind yourself.*

Arthur stood, face hot, appetite gone. "Excuse me," he said. "I'm going to get some fresh air. I'll meet you at the wagon whenever you're ready."

He slipped past Grilsa and out the front door. Just over the top of a rose bush, he spied the stable roof. He took the winding path through the flower garden, hurrying at first but then slowing as his attention was caught by the shape of a blossom here, the curve of a leaf there. His worries faded as tendrils reached out to touch his passing form and dew darkened the toes of his shoes.

By the time he stepped off the garden path to enter the stable, his mind had quieted and he could breathe again.

Everything was fine, and everything would be fine. He hadn't broken any rules by being fascinated by a stranger. Just like the flower garden had a path, so did he. All he had to do was keep his feet on the road of righteousness and his mind fixed on the Bearfolk laws, as Mama had taught him since birth.

He could do that.

On a work table near the stable door, he found a new pencil and a sketchbook labeled with his name. Grateful for Grilsa's generosity, he sat on a bench and started to sketch the scene before him: an old wooden plank door halfway open, and the little cat that paused there to lick one spotted paw. Absorbed by the movements of his pencil, he forgot all else.

Chapter Eleven

Gretchen looked back over her shoulder as the wagon carried her and her companions away from Grilsa's gardens. She hoped she'd remember every detail of the flowers and shrubs when she got home. She wanted to record their strange beauty in her plant journals. They were so different from any she'd ever seen in data collections, books, or in person. She'd have to name them herself—which would be thrilling indeed. *Creeping sun-whisper, golden hens' beak flowers, flaming eye of jasper...*

Too bad she'd never get to revisit the place. Grilsa's estate was utterly amazing—as was Grilsa.

Gretchen touched her cheek where the faerie woman had blessed her with a parting kiss. After breakfast, they'd shared a quiet walk among the magnificent plants. "You, my dear, are more than you know—and not as you seem," Grilsa had said. "Always remember: appearances deceive many. The wise see with the heart and not the eyes."

A peculiar calmness had settled over Gretchen then. A remnant of it lingered still. She wished she could keep it somehow, or tuck it away for later use. Having access to such a feeling when she returned to Stepmother's service would be priceless.

"Feels like rain," Thorburn said as the road inclined before them. The leaves whispered above them in agreement. "If the Gilly Beck floods, as it likes to at the slightest provocation, we'll be hard pressed to find another route."

"Doom and gloom," Lusela said. "And you say I'm the worrier. You heard Grilsa. Our road is 'straight and true,' she said."

"She can coax a road well enough, but no one can coax the weather," Thorburn replied. He flicked the reins to hurry the horse. "Look sharp now, Uffington."

A mighty rumble of thunder shook the wagon. Gretchen gripped the seat with both hands as Millicent the moth perched on her shoulder. The violence of Earth's weather still shocked her sometimes. She turned her face toward Thorburn as the words of her pre-colonization weather safety course echoed in her mind: *If you can hear thunder, you can be struck by lightning.* "Shouldn't we seek shelter?"

Another crash reverberated through the wagon and Gretchen's body. And then another.

"I don't think that's thunder," Arthur said from behind her. The thudding continued, slow but rhythmic.

"Footsteps?" Lusela said.

"Ursa above," Thorburn swore. "You're right, wife. Must be Old Greentoes out for a stroll. Thought he usually slept well into July. Blast it."

"What? Who's Greentoes?" Gretchen asked, regretting her hearty breakfast as her stomach tightened with terror. Anyone whose footfalls shook an entire forest had to be enormous.

"A very cranky old giant who lives in a cave not far from here," Thorburn said. "Well, we'll just keep moving. Maybe he'll pay us no mind." He snapped the reins hard. "Gallop fast as you can, please, Uffington."

A few cold raindrops splattered on Gretchen's forehead and arms. She laughed nervously. "Look. Maybe it *was* just thunder."

The thudding continued. Closer. Louder.

Arthur tugged on the back of her tunic. "Hurry," he said. "Under the blankets with the provisions."

"Good idea, lad," Thorburn said. "Old fellow's lost his sense of smell mostly, but if he sees a human, well…"

She didn't need another invitation. She leapt from the wagon seat into the bed, landing hard between a wooden crate and a lidded basket. If she lived, she'd have bruises for souvenirs. She crouched down. Arthur tossed a woolen blanket over her and tucked it around her and the crates.

Thud… thud… thud… thud…

How had the story of Jack and the Beanstalk gone? A magic harp and a golden goose, "Fee, fi, fo, fum," and threats about crunching human bones?

She had a terrible feeling she was going to be lunch.

Arthur exchanged worried glances with his mother. There were fae you could ignore, fae you could outwit, and many tribes you could co-exist with—but there were also creatures that would seize any opportunity to swallow you whole or set you ablaze with a breath. Finally, he understood why Mama had insisted he stay home when he was a boy, instead of letting him travel to the faerie markets and fairs to sell fruit with Papa. Risking her only child's life just so he could keep Papa company would have been foolish.

The thunderous footsteps grew closer. Arthur's mouth went dry. Mama reached for his hand and gripped it hard.

Papa started to sing. Rather cheerfully, given the situation.

"Old Greentoes was a happy chap
Hey diddle dee, hey diddle doe

Wore a storm-cloud for a cap
Hey diddle dee, hey diddle doe
Picked his teeth with trunk of ash
Hey diddle dee, hey diddle doe
Used a moonbeam for his sash
Hey diddle dee, hey diddle doe."

The earth-shaking marching ceased, only to be replaced by an equally reverberative voice calling out, "Hark me! What good fellow doth sing my praises 'neath the noonday sun?"

"Thorburn Woodley of the Bearfolk, Master Greentoes," Papa answered boldly. "I beg your pardon if I've disturbed you, sir. Just passing through on our way north, my family and I. We'll move along and trouble you no further, if you please."

Rain pattered harder and harder on the blanket concealing Gretchen. It slid down Arthur's face in tiny rivulets and dripped off his chin. Mama whipped her shawl off her shoulders, wrapped her head with it, and frowned—either at the storm or at Papa's way of dealing with the giant. Perhaps both.

"Thorburn Woodley," Old Greentoes said. One more giant-sized step brought him into view—his hairy bare feet and calves, anyway. His head was high above the treetops, too far off for Arthur to glimpse clearly. "Art thou the very one who gave unto me a fine hive of honey autumn last?"

"The very one and the same," Papa replied, head back, squinting upward. "I do hope it was to your liking."

"Forsooth, 'twas the best honey ever to bless my lips. Tell me true, now. Have you any more of the bees' sweet liquor, Bear-fellow Thorburn?"

Papa looked at Mama questioningly. She lifted the edge of the blanket and peered into the crates of food Grilsa had provided.

"Arthur," Mama whispered. "Help me with this barrel."

Arthur was certain he'd seen no such thing when he'd

eyed the supplies earlier. But he crawled to Mama's side and looked under the blanket, and sure enough, there was a two-gallon-sized oak barrel labeled "honey." He pulled it out and lifted it to show Papa.

"Why, yes I do!" Papa said. "Only a small barrel, sir, but honey nonetheless. You're welcome to it."

A huge hand descended from above, palm open. Arthur stood and tossed the barrel into its center. To such a big man, it would provide no more than a mouthful.

"Two Thorburns I see," the giant said as he lifted his hand away from the wagon. "And a Bear-woman. Unless my failing eyes deceive me? Old I am, and time doth plague me from top to toenail."

"My lad and wife are with me, good giant." Papa said. "As I said, we mean no trouble, sir. Just passing through on our way to the lakes."

Lightning flashed above them, followed by a gentle rumble of real thunder. Rain poured from the heavens as if the skies' floodgates had failed.

Old Greentoes bent low, poking his broad, bearded face between the tree limbs. His dark eyes were cloudy, his face freckled with age and as furrowed as a newly plowed field. "North, thou sayest? River Tumfrees and Gilly Beck shall hinder thee if the gods' tears continue thusly."

"We must hurry, then," Papa said.

"No need, little Bearfolk," the giant replied. "As thou hast shared thy bounty with me, my strength shall I share with thee."

Before Papa or Mama could object, Old Greentoes reached down and, deftly, gently, scooped up horse, wagon, and all. Mama shrieked and the horse whinnied with dismay, but the giant started walking anyway, cradling them carefully in his massive arms. Each of his steps covered a quarter mile by Arthur's reckoning.

"Thank you," Papa said. "You're very kind." To use one's manners in every circumstance—especially when dealing with giants and royalty—was advice he'd given Arthur countless times since birth.

Old Greentoes chuckled, causing the wagon to jiggle and the horse to squeal. "Kind? Thou makest my heart jolly, Bear-fellow. My name was Redfoot Baz in days of yore, when both giants and men did dwell upon this isle. For by my might did I squeeze the blood from many men, and in my kettle did I stew their bones."

Under the blanket, where Arthur's foot had slipped to rest against Gretchen's, he felt her tremble.

"To be young again," Old Greentoes said as he stepped across a rushing stream. He drew a deep breath then sighed it out as a breeze. "The very thought of youth's joys stirreth my feeble senses, for on the air methinks I smell human flesh just now, and such a thing couldst not be so."

Arthur felt the blood drain from his face.

"Ursa help us," Mama whispered.

Chapter Twelve

Gretchen held her breath and kept still as a terrified person could. Arthur's foot shuddered against hers. Would the giant kill him, too? Or did giants not eat "Bearfolk," whatever that meant?

"I've heard tales that the humans have come down from their floating ships to colonize the land across the sea," Thorburn said, responding quickly to the giant's remark about smelling a human. "Do you think they'd dare come here and face the peerless power of faeriekind?"

"Mankind doth not abound in wisdom," Old Greentoes said. "Nevertheless, Bear-fellow, my nose doth tell me something…"

Gretchen felt the wagon move upward. The giant sniffed, and the force of his inhalation lifted the blanket. She grabbed hold and tried to stay covered.

But it was no good.

His unblinking eyes, each bigger than Thorburn's head, took her measure as she stared back in terror.

Old Greentoes gripped the wagon with one hand now. The horse squealed and roared, and Gretchen imagined the poor animal dangling from its harness. "What be this?" Old Greentoes asked angrily. "Thou hidest a human from me, Bear-fellow?"

"I cannot deny it, sir," Thorburn said. "But please! Have mercy on us, and I swear I'll bring you all the best fruits and vegetables I grow, and all the honey I can find, for as long as you shall live."

"Have mercy? Dost thou dare deride me and my forefathers besides? Giants show no mercy to mockers!" He held the wagon closer to his eye and examined Gretchen. "Little girl," he said, "a sweet morsel such as I've not tasted in the span of a hundred years or more." His hot breath further moistened her rain-spattered clothes.

"I'm far from sweet," Gretchen said in a shaky voice. "Probably bitter. We have other food—"

"Please," Arthur begged. "Put her down, Sir Greentoes. We'll find you a better meal."

The moth flew between the giant's eyes and the wagon, buzzing back and forth quickly.

"To the devil with thee, bug!" Old Greentoes roared. He blew hard and propelled the moth across the forest. "Now, shall I eat thee raw or toasted, girl?"

"Put us down this instant," Lusela shouted. "She's not for the likes of you. Are your eyes so bad that you can't see that plain as day?"

"Hush, Bear-woman, or thou shalt follow her down my gullet." He bent and set the wagon down hard. The wheels splintered and the traces snapped. He picked Gretchen up, gripping her waist between his thumb and forefinger, and once again brought her close to his hazy eyes. "Ugly as mud, like all humans. Smooth skin. Spindly limbs. Useless little nose. Golden hair fine as spider's silk. But what be this?"

He practically poked her into his right eye as he examined her head. And then he swore.

"Ruined my good lunch, Bear-woman! Curse thee! Take thy Silverhair and go."

He set Gretchen on the ground as if she were made of glass. And then he turned and stomped away through the forest, muttering and swearing and snapping trees like twigs.

Gretchen fell to her knees, heart racing impossibly fast. Arthur jumped off the broken wagon and hurried to her side. He offered her a jug of water. "Are you all right?"

"What just happened?" Gretchen asked as soon as she found enough breath to speak.

Arthur held the jug to Gretchen's lips. "Drink."

She took a few swallows of water and then pushed the jug aside. Pale and dripping, she gazed at him intently and rather accusingly. She'd surely heard the words "Bearfolk" and "Bear-woman" in the conversation with the giant. He had no idea how to explain the fact that he sometimes wore a magic bearskin and transformed into a wild animal without causing her more alarm. Merely mentioning that they were not actually human might be enough to make her run off into the dangerous woods alone.

"We need to keep moving," Papa said, offering his hand to help the girl to her feet. "We've made good progress, but we're not there yet. This isn't a good part of the forest to tarry in."

She shook her head, refusing help. She stood and wiped pine needles off her damp tunic. Her moth friend returned and hovered over her shoulder. "I don't know what you are or what you want from me, but if you're not going to help me find Ruby, please just go away."

"Lass," Papa said, laying a hand on her shoulder, "we do want to help. And we mean you no harm, I assure you."

"See to the horse, Thorburn," Mama said as she

approached him. "He needs untangling, and your blessing to return to his master."

"Of course," Papa replied. "Arthur, aid the women in gathering whatever supplies you can carry. We can talk once we're walking again. And thank Ursa, the rain has stopped." He pulled a short knife from his belt and set off to free Uffington.

Gretchen crossed her arms and stood her ground. She looked almost as threatening as Greentoes. "I want answers now," she said.

"Linger here if you'd like," Mama said. "But when the woodlings come and snatch you, or some black dog drags you off to feed her demon pups, you'll wish you'd done otherwise."

"Don't bother trying to scare me like I'm some kid who doesn't want to go to bed," Gretchen said, taking a step toward Mama. "I was almost eaten by a giant a few minutes ago. I flew thousands of miles, by myself, to rescue my stepsister from a faerie prince on a faerie-infested island. Go ahead and boss your little boy around all you like, but don't begin to think you can do the same to me. Besides, compared to my stepmother, you're nothing but a yarn-wrapped kitten."

Mama's jaw dropped. She sputtered as if she'd lost all command of language. After a few seconds, she turned and stalked off toward the remains of the wagon.

Gretchen straightened her tunic and glared at Arthur. "What are you looking at?"

"Sorry?" Arthur said sheepishly, hoping not to rile her further.

Her expression softened. She huffed out a slow breath. "Um. Yeah. I guess that giant got me a little worked up."

He smiled. "Getting almost eaten can be unsettling. Or so I've heard. And Mama can be…"

"You must have a lot of tolerance. Unfortunately, I'm well acquainted with the whole overbearing parent thing."

"She means well."

The horse whinnied and galloped away from Papa. Arthur watched Gretchen turn her head to observe the animal disappearing into the forest.

"You could do that, you know," she said quietly. "Run off. Start over. You're not a child anymore—even if they treat you like one."

"It wouldn't be that simple. And I don't want to leave my home and my kind. I love our way of life." It was true, but his heart skipped a beat at the thought anyway. What would it be like to be just himself instead of Lusela and Thorburn's son?

"About that," Gretchen said. "Your kind? The giant called you 'Bearfolk.'"

Arthur swallowed hard.

Papa returned and clamped a hand down on his shoulder. He leveled his gaze at Gretchen and said, "That, lass, is nothing we have time to explain now. Help us gather some food, and I promise to answer your questions before we retire for the night."

As if to endorse Papa's proposal, something howled nearby and a chilly breeze swept through the woods.

"We never make idle promises," Arthur said when she looked at him with questioning eyes.

"Oh, all right," she said. "But I'll hold you to it."

"Of that I have no doubt," Papa said.

Chapter Thirteen

With a finger on his lips and a warning look, Thorburn quieted the travelers soon after they abandoned the wagon. For safety's sake, they stayed silent mile after mile. Other things in the forest did not. Hardly a minute passed when a creature didn't howl in the distance, shriek in the treetops, or grunt in the brush along the narrow path—and every time, Gretchen startled.

The strap of her pack dug into her shoulder as she followed Lusela and Thorburn. She'd crammed the bag full with fruit, bread, and cheese—on top of the things she'd already been carrying. She probably ought to have thrown out the anti-faerie charms she'd brought from the colony. As far as she could tell, toting them around had done her no good whatsoever. They hadn't repelled the giant or the "Bearfolk."

Maybe she wasn't the cleverest girl in the world, but she was smart enough to figure out that "Bearfolk" meant "not human." She knew it, felt it in her bones, even without Thorburn's promised explanation. Darn the tricky faeries.

She glanced over her shoulder at Arthur. If there was one thing he excelled at, it was looking guilty. He had the eyes of a dog caught chewing its master's best shoes. She felt almost sorry for him—although she wanted to hate him for letting her believe he wasn't fae.

He met her gaze and the corner of his mouth lifted in what might have been an attempted smile. She turned her head quickly, returning her attention to Lusela's back and the path ahead.

Millicent bobbed in front of her as if anxious to tell her something. "Sorry, I don't speak moth," Gretchen whispered.

"Mind your feet," Lusela said, raising an arm like a barrier. The volume of her voice was shocking after so much silence. "Those black mushrooms'll burn a hole straight through your shoes if you tread on them."

Just in time, Gretchen stopped her boot from squishing down on a slimy, ink-black mushroom. The truth was evident: she needed her three companions—like it or not. How long would she last without them warning her not to touch dragonfaeries or to avoid stepping on toxic fungus?

A crackling, sputtering sound came from her wrist, and then two static-laced words, "Hurry, daughter."

Father's voice. Or was it faerie mischief?

She stopped walking, and Arthur collided with her back. She tapped the device, hoping to get enough signal to answer her father, if it was truly him. Her pulse raced as tears misted her eyes. "Come on," she begged the comm. "Father?" she said desperately, knowing in her heart that he couldn't hear her. "Hold on, Father. Please."

The comm screen glowed faintly as the message repeated, and then went dark. Gretchen shook her head in frustration. "No."

"Is there anything I can do?" Arthur asked.

He stood too close to her. She could smell his musky pine-and-boy scent over the musty dead-leaf-and-fungus scent of the woods. She took a step away from him. "Not unless you can make this blasted comm work."

"No time to dawdle," Lusela said over her shoulder. "I smell woodling scat, so they're lurking nearby, I reckon."

"How much farther?" Gretchen asked. She started walking again, following Lusela around the trunk of an enormous oak tree.

"Could be an hour, or another day," Thorburn said. "But, wait—" His eyes lit up as he pulled a map from his pocket, unfolded it, and pressed it flat on top of a fallen tree trunk. "That Grilsa's a sly one. Gave me this map and made me forget it until now."

Lusela pointed a fat finger at a blue wavy line. "There's Morris Brook. So we must be about here."

Thorburn traced a path across the parchment. "Almost to Hayslip Meadow. A safe place to spend the night. My grandfather took my brother and me there to camp when we were wee cubs."

Gretchen fingered the wrist comm. Her father's words echoed in her mind, and the thought of another delay made her jittery inside. "As lovely as camping sounds, I need to hurry."

"I know that, lass," Thorburn said kindly. "I'm doing my best, by Ursa. Some journeys can't be rushed, I'm afraid. And when night falls, we'll be thankful for the ancient pact that makes Hayslip a refuge for travelers."

"You don't understand. It isn't just Ruby. My father is in danger, too. He's all I—" She choked on the words she hadn't meant to speak aloud. Darn it, she hated being emotional in front of strangers. She took a breath and started again. "I need to get home. With Ruby. Like yesterday."

Thorburn patted her shoulder. "I swear, lass, as much as it's in my power, I'll get you home as quickly as I can."

Lusela grunted. "Meanwhile, we're standing here wasting time."

"Onwards, then," Thorburn said.

Gretchen shifted her pack from one shoulder to the other. She rubbed the sore spot it had left behind.

"Let me carry that for a while," Arthur offered.

"I'm fine," Gretchen said. "But thanks."

Arthur fell into line behind her again. Sometimes he was too nice. He took after his father, obviously. Even when Lusela seemed to be trying to act friendly, the scowl never quite left her face. Good thing she and Stepmother would never meet. The Earth might need to be regenerated all over again if two such stubborn forces collided.

Arthur opened his mouth, wanting to say, "Just being polite," but he found he couldn't. Bearfolk couldn't lie.

The truth was he wanted to help her because it was the honorable thing to do, but also because he admired her. She was risking her very life for her family and not letting anyone or anything stand in her way: not technology-disabling magic, not the perilous faerie forest, not even his difficult mother. He didn't know if he could be that brave.

He followed her, ducking under a low-hanging vine and then straightening again. The silver strip of hair beside her left ear caught an errant ray of sunlight, and for a moment, he wondered if Mama could be right about the girl being the Silverhair of legend. It had been years since he'd heard the story, but he remembered bits and pieces. A young woman was supposed to come from afar—one who would ride bravely into battle, one who'd bring peace to the Bearfolk and earn the blessing of the faerie high king.

Could such a hero be unaware of her mission? It seemed improbable. And Gretchen was absolutely focused on finding her sister and leaving quickly.

No, he thought. Some stories were only stories.

Gretchen tripped, but he reached out and caught hold of her arm, preventing her from falling into another patch of slick, black mushrooms.

"Thanks," she said, eyeing the insidious fungus before turning to face him. "I owe you one."

"One what? A mushroom?"

"No. A favor," she said, smiling. She didn't smile often, but by Ursa, her smile was a lovely thing. "You don't know the expression?"

"No," he said, smiling back. "But I'll gladly accept the favor if I happen to need it."

"You never know. You might need me to scare a giant off for you again sometime. What happened back there, anyway?" She started walking again, and the wider path allowed him to walk next to her instead of behind her. "Why did the giant change his mind about eating me?"

"I think that—" Arthur began slowly, struggling to think of the proper words.

"Look," Thorburn interrupted, pointing to a wooden gate set in a five-foot-tall stone wall. "The entrance to Hayslip Meadow. That's a grand sight if ever I saw one." He pushed the gate open, held it, and gestured for them to enter. "Come on, come on. Time for a rest and a hot meal, thank Ursa above."

"And time for questions to be answered," Gretchen added as she approached Papa. "You promised."

"Aye. A long talk we shall have, lass. As long as you require."

Arthur trailed behind Gretchen. Papa patted his back as he passed. "Don't look so worried, son. This meadow's far safer than our cottage."

Arthur didn't mention that his concern wasn't for their safety, but for how Gretchen would respond to the fact that they weren't human—that magic-rich blood flowed through their veins, just as it flowed through the veins of every faerie creature on the island.

As it flowed through Barrett Turnleaf, the sly prince who'd lured her stepsister into danger.

Chapter Fourteen

Bright moonlight streamed down to silver-coat the meadow grass and wildflowers around Gretchen's ankles. She held up a small brass lantern while Thorburn lit its wick—although the extra light hardly seemed necessary. Millicent circled them with humming wings, as if rejoicing in the safety they'd found.

Nearby, Arthur and Lusela sorted through their packs, picking out things they'd need for the night.

"Well, I'll be a striped newt. If it isn't a dinner-wish blanket," Lusela said. In one hand, she held the corner of the blanket Grilsa had included with their provisions. At her feet, almost obscuring the plaid fabric, were all the components of an elaborate meal. "That explains how the barrel of honey showed up in the wagon."

Gretchen marveled at the steaming dishes of food, platters of cakes, bottled drinks, gold-edged plates, and shiny cutlery spread out on the cloth. Her stomach growled in anticipation. Thank heaven for that magic marble she'd swallowed. She wanted to taste every single thing she saw.

Millicent zipped to the center of the picnic cloth where

a vase of yellow flowers awaited her. She perched on a bloom, unfurled her long proboscis, and started sipping her supper.

Setting the lantern on the ground, Thorburn said, "We'd best be careful not to squander the third dinner wish. 'Tis a long road home, after all." Grinning with delight, he sat down and grabbed a plate.

Lusela knelt beside her husband and took a flaky, golden brown pasty from a tray. "Home," she said. "I do like the sound of that. And to think, Arthur will have a home to call his own, come spring. A fine home and a fine bride."

Arthur's face flushed, and he coughed as he took a seat on the edge of the cloth. He stuffed a biscuit into his mouth and reached for another as Gretchen sat an arm's length from him. "You're engaged?" she asked, genuinely surprised Lusela would let her baby boy go so soon.

Arthur coughed again, harder. Thorburn passed him a bottle of juice.

"Not yet," Thorburn answered for him. "He's on the list for possible autumn betrothals. Our elders match up the young folk when they come of age."

"Oh." As intrigued as she was by the topic arranged marriage, Gretchen had more pressing matters in mind. She swallowed a bite of strawberry tart and then asked the question she'd been holding onto since their encounter with Old Greentoes. "Thorburn? What did the giant mean when he called you 'Bearfolk?'"

"That's what we are, lass. Bearfolk. An ancient and honorable tribe of fae. It's like this, you see." Thorburn held up a chunk of bread. "Usually, we live and work in human form. We have houses, grow food, make crafts, trade goods—just as your own kith and kin do. But there are occasions," he said, picking up a thin slice of ham and draping it over the bread, "when we wear fur. When the magic calls, or in times of war, we don our pelts and we are changed, transformed. Made into bears, from teeth to toes."

Gretchen tried to picture such a thing in her mind—and it was surprisingly easy. Thorburn was a tall, broad man, and Lusela was sturdy and wide-shouldered. As trim as Arthur appeared, she suspected he hid lean muscle under his modest clothes.

Maybe she wasn't too shocked by the revelation because she'd been given a clue and had time to consider it. Not that it wasn't a bit disconcerting that they could change into bears—but *everything* in Britannia was a bit disconcerting. In the end, she was there to find Ruby, not to judge foreign cultures. As long as they had no plans to transform and attack her, what difference did it make to her that they occasionally ran around shaped like animals?

Thorburn continued. "On our sacred days—the solstices and equinoxes in particular—we gather together as bears and celebrate with dancing and feasting. Those are the times, I feel, that we are our true selves, carefree and wild and utterly blissful."

"Fetch your pelt and show the girl," Lusela commanded Arthur.

"She doesn't need to see that, Mama," Arthur said. "She's clever enough to imagine it, certainly."

"Obeying your elders is part of your Bearfolk duty," Lusela said, nostrils flaring. "Go on. Do as I say."

Red-faced, Arthur stood and walked to the place where they'd piled their packs.

Why didn't he stand up to his mother? He wasn't a child anymore, for goodness sake.

Gretchen's own face grew hot as she realized how often she'd been in the same situation—and obeyed Stepmother when she could have objected.

Maybe they were more alike than she'd thought.

Maybe she even envied him a little. She'd never once spent

a night feasting and dancing with her friends. Stepmother never invited Gretchen to the parties she hosted, and besides, she rarely had enough energy to do anything but fall into bed with a book after finishing all the errands and chores Stepmother assigned.

Arthur returned, cradling a mass of thick black fur against his chest, his expression inscrutable. There was something in the way he held the pelt that reminded her of a child clutching a security blanket, something of affectionate ownership and maybe a hint of pride. Yet his eyes—they told another story, even as he refused to look in her direction. Unease? Confusion? Resentment for his mother's demands?

Lusela's set jaw and cold gaze sent a shiver through Gretchen. How could she look at her good-hearted, dutiful son like that?

Maybe she shouldn't envy him after all. Any joy he experienced, whether as a bear or a boy, was surely hard-won with such a harsh mother directing his days. Gretchen had seen enough hints of Lusela's character to know she was as much of a storybook wicked queen as her own stepmother.

And that knowledge begged a question of its own: Why was Lusela really on the quest to find Ruby? Because "out of the goodness of her heart" was definitely out of the realm of possibilities.

Sometimes, sinful as it was, Arthur hated his mother.

Standing before Mama, wincing like a shamed child, forced to show Gretchen his most personal, most treasured possession, he allowed himself to entertain the forbidden emotion for half a minute. He hated her callousness, her selfishness, and how she treated him like a five-year-old instead of a grown man. He hated her icy smile and her haughty stare.

"Touch it," Lusela urged the girl.

"There's true magic in that fur, beautiful and age-old."

"No," Arthur said, taking a step backward. "She shouldn't. It's sacred, not a plaything."

"The lad's right," Thorburn said firmly. "Put it away now, Arthur. She's beheld it with her eyes, and that's more than enough as far as I'm concerned. Magical things are not meant to be trifled with."

Lusela scowled before offering a tight smile. "Of course," she said, too sweetly to be believed. "Do as your father says, Arthur. I've had enough chitchat and rich food for one night. I'm going to bed."

"Good night, my love," Thorburn said as she plodded over to the bedroll Arthur had prepared near the stone wall. "I shall join you soon."

In Mama's absence, the tension lifted from Arthur's body. He put away his pelt and returned to sit with Papa and Gretchen. Papa, unmoved as usual by Mama's dramatics, nibbled on a pheasant leg while Gretchen picked apart a honey glazed pastry. Arthur looked at the food without interest. It was pretty enough to be painted as a still life, and it smelled heavenly, but Mama had quashed his appetite.

Papa addressed Gretchen. "My wife is fierce," he said in a quiet voice. "Descended from our royalty, so she does like to rule the roost."

"I'm familiar with the type." Gretchen whisked a few crumbs off her tunic. "So. I know it's getting late, but there's another question I need to ask. What does 'Silverhair' mean?"

Papa scratched his bearded chin. "Ah," he said. "You've keen ears, Miss Gretchen."

"It's a legend," Arthur said, eager for Gretchen to know what Mama not-so-secretly believed. "About a woman sent by Fate to help the Bearfolk win a war. A human with a lock of silver in her hair."

Her eyes widened. "And you think that's me? You think I'm this Silverhair?"

"No, I don't," Arthur said with conviction. He looked her straight in the eye. "I think you're a girl with unusual hair who came here to rescue her stepsister, and that's all."

"It does seem improbable," Papa said. "The tale is old, passed down through many generations. It's likely changed fifty times since its first telling. Myself, I tend to think it's more story than prophecy. Not that I don't think you're capable and brave enough for heroics, mind."

Gretchen ran her fingers over her silver-streaked braid, her brow creased. "Lusela thinks differently, doesn't she? And the giant. That's why he let me go."

Arthur nodded. There. Now she knew. Now, if Mama tried to force her to be part of some Silverhair-inspired scheme, Gretchen would at least be ready for it.

Papa lifted a goblet as if to toast her. "Yes, my clever lass. She does. But just because a few folks believe a thing doesn't make it true. There are as many legends in the world as there are fish in the rivers, and only a fool or a madman would expect them all to come to pass. Now, don't waste your time fretting over my wife's flights of fancy. We'll find your sister and have you off home soon as can be."

The moonlight reflected off the gold plates and silver serving dishes. Papa glanced skyward and said, "If you're still hungry, best be quick and eat your fill. The feast will disappear come midnight, if I rightly recall the ways of the wish-blanket." He stood and patted his belly. "As for me, I'm stuffed as a new-made mattress. I'm off to bed."

"I'd like to see it," Gretchen said. "The food disappearing."

Papa chuckled. "Please yourself, lass. Good night."

Arthur's heart fluttered in his chest at the thought of being alone with Gretchen. With a pang that felt like guilt, he remembered Birna and his upcoming betrothal. "I should go, too." He started to stand, but she caught his sleeve.

"No, stay. Please? I mean, have you ever seen a disappearing feast before? If that's not worth losing a few minutes of sleep over, I don't know what is. It will be something to tell your kids about someday. Your cubs, I mean. Come on, Arthur."

He sat.

The flutter in his chest continued, expanding like a hundred-petaled flower blossoming behind his breastbone. It was sweet and suffocating, wonderful and frightening. As magic-tinged as the moment just after shifting from boy to bear.

Oh Ursa, he prayed. *Help me stay true to my kind.*

He stared at Gretchen, trying hard to find something in her worth loathing. Her gaze was fixed on the remains of the feast. As the food and dishes shimmered and dissolved into a cloud of sparkling dust, her face practically glowed with delight. She clasped her hands over her heart and turned to face him.

"Did you see that? That was amazing!" she said.

He'd never seen anything more beautiful.

Chapter Fifteen

24 June, 170 N.E.

Birds twittered and poked their beaks into the soft earth in search of breakfast worms as morning light kissed the meadow. Gretchen stood ready to go, her pack at her feet, Millicent bobbing over her left shoulder. Nearby, Thorburn turned out his pockets for the third time.

"The map has disappeared," he said, throwing up his hands in frustration. "Utterly and completely."

"One can never rely on gifts from strangers," Lusela said. "No matter. I spied out the best route when we last looked at it. North to Fiddlesworthy, then the Howlers' Hollow Road."

"I don't recall anything about Howlers' Hollow," Thorburn said. "But if you say so, my love. Off we go, then."

They shouldered their packs and Thorburn led the way out of the pleasant meadow. The path soon split into two, and Lusela pointed to the wider, less welcoming trail. Thorburn followed his wife and gestured for Gretchen and Arthur to follow.

Gretchen soon regretted Lusela's choice of route. It was

dim as twilight and smelled of decay. Gnarled, leafless trees overarched stony ground, and beady eyes glinted at them from patches of black, thorny brush.

"What are they?" Gretchen whispered over her shoulder to Arthur.

"Bramble pixies. Watch your ankles. They may grab for you. They're small but strong, and I think they used to take humans for brides before the regeneration."

"Nice," Gretchen said wryly, wishing her blaster was functional instead of useless and tucked away in her bag. "You don't mind if I walk beside you, I hope. At least one of my ankles might stand a chance with you between it and them."

"Happy to be of service," Arthur said. He looked more nervous than happy, in Gretchen's opinion. But who could blame him for not liking this part of the forest? She certainly wasn't a fan of the sulfur-scented air and the jagged terrain.

From a branch dangled a strip of pale rose fabric, its edges frayed. "Ruby's favorite color," Gretchen said, stopping to finger the silky material. "You don't think—?"

Before Arthur could answer, needle-sharp claws seized her calf and dragged her over the sharp path and into the tangled bramble bushes. She didn't have time to scream before a bony hand clamped over her mouth. Other hands and claws gripped her arms and legs and throat.

"Pretty, pretty," one pixie said in a high-pitched, sing-song voice. "Mine, mine." Its breath burned her ear. She thrashed, trying to free herself, but only earned more wounds from stubborn claws.

"Hush, hush. Little bride, little bride. My own, my own."

Numbness spread through her body. Poison from their claws, or magic? She ceased fighting and closed her eyes as euphoria rushed through her veins and eliminated all fear. Why had she been afraid? A laugh bubbled from her lips. She'd never felt lighter or happier.

Who was she?

Oh, yes. The pixie's bride. She'd have a bouquet of daffo-dils and a cherry cake, and always, always be completely happy from her head to her toes.

A chorus of terrible shrieks interrupted her wedding dream, but she couldn't open her eyes to see what was hap-pening. There were fighting sounds, grunts, and shouts. She didn't care much. She was going to be married soon, and have cherry cake and ice cream. Soft shoes made of cloud-silk, and a cloak woven from starlight.

Someone picked her up. It made her stomach lurch pleas-antly, like diving through clouds in an airskipper. She felt his heart beating hard against her side. "My love?" she said, eyes still closed and limbs still floppy. "Is it time for the cake? Kiss me first, or the marriage won't stick."

"Gretchen?" a familiar voice said. A boy voice. He sounded worried, even though everything was nice in the world. "Stay awake."

"Mmm-hmm," she answered, snuggling her face against his warm chest. "Anything for you."

She returned to thinking about cake. Other voices blended with the boy's. They sounded far away. She wanted to ask them when she'd get her piece of cake, but her mouth refused to speak.

Millicent flew back and forth in a state of moth panic as Arthur stumbled toward his parents with Gretchen lolling in his arms. Mama and Papa had climbed out of the brush just before he did. Mama's hair was mussed, but otherwise she looked no worse for wear. Papa's sleeves had been sliced by thorns or claws, and his face bore a couple red, seeping scrapes.

"Ursa above," Papa swore. "They put up quite a fight for such wee beggars. And look at the lass. They've spelled her good, haven't they?"

"Do something, Mama," Arthur said. "Help her, please." He looked down at the girl he held. Her face was scratched, her clothes torn. Bite marks pocked her legs and arms, oozing blood. In spite of her injuries, she was grinning and rubbing her cheek against his chest.

"We can't stop here long," Papa said. "Or we might all end up in that state." He picked up Gretchen's pack from where it had fallen when the pixies grabbed her.

Mama reached into her bag and rummaged around before pulling out a corked bottle. "This might help. But I can't promise." She uncorked it with her teeth. "Tip her head back, Thorburn, and I'll sprinkle some on her tongue."

Gretchen murmured something about daffodils as Papa maneuvered her chin to open her mouth. Mama dumped a little purple powder onto her tongue and then a splash of water. The girl swallowed and sighed.

"It could take an hour or two to work, if it works at all," Mama said. "We'll have to take turns carrying her until she comes around."

Suddenly feeling protective, Arthur clutched her tighter. She squeaked like a mouseling. "I have her for now."

"Onward, then," Papa said. "Before the pixies return with their myriad relatives and do violence against us as well. They've never had a fondness for us Bearfolk to begin with, and given the excuse—"

"Yes, yes," Mama said churlishly. "Let's just move on and save the chatter for later, shall we?"

They followed the rocky path for mile after mile. Arthur's arms and back ached and then throbbed, but he refused to complain or hand her off. He trailed behind his parents, surrendering to his desire to study Gretchen's face as she dozed. He fell in love with the freckles on the bridge of her nose, the curve of her eyebrows, the one faint crease on her forehead, the shape of her earlobes. It made it hard for him to breathe, having her nestled against him, and it was the best and worst feeling at the same time.

He knew it was utterly stupid and altogether wrong.

Stupid because he'd known Gretchen for less than a week. They'd spoken only a few times. He didn't even know her father's name, what color she liked best, or if she already had a suitor back home.

Wrong because Bearfolk law forbade him to form any bond with a human.

Wrong because he was as good as betrothed to Birna.

Wrong because it could cost him everything he held dear.

He could be cast out of his tribe, stripped of his sacred pelt, and doomed to suffer the pain of not being able to Change when the magic demanded it. He'd been told words did not exist to describe the horror of such an experience.

If all went as planned, she'd be gone soon. In time to keep him from ruining his life.

His foot caught on a root. He lurched forward and almost collided with a tree—but he did not lose his grip on Gretchen for half a second. He kept her close to his heart, where he wished she could stay.

She wriggled, yawned, and opened her eyes. Grinning like an inebriated elf, she gazed up at him. "I'm really starting to like you," she said. "You have nice eyes, and—hey, did you bite my ankle? Because something bit my ankle, and it itches like crazy."

Arthur stopped just short of running into Papa, who'd stopped and turned to face him.

"Your mother and I think it would be best if I carried the lass for a while," Papa said. He scooped Gretchen out of Arthur's arms. She giggled when his beard brushed against her forehead.

"Do I know you?" she asked, gazing up at him.

"Hush, lass," Papa said. "You're under an enchantment. The less you speak, the less you'll regret later."

Arthur crossed his arms over his ribcage, missing her although she remained in full view.

Mama's slap was unexpected and forceful.

Her face and neck reddened as she pressed a finger into his chest. "Do you think I don't know what that look on your face means? Keep your eyes on the path and your mind on decent matters. I've worked too hard for too long to gain the elders' respect. I'll not let you and your youthful fancies bring ruin on this family. Do you understand me, son?"

He didn't answer her. He returned her glare until she stepped away from him with a huff. Standing up to her made him feel strong—and terrible.

Millicent landed on his shoulder, her touch light and gentle and somehow comforting.

Having a moth for a mother seemed preferable to having a Bearfolk mother.

Chapter Sixteen

Gretchen awoke with a pounding headache and ankles and hands that itched like mad. Adding to her discomfort, someone had slung her over a shoulder and was carrying her with her head hanging upside down.

It took her a minute to be able to speak. "Could you please put me down?"

"Glad to," a woman's voice replied. Lusela's voice. "You're not as light as you look, to be sure. Probably ought to eat less like a half-starved giantess, if you ask me."

Gretchen's memories returned as her feet met the ground: the Bearfolk, the pixies yanking her into the brambles and biting her, being in Arthur's arms, snug against his chest.

Good heavens, did she actually tell him she liked him *out loud*—and that he had nice eyes? Those pixies must have seriously messed her up.

She swayed for a moment and spread her arms to regain her balance. She was thankful to see that they'd exchanged the dark, tangled wood for a grove of birch and shafts of sunlight.

"You feeling better, lass?" Thorburn asked. He offered her

a jug of water and she gulped down every drop. "Pixie bites contain potent magic. Can make a person lose their senses for good, I've heard. Lusela's tonic worked against it, praise Ursa."

"Thank you for saving me," she said. "I think I'll be fine once my knees stop shaking." She looked toward Arthur and tried to forget how she'd embarrassed herself when under the influence of pixie magic. "It was you, wasn't it, who got me away from them?"

He smiled and opened his mouth to reply, but Lusela stepped in front of him.

"We all did out part, as you can tell by the filthy state of my husband's shirt," Lusela said, gesturing for them to follow her along a mossy path. "Now, just over that next ridge we should come to the gray faeries' village, and then—"

Faint echoes stirred the air—hints of shouts and clangs. Thorburn stopped and raised a hand to halt and silence his companions. After a moment, his face blanched and he shook his head in disgust. "By Ursa, woman," he said to Lusela. "What have you done?"

"Only what you weren't bold enough to," she replied, chin held high.

A far-off, rumbling sound filled Gretchen with dread. "Another giant?"

"Another giant might have been preferable to what's ahead," Thorburn said.

"Shut your mouth and keep walking," Lusela said. "No use frightening the girl. We've come this far, and we've a duty to continue and see the job done."

"Wait," Arthur said. "Are you talking about the Silverhair legend again? Mama! It's just a story! Tell me you haven't brought us to the Red Meadows."

"Fate is fate, son. Destiny is destiny. Your lack of faith has no effect on either. Now, we're going to cross that ridge, find the girl a mount and standard, and win the blasted war once and for all."

"I won't allow it," Arthur said.

Millicent zipped back and forth frantically in front of Gretchen. Her wings buzzed like a hive of angry bees.

Lusela reached down and pulled a long knife from a sheath strapped to her leg. Her lower lip trembled as she pointed it at her son. "I would hate to have to kill you, son, but if it's what I must do to please Ursa and see the prophecy fulfilled…"

"You've lost your mind," Thorburn said. But he made no move to challenge his knife-wielding wife.

Lusela waved the blade. "Arthur, get the chain from my bag. I want the girl bound close to me until we see the fields."

When Arthur hesitated, she took a threatening step toward him and pressed the tip of the knife into his shoulder. "You know what the law says about obedience, son."

Shaking, he bent and opened his mother's sack.

"No," Gretchen said. "You said you'd help me find Ruby, and you're not allowed to lie."

"I said no such thing," Lusela said coolly. "My husband and son spoke for themselves, not for me. I have a higher calling than rescuing fools from fae princes."

"A higher calling to try to make me act out some old story just because I have odd hair? Are you serious?"

"As serious as the dead," Lusela replied.

Face grim, Arthur handed a golden chain to his mother. Without putting down her knife, she managed to loop the chain around Gretchen's throat and fasten the other end to her own wrist. "Walk, lass. The sooner we get there, the better."

The chain was light about Gretchen's neck but somehow made her unable to move her arms. Magic. She hated magic more with every passing minute.

Lusela tugged the chain, and Gretchen started to walk.

With every step, she tried harder to think of something she could say or do to help herself—but came up with nothing.

She had no choice but to go along with Lusela's plan for the time being.

Millicent hovered above, out of Lusela's reach. The moth was a comfort, Gretchen thought, a constant friend—just as Thorburn had told her back at the cottage. It seemed like a year had passed since then.

Arthur met her glance as she passed him. "I'm sorry," he whispered, his voice cracked with despair.

"Me too," Gretchen said.

She'd been right about Lusela all along. Arthur's mother was the image of her self-serving, manipulative stepmother.

But being right this time gave her no satisfaction. In fact, it only made her feel worse. For if she was forced into some battle and killed, Ruby and Father would be doomed as well.

Arthur tried not to look at Gretchen as he followed her up the fern-covered slope that led to the ridge. Seeing her chained made him sick to his stomach—as if being betrayed by his own mother wasn't enough to sicken him. Having to obey Mama and give her the chain had made him tremble with anger. He wished he had not been cowed by her threats, her knife, and her mention of the Bearfolk law which required him to obey her.

If keeping the laws meant being cruel and compassionless, he'd just as soon cast them all away.

He stepped over a silver caterpillar, minding the Bearfolk's code of respect for its tiny spark of life and its share of the world's magic. If it was right to make an effort to save such a little thing, surely it would be right to help an innocent young woman avoid an untimely death.

Because that was what Gretchen was heading for if Mama forced her to ride into the midst of a faerie war.

There had to be a way to free the girl. If he kept his eyes open and waited in readiness, perhaps he'd catch Mama in a moment of distraction or weakness. The odds were against him, certainly. Mama was a shrewd one, especially when focused on something she desperately wanted.

Papa trudged beside him, not saying a word. Bearfolk men knew better than to oppose the will of a strong-minded Bearfolk wife. History had taught them that to do so proved costly more often than not. A line of fierce warrior queens had been their rulers from the beginning of time until the days of the first English king. Although councils of male elders had replaced the monarchy, every Bearfolk citizen knew who really continued to run their society.

So, when Mama's queenly blood began to simmer, there was little Papa could do but yield to her.

It might be better, Arthur thought traitorously, *to remain unmarried.*

Standing on the crest of the ridge, Arthur surveyed the valley. There was the gray faeries' village, all stone spires and glinting windows of colored glass. Beyond it, puffs of black smoke and showers of sparks rose up from behind another ridge.

The war.

No one remembered exactly how it had begun, but no one wanted to admit defeat, either. Therefore, tribes of Bearfolk, green elves, and meadow fae had fought against battalions of woodland fae, hobgoblins, and northerly dwarves year after year. They knew how to destroy one another, how to crush the magic out of even the immortal fae among them.

And Gretchen was supposed to stop them?

Arthur shivered and wrapped his arms tightly about his

ribcage. He wanted to weep, to throw up, to grab Gretchen and run far, far away.

Mama laughed low, a madwoman ready to do mad things. She shook the chain and it tinkled like tiny bells. "Look, Silverhair. Your true destiny, laid out before you like a glorious, bloody feast."

Arthur made his decision then. He would give his life for Gretchen if that's what it took to save her. He would do what was truly honorable and good. In his heart, he wrote a new law for himself, one better than all the other Bearfolk laws: a law of steadfast, selfless love.

Chapter Seventeen

To Gretchen, the sounds of the faeries' war were, strangely, almost beautiful.

Songs rose up from the battlefield, songs heavy with magic and intertwined melodies, and when the warriors' swords met, the metal rang out clear and bright. Balls of colored flame hissed and whirred, soaring in vivid arcs before exploding into popping bits of glitter.

She couldn't see the actual fighting yet. One last hill stood in the way. One hill over which huge black birds circled, beaks snapping hungrily.

One hill between her and…

Millicent brushed against her cheek, blessing her with a moth-kiss. She wanted to thank the moth for it, wanted to beg her to somehow find Ruby and express her regret, wanted the miracle of being able to commission the moth to go to her poor father's side. But her mouth, like her enchantment-stricken arms, refused to move.

Swallowing hard to hold back tears, she followed Lusela over the hill, to doom or destiny.

A horn blast ended the fighting just as Arthur caught sight of the camps across the valley. The soldiers abandoned the muddy, red-stained field and walked, hobbled, rode, or crawled toward one camp or the other: to the east, the blue tents of the Bearfolk and their allies, and to the west, beyond where Mama stood, the green tents of the woodland fae and their cohorts.

Wind whipped through the valley, making the pennants atop the biggest tents snap. The air smelled of spent spells and spilled blood, bitterness and bile.

Mama stopped, and so did Gretchen. The girl fidgeted with the chain around her throat, exposing the scarlet welt the thing had caused.

"We've come in on the wrong side," Mama said. We'll have to go around, through the wood there, and do our best to avoid the enemy."

"Is that part of the so-called prophecy?" Arthur asked cynically.

Mama's glare was sharp enough to slice rock. "Watch yourself, lad. You weren't raised to scoff at holy things, and I'll not tolerate it here."

Unrepentant, he blinked at her and held his ground.

"This way," Mama said finally. She yanked the chain hard. Gretchen gasped in pain. Arthur started toward the girl, determined to loose her or at least take the chain from Mama's grasp, but Papa put an arm out to stop him.

"Gently, my love," Papa said to Mama's back. "If she's the savior, should we not treat her as kindly as possible? We'll owe her much if you're right about her."

Mama glanced over her shoulder and scowled. "Oh, so you doubt me, too? Well, you'll be singing a different tune soon enough, Thorburn Woodley. You and your insolent son."

They slipped into the cover of a thick grove of smooth-barked, gray trees. The trunks grew close together, leaving only enough space for one at a time to pass through. The ground was an uneven mass of roots and rocks, ready to inflict twisted ankles and stubbed toes. Arthur rejoiced in the slow pace they were forced to adopt. Let it take all night. Gretchen was still alive. He could still see her ahead of him through the branches, her honey-colored braids half undone, her shoulders still proud even in her captive state.

As long as she was alive, he would not lose hope.

At the grove's edge, they stumbled to a stop. In front of them, a raging river of green water churned and rushed, half a mile wide—and completely soundless.

Mama swore and stomped her foot.

And that was when the nets fell over them, trapping them like unsuspecting butterflies.

Chapter Eighteen

"What's this fine catch?" Gretchen heard a masculine voice say from somewhere behind her. She watched as several pointy-nosed, green-skinned, warty fellows worked to untangle her and her companions from the net. The short-statured creatures wore leather breastplates and knee-length fur breeches.

For the hundredth time, she wished she had a functional blaster at hand. Not that she really wanted to shoot anyone. It just would have been convenient to be able to *threaten* to shoot someone.

"We are weary travelers, good sir," Lusela said breathily. "Thank you for your aid. We'll be on our way and out of yours as soon as we're free from this wretched net."

"We shall see about that," the man behind her said.

As the green-skinned fae carried the bundled net away, Gretchen noted that they were surrounded, not only by other green-skinned soldiers, but also by some very tall men with pearlescent skin and aquamarine eyes. Their hair varied in shades of gold, silver, and copper, and their richly embroidered leather tunics were shades of green and brown. Turning her head a little, she noticed the tallest of them standing a little apart from them. A circlet of twisted gold crowned his corn silk hair, and he was possibly the most beautiful thing she'd seen in her life. Looking at him made her insides quiver and her vision blur—sure warning signs of enchantment trying to take hold. She made herself return her attention to the green guys—although it took a lot of effort.

"A human maiden," the tall one said, and Gretchen recognized his voice as the one she'd heard while still inside the net. "Tied with a chain of Densmoor gold. Surely there's a tale behind such a spectacle, Bear-wife."

Lusela curtsied. "Found her trespassing in our cottage, Prince. Your Highness. She needs a bit of discipline, not being accustomed to our ways. Why, she'd wander into mischief before you could say 'gillyflower,' and that would be the end of her."

The prince came close. He lifted Gretchen's chin with his gloved hand as Millicent hovered a few inches above her. "She's already been in a scuffle, I see. Unless you left these marks on her fair face, Bear-wife?"

"Bramble pixies, Your Highness," Thorburn said, bowing. "As my good wife said, the girl does seem rather prone to mishaps."

At the prince's touch, Gretchen's heart had skipped a beat. Definitely magic, the hateful stuff. He stood close enough that his sweet breath warmed her face, but she avoided looking him in the eye. It seemed like a bad idea, given what she'd learned in school—and firsthand—about fae trickery.

He took his hand away from her chin, and right away she missed it—although she didn't want to. He said kindly, "Tell me your name, girl."

Eyes lowered, she answered, "Gretchen Werner, Your Highness."

The prince laughed, throwing his head back as if he'd

heard the best joke of his life. When he regained his composure, he said, "Well, Gretchen Werner. My name is Prince Barrett Turnleaf, and I have heard many things about you from my darling bride. Never did I dream you would come to join my household as well."

Gretchen's knees buckled, and Arthur caught her under her arms. "Ruby?" she cried. She looked into the prince's face then, and found him smiling benevolently. She wriggled free of Arthur's grasp as tears filled her eyes. "You have my stepsister?"

"She is well and happy," Prince Barrett said. "The true treasure of my heart."

"Please, Your Highness, may I see her?" Gretchen wished she wasn't weeping like a baby but she couldn't stop. The news that Ruby was alive combined with standing in the magic-saturated presence of a faerie prince had undone her.

"Of course. She is in my quarters with her maidservant. Come with me, and her maid shall dress your wounds and mend your garments." The prince caught one of her tears on the tip of his finger. "Tears of happiness are like perfect diamonds, are they not? Precious and rare."

Gretchen felt Millicent land in her hair just above the nape of her neck between her braids. The moth's little feet tickled as they sought places to grip. A light humming transferred from the insect's body into her skin, and suddenly the prince's magic lost its hold on her. He remained almost unbearably beautiful, but she no longer felt compelled to please or obey him. Gretchen revised her opinion of magic. She still despised most of it—but the kind wielded by hummingbird-shaped moths had won her approval.

"Begging your pardon, Highness," Lusela said. "The girl is ours. A trespasser. A lawbreaker. Not fit company for your good ladies."

The prince straightened his back and spoke like the royal he was, saying, "Remove that chain immediately, Bear-woman. This girl is no longer your concern."

Arthur watched Mama slip the chain over Gretchen's head and step aside. Gretchen's tear-streaked face was lit by a perfect smile. Mama, however, had turned radish-red, her nostrils flaring with barely contained rage. Thank Ursa she knew better than to defy a powerful faerie prince.

Barrett Turnleaf offered his arm, and Gretchen took it. He addressed Papa and Arthur, for Mama had slunk away to pout on the riverbank. "If you're headed toward the Bearfolk camp, make haste. There's a bridge across the river half a mile to the south. When the horn sounds, fighting resumes, and nowhere outside the camps is safe ground for spectators."

"Thank you kindly, Your Highness," Thorburn said.

The prince's lips curved into a sneer. "You do well to thank me, Bear-fellow. As your kind opposes mine in this war, I show you inestimable mercy by not striking you down where you stand. Go. If we meet again, you will find my mercy spent and your deaths certain."

Arthur bowed his head in respect but said nothing. He hadn't expected to be parted from Gretchen yet. He'd imagined there would be time for a proper farewell at least. Instead, all he could do was watch her leave with someone who probably planned to subdue her with magic and force her to become one of his many wives. She'd never leave Britannia—and she'd soon forget to care about the father she'd left behind. Eventually, she'd forget she'd been human at all.

"Arthur?" Papa gripped his shoulder. "Time to go, lad."

"We have to help her," Arthur said. "We promised."

"We promised to help her find her stepsister, and that

we've done. Whatever becomes of her now… Well, I'd say that's your mother's fault. You mustn't blame yourself, lad."

"Papa," Arthur began, voice cracking with sorrow and regret. He wanted to tell Papa he loved the girl. That losing her felt like dying.

"Hush now. 'Tis better not to speak one's heart sometimes." Papa put an arm around Arthur and guided him toward Mama. "As my father used to say, 'We cannot always steer our hearts, but we can choose to steer our actions toward the right.'"

"What's right is saving Gretchen from Barrett," Arthur said. "So she can take her stepsister home and save her father."

"Bearfolk must attend to Bearfolk matters," Papa said. "Our law is plain. Helping the girl for a few days was an act of honor, I grant you. But meddling further, provoking the faerie high king's son—that we cannot do."

Mama marched toward them, skirt muddied to her knees, seething with anger. "That prince crossed the wrong Bear-woman today. I swear, by all that's holy, he'll regret it."

"We'll speak of it once we've reached the camp, my love," Papa said soothingly. "Let's gather our things and be away before the battle horn sounds."

"Oh, it's sounded already, far as I'm concerned," Mama declared. "And it will keep sounding until I spill some royal blood and have the Silverhair back on my chain."

Chapter Nineteen

The camp was bigger than Gretchen had expected. Row after row of dark green tents encircled a large pavilion striped in gold and emerald. A silver pennant embroidered with a dragon's head flapped from a pole at the pavilion's peak. Soldiers milled throughout the lanes between their dwellings; some, the short green-skinned guys, some tall and lithe like the prince, and others brawny, bearded fellows with oversized axes and hammers strapped to their backs.

Gretchen trailed behind Prince Barrett, hoping she wasn't breaking any etiquette rules by not maintaining a wide enough distance between herself and royalty. She didn't want to get lost now. She was too close to meeting Ruby.

Of course she had no idea yet how she'd get Ruby away from the camp and back to the airskipper—but at least they'd be together, right?

Flute music drifted through the camp along with smoke from cooking fires and the scent of roasting meat. Gretchen's stomach rumbled. The silly thing didn't care if she was home or captive to a fae prince; it wanted what it wanted. At least the music and the conversations going on around them made it unlikely that anyone else could hear her hungry gut's obnoxious song.

As they approached the pavilion, a blonde girl peeked out the door-flap. When she saw them, she lowered her gaze, bowed her head to the prince, and then slipped back inside. Seconds later, the door-flap was held aside and Ruby stepped out. This glitter-skinned Ruby was rosy-cheeked and dressed in shimmering faerie finery from head to toe, but she *was* Ruby.

Her Ruby.

Every argument, petty jealousy, cruel word, and hair-yanking scuffle they'd ever had disappeared from Gretchen's memory as, sobbing, she ran past the prince and into her stepsister's open arms.

"Sister," Ruby said, stroking Gretchen's back. "I'd almost forgotten you, but here you are." Her voice was airier than Gretchen remembered, her speech slower. "I do believe you need a bath."

Gretchen laughed and stepped out of Ruby's arms. She wiped her tears with the side of her hand. "I'm afraid I can't disagree with you about that."

"My beloved," Prince Barrett said from behind her. "I must attend to my duties. I'll return to sup with you when night falls."

Ruby brushed past Gretchen, her gown of petals giving off the scent of a hundred roses. Gretchen turned and regretted it. Ruby was in the prince's arms, kissing him passionately and noisily—and it looked like she didn't plan to stop anytime soon.

Gretchen stepped into the pavilion. Inside, it was as big as the ballroom Stepmother rented for parties. She could have parked a dozen airskippers in there and still had room for a dinner table and a dance floor. Layers of colorful rugs covered the ground. Silken cushions and gilded trays were arranged in several areas so groups of five or ten could socialize separately.

Brass and stained glass lanterns hung from poles and dangled from a wire that spanned the room.

Part of the pavilion was divided off by tall screens painted with scenes of water nymphs and mystified youths. Another section was hidden by screens painted with entwined dragons. Some of the screens probably formed the walls of Ruby's bedroom. She tried not to wonder if Ruby shared sleeping quarters with the prince. If "bride" meant to fae what it meant to humans… Well, she *really* didn't want to think about that.

The blonde girl Gretchen had seen earlier glided out from behind one of the dragon screens. She was willowy and a shade fairer than the prince, with eyes the color of a clear sky over water. Her dress looked like thousands of pale violet petals stitched together. She curtsied to Gretchen and said, "I am Asphodel, mistress. How may I serve you?"

Gretchen's stomach volunteered an answer by growling like an angry beast. "Um—sorry about that. I'm Gretchen. And apparently hungry."

Asphodel laughed, a bright sound that made Gretchen think of swarming butterflies. She gestured toward a group of cushions. "Sit, and I shall bring you refreshments, mistress. And then, perhaps, a bath would please you?"

Gretchen flopped down on a small mattress and sank into its soft fluffiness. It made her bed at home seem like a slab of marble. "Yes, thank you, Aff-so-deel?"

"Asphodel," the girl said, smiling so widely that her pearly teeth reflected the lantern light. "Wait there while I fetch your meal."

As she waited, Gretchen reached back and touched Millicent. Good. She hadn't moved. The moth purred under her fingers. "I hope you can keep up whatever you're doing," Gretchen whispered. "Heaven only knows how long I'll be stuck here with Prince Handsome-and-Way-Too-Charming."

Asphodel returned with a tray of fruit and cakes and a steaming glass of tea. "Pardon me, mistress," she said as she set the tray at Gretchen's feet. "But do you know there's a hummingbird moth faerie in your hair?"

"I'm well aware, thank you. She's a friend."

Asphodel giggled as she backed away. "I'll prepare your bath, if you require nothing more?"

"Thank you," Gretchen said, trying not to drool as she reached for a flower-shaped cake coated in sugar crystals. "I think I have everything I need here."

Asphodel left her side as Ruby strode into the pavilion, glassy-eyed, blushing, and smiling.

"So, you've met Asphodel," Ruby said. She sat close to Gretchen and grabbed a cream-topped pastry from the tray, every bit as calm and casual as she would have been in their sitting room in the colony. "These berry filled ones are my favorite snack. But oh! Wait until you taste what our cook's making for supper. Then you'll want to stay forever, too."

Gretchen set down the cake she'd been nibbling. She reached out and took Ruby's hand. "Ruby, I'm not here to stay, and neither are you."

"Why would I leave? Barrett loves me, and I love him. I have gowns and servants and crowns. Back at the palace, I have my own griffin, and a winged horse to ride. This is my home now."

"Ruby, he's enchanted you. Used magic to manipulate you."

"That isn't true," Ruby said. "You're jealous. That's only natural. But you don't have to be, sister. Barrett says you can marry his brother Adken. And if you'd rather not marry, you can be my servant, and I'll let you eat as much as you like."

"Millicent," Gretchen whispered. Maybe the moth could loosen the magic's hold on Ruby so she could think straight. "Could you help her? Show her the truth? Even just for a minute?" She didn't want to risk a long separation. If Prince Barrett or one of his brothers came in, she needed to be able to hold her own against their mind-melting magic.

The moth fluttered against the back of Gretchen's head and then flew to Ruby. She landed on top of Ruby's black curls. Ruby froze. "Is that a bug? Get it off me!" Her pale skin paled further. Gretchen had forgotten how much her stepsister hated insects.

"I will. In a minute." Gretchen watched Ruby's face. Sure enough, her eyes lost some of their glassiness.

"What is it doing to me? Is it poisonous? I feel…strange." Ruby blinked a few times. "Everything looks so dull."

"You were under the prince's enchantment. He lured you here and then kept you with his magic."

"No. I—" Ruby shook her head, her expression troubled. "I love Barrett."

"Do you, Ruby? Take a deep breath and try to think clearly."

"Maybe. I don't know."

Gretchen squeezed her sister's hand. After a few seconds passed, Ruby said slowly, "It was a secret mission. Mother sent me to arrange a treaty with the fae. She said that if I got the faerie high king to agree to an alliance, our nations could help one another—and she'd be a shoo-in for prime minister."

"But you knew the prince before you left the colony. You wrote his name on your arm. I saw it."

"He was my contact, the intermediary between us and the high king. At least that's what he claimed at the time. He was really acting behind his father's back. Anyway, I met him at the new colony up north a few months ago. Mother had him flown in so we could talk strategy face to face. And, well, you know I've never been able to resist a handsome guy. He was sweet, polite, and that accent… I fell hard. But I swear he never made a move that week. Maybe his magic didn't even work in Old Canada. Anyway, he was different when I landed here. More serious. More prince-like. He took me to his palace and gave me wine and started flirting with me like you wouldn't believe. And then—honestly, I can't remember much between then and now. It's all kind of a blur, but—oh my heck! Gretchen! Am I married to a faerie?"

They both looked at Ruby's left hand. A band of platinum encircled her ring finger.

"No, no, no. I'm never going to be able to leave here," Ruby said, shivering and tearful as she pulled and clawed at the immovable ring. "And what's worse is that you're going to be stuck here with the faeries, too. I'm so sorry, Gretchen."

Gretchen took her stepsister's face in her hands. "No. We're both going home. I promise."

"Mistress Gretchen?" Asphodel called from beside the water nymph screen. "Your bath is ready."

"She'll come to you in a moment," Ruby said dismissively. "Go fluff the towels or something."

Gretchen hoped the maid hadn't overheard much, but she had no time to worry about it. Things were looking hazy and whimsical without Millicent's contact, as if the pavilion itself contained some sort of mind-altering magic. She tapped her temples and tried to refocus her eyes. "Ruby, I have to take back the moth now, so you'll probably forget everything we just said. But if you can remember anything at all about this conversation, try to remember to be ready to run with me when I say it's time."

"I'll try my best. And Gretchen? Thank you for risking your life for me. I know I haven't been the greatest sister, but I do love you, you know?"

"It's okay. I love you too." She was sorry that she hadn't loved Ruby more, sorry that what had driven her to search hard was more the threat to Father than anything. When they were free, she'd make it up to Ruby somehow. She'd be the kind of sister she'd always dreamed of having: thoughtful, fun, a good listener, and a reliable friend.

Ruby kissed her cheek and Millicent buzzed from one sister to the other. She settled on the back of Gretchen's head again, renewing the clarity Gretchen had lost in her absence.

Ruby shoved her stepsister playfully. "Go. Get your bath. You smell like that time a mouse died in the ventilation system. Only ten times worse."

Gretchen stood, smiling. "I'm going."

Heavens, she hoped the moth could implant some escape plan into her brain before morning. Otherwise, Ruby might end up being right about them both being stuck there forever.

Arthur lay next to the tent wall on a thin mattress, sweating under a woolen blanket but too soul-weary to bother kicking it off. Papa snored nearby, and across the tent, Mama snored even louder. He was certain he'd never sleep at all, and the snoring had nothing to do with it. Until he knew Gretchen was safe, he'd keep his eyes open and his mind working.

They'd eaten supper with the troops a few hours ago, and afterwards, Mama had taken the Bearfolk general aside. Arthur had not heard what they'd said, but he knew nonetheless: Mama had told the general about Silverhair and tried to convince him to take Gretchen back from Prince Barrett. He wondered how the general had reacted. Perhaps he'd thought she was a madwoman. Perhaps he'd believed her and was already planning an ambush or kidnapping.

Either way, Gretchen was in danger.

He rolled over to face the wall. His chest hurt, as if his actual heart was breaking in two. If there'd ever been a moment when he wished he was simply a wild bear, free of all care and emotion, it was then. But no. He refused to regret loving her. It had been a privilege, an honor, the grandest and most terrible thing that had ever happened in his life.

And he couldn't let it be over. Not yet.

He crawled out from under the blanket, grabbed his boots, and snuck out of the tent. He didn't know exactly where he was going or what he'd do when he got there, and he was probably about to break many of the rules he'd always held dear, but by Ursa and all the stars above, he was going to do *something*.

This time, he was going to do what his heart said was right instead of what the old rules said was right. He felt brave and completely scared—and as if he'd stepped into a new legend in which he might be the unlikely hero.

Chapter Twenty

Gretchen emerged from behind the screen feeling like a beautiful butterfly newly emerged from an unsightly chrysalis. She'd been scrubbed, massaged with lotion, spritzed with wildflower essences, and dressed in the simplest outfit Asphodel had offered: a pale green linen blouse embroidered with leaves and berries and a matching pair of baggy pantaloons with pink ribbons cinching the ankles. Not her style, but clean and comfortable.

Millicent perched like a fanciful ornament near the silver streak in Gretchen's almost-dry, freshly braided hair. During the bath, the moth had given up contact with Gretchen only long enough for Gretchen's hair to be shampooed. Magical moths were both steadfast and faithful, and for that, Gretchen was grateful.

"Why are you wearing my dowdy traveling clothes?" Ruby asked dreamily from her nest of cushions. "You'd look better in a real gown. Princes like girls who look princessy."

"Well, it's getting late. We'll soon be in bed, and it won't matter what I'm wearing, will it?" Gretchen found a seat near

Ruby and decided to test her. "Remember the matching yellow dresses Father gave us for Christmas when we were little? We looked like a pair of exploding dandelions."

"I don't remember," Ruby said. "But Prince Barrett doesn't like me to wear yellow. Most of my dresses are pink. Pink like summer rosebuds. Pink like the insides of seashells. Have you ever seen a real seashell? Prince Barrett gave me one as big as your head. He's good at gifts. Isn't he wonderful, Gretchen? I hope he comes back soon." She sighed like a besotted schoolgirl.

Gretchen frowned. Ruby, the real Ruby, had slipped away again under the tide of faerie magic. If only Millicent had brought a moth friend along, it would have been easier to deal with her.

Ruby yawned. "I'm going to bed. Asphodel? Attend me in the bedchamber." She covered her mouth as she giggled. "It isn't really a chamber. Just a place behind a screen. But it sounds much grander, don't you think? To the bedchamber, maid!"

She continued to giggle as Asphodel came and pulled her to her feet. The faerie handmaiden said to Gretchen, "I've prepared a bed for you behind the screen where you bathed, mistress, and laid out a nightgown for you. Would you like me to help you change as well?"

"I can manage," Gretchen said.

Asphodel curtsied. "As you wish. Rest well. The pavilion is guarded on all sides by the prince's most skilled sentries, so you need not worry. No one comes or goes without the prince's permission."

"Thank you." Gretchen watched the maid escort Ruby to her sleeping area, wondering if her words were meant as comfort or a warning. They felt more like a warning.

Her hopes sank. Royal sentries would be highly trained and ready to nip any amateur escape attempt in the bud. To flee unnoticed with a magic-intoxicated princess in tow seemed like a challenge beyond her abilities.

She heard voices outside the pavilion. The prince had returned. She got up quickly and dashed behind the screen, praying he wouldn't pay her a visit and try to woo her with his faerie charms.

"Where are the ladies, Asphodel?" Gretchen heard the prince ask.

"Gone to their beds, Your Royal Highness," the maid replied.

"Then I shall retire as well. Bring wine to my chamber and then put out the lamps. Sleep at Gretchen's feet. She is not accustomed to our ways, and we do not wish her to wander off in the night."

"Yes, Your Highness."

Gretchen groaned and sat hard on her mattress as what was left of her dream of getting away before dawn evaporated.

Clouds drifted over the moon, making it difficult for Arthur to see where he was going.

He should have brought a lantern, but he'd been in such a hurry to set out on his heroic quest to save Gretchen. Halfway to the bridge that led to the prince's encampment, it was too late to turn back.

Something clattered in the underbrush, perhaps a lonely insect or the bill of a night bird. Or some type of fae he'd never encountered before. There were hundreds of kinds, many of which kept to their own little territories—which seemed so much wiser than traipsing about on enemy land in the middle of the night.

He adjusted the strap of his pack on his shoulder and took a few cautious steps forward as his eyes became accustomed to the darkness. He thought he could smell his pelt through the closed bag, a musky, sweet scent that brought memories of feasting and dancing with his kinfolk. Less than a week had passed since the last solstice, but he was hardly the same person he'd been that night. Then, he'd been content and compliant. Now, he was a mess of emotions and new ideas—and risking his life and future for the sake of a human.

He'd never felt more alive.

The moon's light returned, casting shadows on the path before him. He moved faster, mind awhirl with possible scenarios. Perhaps he'd find Gretchen alone and shackled. Perhaps she'd be in her sister's company, watched over by armed guards. Perhaps she'd already escaped on her own and was rushing to her airskipper. Or, perhaps the prince had coerced her into becoming one of his many wives.

That was a thought that turned his stomach.

He tried to pick up his pace, but the wooden bridge was slick beneath his boots, almost as slick as the ice-covered pond he and his friends had played on as children when brought together to celebrate the Yuletide and that year's Bearfolk weddings. Yuletide was the best time of the year for a Bearfolk child, for they'd meet when they Changed for the solstice and then remain together for an entire week afterwards, eating, dancing, playing, and camping in the cozy shelter of a couple of huge caverns. Yuletide—and childhood—seemed centuries ago.

He slid down the last few feet of board and fell. His landing was soft, thanks to the pack he landed on. Thanks to his pelt.

He stood and shouldered the pack again as a question formed in his mind. If the soldiers Changed to fight in the war, why shouldn't he Change into a bear to rescue Gretchen from the enemy? His purpose was every bit as honorable, if not more. It wouldn't be pleasant, of course; forcing the Change at the wrong time of year was said to cause excruciating pain.

Bearfolk soldiers relied on strong herbs to help them endure donning their pelts at the dawn of each battle day—and he had no such medicine. But as a bear, he'd be strong and fierce. A better fighter, a faster runner, a more formidable opponent.

A faint glow along the path ahead drew his eye. As he got closer, he saw a patch of ghostly mushrooms giving off a cool blue-gray light. He took a handkerchief from his pocket and wrapped it around his hand in case they were dangerous to touch, and then he bent down and plucked a few from the damp earth.

In his grasp, they brightened, throwing off as much light as a dozen candles. Too much light. He didn't want anyone to see him coming. He put all but one of the mushrooms back, pressing the soil around their stalks to replant them.

Now, with enough light to see any roots or rocks or creatures in his way, he could move much faster. As he jogged along, he made his choice. He would Change before entering the enemy's camp. His keen bear's sense of smell would help him find the girls. His teeth, claws, and brawn would help him fend off the opposition if necessary.

Arthur pictured carrying Gretchen and Ruby on his broad, furry back. Delivering them from danger. Being brave and strong and honorable—a true Bear-fellow, worthy of his pelt and heritage. So valiant that the elders could perhaps forgive him for breaking a few archaic laws.

The sound of light hoof beats made him stop and turn. Not ten feet away from him, a speckled faerie pony pranced. Arthur's father sat up in the saddle, lantern in one hand, reins in the other.

"Thought you'd go adventuring without me, did you?" Papa said with a grin.

Chapter Twenty-One

25 June, 170 N.E.

Gretchen lay wide awake on her bed, watching the slanted canvas ceiling of the pavilion for any hint of daylight. It had been a long night. She might have fallen asleep for a few minutes. Otherwise, she'd spent the slow, dark hours trying to think up a way to escape. She was almost jealous of Asphodel. Curled up on a mat near Gretchen's feet, the maid breathed the deep breaths of profound sleep.

Beyond the screen, feet pattered and voices whispered. Pale light seeped into her corner of the room from a lamp or candle. Still attached to the side of Gretchen's head, Millicent stirred. Her wings hummed and her little feet tickled Gretchen's scalp as she repositioned herself.

Ruby's voice carried from the other side of the pavilion. "Don't go, my beloved," she said like one of the coy starlets from the 1930's films she used to worship.

Ugh. Gretchen didn't need to hear any more of that.

"A prince has duties, as you well know," Barrett said. "I'm

going to win this war for you, and then we'll go back to our palace and—"

Slurpy noises interrupted the prince. Gretchen interpreted the sound as kissing. She wanted to cover her ears with her pillow but didn't want to miss any part of the conversation that could prove useful.

"Enough," the prince said finally. "Let me go, little vixen. The generals await me with the morning reports. Go back to sleep and dream of me, and soon I shall return."

Ruby whined and sighed.

The light shifted and disappeared. A breath of fresh air hinted that the door-flap had been opened and that the prince and his lamp-bearing assistant had exited.

"Get up," Asphodel whispered urgently, startling Gretchen. "Dress and ready yourself. If your plan is to rescue your sister, you must hurry."

Gretchen sat up. "What? You want to help? Why?"

"Time is too short for me to explain it fully. But this I will tell you: I am not a maidservant, but a princess of the north in disguise. The two guards who remain outside are my trusted companions. Before this day ends, Prince Barrett will be either dead or taken captive as my royal father has commanded. But I would like to spare Ruby. She is not guilty of his crimes, and I have grown fond of her, human though she is."

"Thank you," Gretchen said. "Tell me what to do, and I'll do it."

Asphodel lit a small oil lamp. "Wait here while I dress your sister and serve her breakfast. I will add a potion to her tea so she won't fight being removed from here. Her love-bond with the prince will only dissolve once she's off the island. Until then, unless sedated, she would commit murder to stay with him."

"She's eaten faerie food, too. Is that going to be a problem?"

"I've put a remedy for that in your traveling bag. In a blue bottle. Give her three drops twice a day until it's gone." The maid started to leave, but hesitated. Her brow furrowed as she said, "One more thing. I do not think Ruby is aware of it yet, but she is carrying the prince's child."

Gretchen flinched. Could things get more complicated? "Will it…? I mean, will the baby be human, or…?"

"The baby will be half-fae. There have been many babes born with mingled blood throughout the ages, children who lived amazing human lives as artists or musicians or seers. There is no reason to fear for the baby's future—as long as he or she never returns to Britannia. Now, I must hurry. When the true battle of the day begins, I will be unable to aid you further." Asphodel left, taking the lamp with her.

In the shadows, Gretchen put on her shoes and grabbed her bag. She stood ready for Asphodel's call, wishing she knew more of the pseudo-maid's plan so she could be prepared to run or crawl or play dead or whatever else she'd have to do. Knowing about the baby made Gretchen ten times more determined to get Ruby home safely.

It was terrible of her, but she couldn't help but smile as she imagined what Stepmother's face would look like when her darling Ruby returned without the faerie alliance agreement but with a faerie wedding ring glued to her finger and a half-fae baby in her belly. Stepmother was going to hate being called grandma.

"Come now," Asphodel called. "It is time."

Gretchen took a deep breath and stepped out from behind the screen.

The sky lightened by small degrees, and the forest birds celebrated with a frenzy of chirping and twittering. Arthur stumbled along beside his slow-gaited father and the weary pony. They'd walked for hours and couldn't afford to sleep now. Smoke from the enemy's morning cook fires stung his eyes, and the reality of what he needed to do pricked his heart.

He stopped beside an oak tree that looked far older than the regenerated Earth. Magic must have hastened its growth. It seemed fitting to Arthur that he should choose an extra-magical place to don his pelt. His heart pounded as he pressed one hand against the tree's rough bark. He turned to face his father. "Papa, I think I should Change before we get any closer to the camp."

"Are you sure you want to try that, lad?" Papa asked with fatherly concern. "Without the herbs, it's said to hurt like being skinned and boiled alive."

"I'm sure."

"Aye. I expected you'd say as much. I reckon if I were your age and loved anyone half as much as you love that girl, I'd do the same." Papa shook his head as a sad smile lifted the corners of his mouth. "Youth and love together can make a fellow do mad things. Things he'll likely regret later."

"I'm sorry, Papa. I didn't mean to feel this way," Arthur said. "I know it isn't right. The elders—"

"If you mean to rescue the girl, you can't waste time considering the elders. Go. Whatever happens after that is a tale not yet written. Although I hope you realize it will be a short tale. The girl must return to her people, and your life is here."

Arthur threw himself into Papa's arms and hugged him tightly. "Thank you, Papa."

Papa pushed Arthur away. "Go on, now. Into that thicket, pelt and all. I'll keep watch here. Try not to make too much noise, if you can help it."

Arthur ducked into the shoulder-high brush behind the oak. He knelt and prayed for courage and endurance for the Change and success in his mission. Next, he opened his pack and tossed a few things aside: a length of rope, a water flask, an extra shirt. And then his fingers found the thick fur they sought.

The magic within the pelt responded to his touch by sending a warm, tingling sensation through his fingertips and then his entire body. He felt the familiar, achingly sweet desire to be one with the pelt, although it was less intense than at an equinox or solstice. He trembled as want and fear collided in his chest.

He spoke to the fur as he embraced it. "Please. This is not a holy day, but I need your help. Forgive me if my cause is less than holy—although what could be more holy than acting out of love?" He couldn't think of anything more to say other than the ancient words required before every Change.

And so, reverently, he draped himself with the pelt and uttered the ritual verses in the seldom-used tongue of his Bearfolk ancestors.

The first lightning bolt of pain stopped his heart, and the second restarted it and sent it racing. Every muscle twisted and snapped; every bone shattered into white hot shards and punctured his organs. He could hear himself shouting in the Bearfolk language and then simply screaming in anguish. His blood simmered, burning holes in his veins and leaking out to sear his skin like acid.

The torture stopped suddenly, and peace fell over him like a warm blanket. Surely he was dead.

"Arthur," he heard Papa say. "Get up, lad. It's over."

He opened his eyes. He saw his black paws and curved claws. Bear strength coursed through him. He rose up on his hind legs and sniffed the morning air, searching for a trace of Gretchen's scent.

There it was, to his left. Not far.

He took off running.

Chapter Twenty-Two

Gretchen followed Asphodel out the back of the pavilion. She touched Millicent, making sure the moth remained in her hair above her left ear. Although Asphodel had expressed great confidence in her ability to escape with Ruby, the moth's presence was reassuring. Behind Gretchen, one of Asphodel's guard friends carried Ruby—whom the potion had rendered drowsy and amenable.

A black and white horse with two nubby horns between his ears ambled toward them.

The horse stopped and bowed its head before Asphodel, who patted the horse's nose affectionately. "This is Yarrow. He knows every road and path in the land. He'll carry you wherever you wish to go."

"Thank you," Gretchen said. She reached out to shake Asphodel's hand. "Good luck today."

The battle horns signaled the start of the morning's battle.

"Be on your way quickly," Asphodel said.

One guard helped Gretchen into the saddle, and the other set Ruby in front of her. Ruby lolled back against Gretchen's chest as Gretchen shook the reins.

"Yarrow, I wish to go to my airskipper. It's in the forest south of here, not far from the cottage of Thorburn Woodley." She hoped her directions were specific enough. She couldn't do any better.

Yarrow whinnied and surged forward, heading toward the woods.

Ruby laughed and took hold of Yarrow's mane as Gretchen gripped the reins and prayed they'd not be jostled off the horse's back.

A big, black bear loped onto the path ahead of them. Yarrow stopped, skidding on wet leaves. The spooked horse reared and then galloped in the opposite direction as Gretchen fought to keep her seat.

They sped through the camp, dodging tents and smoldering cook fires. Ruby giggled as she held tightly to Yarrow's mane, but Gretchen wasn't enjoying the ride one bit.

"Stop, Yarrow!" Gretchen shouted. "Whoa!" But Yarrow did not heed her.

Gretchen could think of only two things as she held onto the horse for dear life. One: she knew that bear's eyes—recognized them as belonging to Arthur, and two: Yarrow was carrying them straight toward the battlefields.

Arthur stood still on the shady path, breathing the dust stirred up by the horse's flight.

He'd found Gretchen, but by Ursa, he regretted their momentary meeting. He hadn't meant to scare the horse. He'd been so intent on finding Gretchen that he'd focused solely on her scent, ignoring the scent of the horse and assuming the animal was just a nearby faerie war horse. How could he have known she'd be riding the horse—and sharing the saddle with Ruby?

Gretchen had surprised him again, for not only had she managed to escape from the prince on one of his mounts, she'd stolen his bride. Clearly, Gretchen didn't need his help.

If he ruined her getaway with his clumsiness, he'd never forgive himself.

Sounds of battle shook the air and silenced the birds. Gretchen had gone directly toward the fighting, straight into more danger. He couldn't think how he might aid her there, but if there was anything he could do, if the smallest opportunity to help her presented itself, he wanted to be nearby and prepared. All he could do was head toward the battle himself and watch from the tree line. Perhaps she'd fly past the armies unnoticed and journey back to her airskipper. That would be a feat worthy of legend.

He left the path and loped through the woods, following his keen nose on a shortcut to the battlefield. He'd keep his bear form for now; he hadn't time to Change back, nor the inclination to endure such pain again before it became necessary. Come nightfall, he'd take off the pelt and accept the consequences.

Come nightfall, he'd know if Gretchen survived the Red Meadows he'd sent her hurtling into.

Chapter Twenty-Three

"Yarrow! Whoa!" Gretchen yanked the reins with all her strength. Still, the horse galloped down the hillside, ears flattened with fear.

Smoke rose from the meadow, partly obscuring her view of the soldiers. Through the haze, she saw some of the prince's men wielding swords against some similar-looking fae men dressed in lighter tones. Other types of fae launched arrows from longbows; some fought hand-to-hand or walloped their foes with clubs. A few tossed colored globes that exploded into sparks and added more smoke to the air.

And there were bears. Bearfolk. Fiercely, they fought a group of troll-like creatures, using teeth and claws against the trolls' metal weapons.

The bitter scent of blood and ash and the sight of the mutilated dead made Gretchen retch as Yarrow ran across the field, bounding over fallen soldiers. Ruby, unnaturally still and quiet, clung to the horse's tangled mane.

As they neared the center of the meadow, a single shout went up from the ridge on the opposite side, muffled by the noise of battle. More voices joined in until a chorus of voices surrounded Gretchen and Ruby.

"Silverhair!" the chant said. "Silverhair!"

Gretchen thought she could see Lusela and some other faerie women, fists raised to the sky, before Yarrow turned sharply and trotted toward the prince's banner.

"No," Gretchen said. "No! I'm not your Silverhair!" Her words were lost among the soldiers' cries of jubilation.

A deep, collective growl rose from the Bearfolk on the battlefield. Gretchen felt it in her very bones. A horn blasted long and low, followed by more shouts. Yarrow reared again—spurring the onlookers and soldiers to vocalize out all the louder.

Yarrow spun, and one of the faerie prince's men grabbed the bridle. He spoke a strange word and the horse calmed and stood perfectly still.

Dizzy, Gretchen tried to free her feet from the stirrups. She had to run. Ruby had to run.

"I have to find Barrett!" Ruby cried, throwing herself off Yarrow's back. The prince's man tried to catch her, only to end up pinned to the ground by Ruby's squirming body. As he and Ruby rolled about trying to get free of one another, they became more and more entangled by the fabric of her voluminous dress.

Yarrow bucked and whinnied, and then seemed to freeze in fear.

Gretchen could have left then. Could have dug her heels hard into Yarrow's sides and made the horse flee the field. She could have left her sister, and maybe saved herself, but…

The chanting and growling rang in her ears.

Even if she wasn't the Silverhair of legend, she would not be a coward.

She jumped off Yarrow's back and grabbed a bloody knife from a dead soldier's hand. The prince's man flailed on the ground, still ensnared by Ruby's many-layered dress.

"Hands off my sister," Gretchen commanded. "And hold still, or you're going to get cut." The man froze as she slashed Ruby's dress to separate them, and then used the fabric to bind him fully.

Ruby glared at Gretchen. "Have you lost your mind? He's one of the good guys. And thanks for ruining my new dress, by the way. Do you have any idea how much twenty yards of spider-silk costs?"

Gretchen grabbed Ruby's arm. "Up on the horse again. Hurry."

"You get on first and then help me up. My arm hurts."

"Fine." Gretchen mounted the horse. She reached down for her stepsister. "Ruby, come on."

Ruby took a step back and shook her head. "Just go, Gretchen. Go home. I'm not leaving my prince."

"No! You have to come with me! He's used magic on you. You don't know what you're doing, Ruby. Your mother needs you at home. I need you."

"Go," Ruby said. She turned and ran toward the prince's banner, stumbling over bodies and broken weapons. An arrow zipped past her, barely missing her head.

"Follow her, Yarrow," Gretchen shouted over the din of battle. She pressed her heels into the horse's sides. "Yarrow! Follow Ruby!"

The air was thicker now, heavy with smoke, shouts of valor, and cries of pain. "Please, Yarrow! Move!" The faerie horse took a few hesitant steps and then stopped again with a disdainful snort.

Gretchen peered ahead. A light breeze from the south rolled the smoke across the ground in gentle waves. She caught a glimpse of her stepsister. Ruby had made it halfway to the prince's banner. Streaked with soot and soldiers' blood, her dark hair hanging in tangles, she trudged onward.

A flash of silver drew Gretchen's eye. A stocky figure in a green dress was running downhill toward Ruby, uttering a guttural war cry. Gretchen gasped. It was Lusela. Lusela with a short, silver sword in her hand.

"Ruby! Run!" Gretchen cried, but it was too late.

Lusela stabbed Ruby in the chest, and then stabbed her again.

"Silverhair!" Lusela shouted. She held the bloodstained sword high. "Come and claim your glory! I have slain the sister who dared to betray you, as the prophets foretold!"

Gretchen launched herself off the horse. She landed hard on her feet and ran to her fallen stepsister. "No, no, no," she muttered. "Stay alive, Ruby." She fell to her knees and cradled Ruby's body as she exhaled her final, shuddering breath.

"No," Gretchen repeated. This couldn't be real. Ruby had to be alive. She was too young to die. And the baby…

She looked up at Lusela with hatred burning in her breast. "I am not your Silverhair."

"Oh, but you are! Do you not hear them shouting your name? You rode into battle on a Marendall steed and turned the tide of the war, exactly as the legend said you would. And now the Bearfolk shall have victory." Lusela's smile was smug and cold, a witch's grin.

Gretchen stood, hands balled into fists. "All of this was nothing but a horrible coincidence, and you're a madwoman. Now—"

Prince Barrett appeared through the smoke, astride a silver stallion. "My love," he cried as his gaze fell upon Ruby. He dismounted, drew his sword, and pointed it at Lusela. "Did you do this, Bear-wife?"

"I cannot lie," Lusela said, chin held high.

Gretchen squeezed her eyes shut as Prince Barrett swung his blade.

After a few long seconds, she opened her eyes. Lusela lay crumpled on the dirt, and the prince knelt beside Ruby, weeping. He must have heard Gretchen sob, for he looked up at her with accusing eyes. "You brought this upon her as much as the Bear-woman did. Be gone from my sight before I kill you as well."

"If anyone beside this Bear-woman is to blame, it's you. You, with your luring and tricks, playing at politics with Ruby's mother!"

Barrett held Ruby's limp hand against his chest. "I am a prince and need not defend my actions before a child like you. But know this, human girl: How we came to meet ceased to matter when I lost my heart to her. I loved her more than a mortal like you could comprehend, and I shall never love another, even if I live for a thousand years. Now go, before I take your life. I shall not give you another chance."

Gretchen stood as if rooted to the ground. All around her, in every direction, men and creatures fought or lay dying, weapons clanged, arrows flew, and things exploded. Her stepsister lay dead before her. There was no good path she could take—literal or figurative.

A hand gripped her shoulder, and she turned. "Come with me, lass," Thorburn said. He held a huge shield. "Wished the dinner blanket into an invincible shield. Didn't know that could be done, but there it is."

Dizzy with shock and sorrow, Gretchen grabbed his shirtsleeve. "But did you not see? Ruby is dead, and your wife, and—"

"Now is not the time for tears." He put his arm around her back and pressed her forward. "One foot in front of the other. That's the way."

Tears flowed down her face as she walked, in spite of Thorburn's words.

After a dozen steps, she fell. She shut her eyes, too

weary to stand. The fighting sounds drifted over her like a nightmare lullaby.

"Gretchen, lass," Thorburn said severely. "You must get up. It isn't far now, but I can't carry you and hold the shield at the same time. Honor compels me to do what I can, but I will not stand here and invite death to take me next."

She felt him try to lift her, and then heard a low growl.

"Arthur," she murmured.

"Sure enough," Thorburn replied. "Not a horse, but he'll do to carry you a while."

She felt herself lifted and arranged atop a bear's broad back. She nestled her face against warm fur, and let sleep claim her.

When Arthur had come to a place where he could watch the battle, it was already too late for him to stop his mother from murdering Ruby. She already stood over the dark-haired girl, thrusting a sword into her heart as if it meant no more to her than slicing bread. As if she was a hardened criminal instead of a faithful, law-abiding, Bearfolk wife and mother.

When he saw Ruby fall, he'd run as fast as his four legs could carry him. *Please*, he begged the universe as his paws slapped the ground, *please don't let Mama kill Gretchen next*.

By the time he reached the girl, Papa had half-dragged her uphill to safety, protecting her with a big shield. Good, honor-bound Papa.

Now, Gretchen rode upon Arthur's fur-covered back. Her fingers clutched his coat. He could feel her breathing in and out slowly, her chest against his spine, and wondered if she'd fallen asleep. If she was asleep, she was crying in her dreams, for her tears continued to leak through his fur and onto his skin, her sorrow becoming part of him.

He'd thought he could not love her more, but he did—even

in his bear form. In spite of being broken by his mother's betrayal, his heart still overflowed with tenderness and adoration for Gretchen.

At the top of the hill, they rested. The horn had sounded as they walked, marking the end of the battle. Once again, birds twittered in the treetops and rabbits ventured out of their holes to nibble grass—although they gave Arthur a wide berth.

Papa sat at the base of a tree and set his shield aside. Arthur lowered his body to the ground slowly, careful not to disturb Gretchen. The cool ferns felt good under his belly. He would have been content there in the company of his father and the girl—had he not just witnessed such horrors. Murder and heartache, war and grief.

Arthur smelled two Bearfolk in human form approaching, and perked his ears to catch their conversation.

"Ho, there, Bear-brothers!" the bigger Bear-fellow called from twenty feet away. Arthur leaned his body to the side so Gretchen rolled off his back and gently onto the ground. The bulk of his bear form, he hoped, would be enough to hide her from view. He was counting on the smoke and dust from the battle to obscure her scent from their sensitive noses.

The visitor continued, "Have you heard the news, lads? We've won the battle—and not only that! The great fae prince actually conceded right before he was taken captive by some northerly fae and carried off. The Holy Well of Huttlesworth shall evermore belong to us and our allies, praise be to Ursa. Our honor is restored among the faerie nations."

Thorburn stood and went to shake their hands, keeping them at a distance from Arthur. "Praise Ursa, indeed," he said. "My son and I saw part of the battle. Now we can go home without joining the troops after all, eh?"

"Aye," said the shorter Bear-fellow. "So you saw her, then? The Silverhair who rode into battle and roused our lads to victory? Such a scene I'll never forget! I only wish my mam had lived to see the day, Ursa bless her."

"You don't say. The Silverhair came? That must have been a grand thing to witness," Thorburn said.

The bigger fellow grinned. "Indeed. Well, old timer, we're off to celebrate. Care to join us at the camp for a few victory drinks?"

Thorburn shook his head. "Thank you, but we'll be headed home. Crops to see to, and all that."

"Not to mention your Bear-son will have to shift soon," the shorter visitor said. "Changed for the battle and missed out on the final fight, did he? That's rough. Cost a pretty penny in pain, I'd reckon. Well, he'll have a story to tell the cubs, anyway. Changed for Silverhair's day like the rest of our brave lads, ready to do his duty. I wish you both well."

"Safe journey, fellows," Papa said.

The Bearfolk gentlemen wandered away, striking up a song as they disappeared from view.

Papa crouched beside Arthur and rubbed his snout. "You know, lad, I am proud of you," he said, voice thick with emotion. One tear leaked from his eye and he brushed it away as if it were a gnat. He didn't have to say a word about Mama; Arthur knew he was thinking of her and missing her, in spite of her faults and sins. "Well, we're lucky to have each other, and that's the truth. Now, I think those fellows were right. It's time for you to Change, before it starts to get dark. The longer you wait, the worse the shift will hurt. I'll stay here with the girl." He reached into his pack and took out clothes. "You'll have to make do with these. They'll be big on you, but serviceable."

Arthur nuzzled Papa's neck for a moment, and then brushed his nose lightly against Gretchen's cheek before taking the clothes with his teeth. He ambled off into the trees to face the Change alone. To pay "a pretty penny's worth of pain," as the visitor had said, unaware that Arthur had already paid a king's ransom in pain that day when he'd lost his mother. Lost her twice, in fact. Once to her madness, and once to death.

Surrounded by bushes that did not muffle his father's sobs of grief, Arthur summoned the Change.

Chapter Twenty-Four

"Be still, lass," Thorburn said, pressing down on Gretchen's shoulder when she tried to stand. A strange and terrible sound had awakened her. It took a minute for her to remember how she'd come to be in the woods with Thorburn—and that Ruby was dead.

"Oh, no," she murmured as tears stung her eyes. "That wasn't a bad dream, was it?"

Grim-faced, Thorburn shook his head and offered her his pocket handkerchief. "We'll see you to your ship and put an end to this whole ghastly adventure." He turned away from her and rested one hand on a tree trunk. He seemed much older than the gentleman she'd met back in the cottage. His posture and the tone of his voice were unfamiliar. Cold.

He'd lost his wife, and maybe he blamed her a little. Or a lot.

Something moaned nearby.

"What was that?" Gretchen asked.

"Nothing to concern you. Arthur had to shift, and it isn't an easy thing."

"He was the bear who carried me here." Gretchen remembered the texture of the fur in her hands and against her cheek, and how the bear's musky, piney scent and rolling gait had lulled her to sleep.

Thorburn grunted then said, "We've all played our parts in this tragedy. As I said, we'll soon see it to its end."

Branches stirred behind them. Gretchen grabbed a pointy stick and jumped to her feet, pulse pounding.

Yarrow pranced into view and greeted them with a whinny.

"No way," Gretchen said. She waved the stick. "Shoo, pony. You've caused me enough trouble. I'd walk all the way to North America before I'd get on your back again."

The horse shook his mane. A rectangle of parchment rustled against its neck. Thorburn slid the envelope out from under the strap and handed it to Gretchen. "It's addressed to you."

She broke the green wax seal and unfolded the note. "Salutations," she read aloud. "Yarrow offers his deepest apologies for how he behaved earlier today. Upon seeing the bear, he forgot his duties and let fear rule him. When he came to his senses, he found himself unable to aid in your escape from the meadow. As penance, he offers you his service. He beseeches you to allow him to carry you to your desired destination. If not, he will bear a mark of shame and be shunned by his kind until death claims him.

"This message was written by the hand of Asphodel of the northern fae, who bids you safe travels and good fortune."

"Oh, no," Arthur said, stepping out of the bushes with his pelt bundled in his arms. "Not that horse."

"He's repented," Thorburn said. "And if he's here to guide us quickly to the girl's ship, I'm all for it. Now that she's helped win the war, the Bearfolk might well try to seize her and make her a saint, given the opportunity. As for me, I've had enough excitement."

Arthur walked up to Gretchen. His hair was a mess of wild waves. A baggy striped shirt and wide-legged trousers hung loosely on his frame. A piece of knotted vine encircled his waist as a makeshift belt.

"What in the world are you wearing?" Gretchen asked, surprised to find herself wanting to laugh.

"Beggars can't be choosers," he said, smiling feebly.

"Which is the exact reason we'll be following this beast," Thorburn said. "A Marendall stallion knows shortcuts even the elves haven't heard of. Why, we might even be home in time for supper."

Gretchen looked at Arthur. He shrugged. "Beggars?"

"Fine," Gretchen said. "But I'm walking behind him, not riding."

Arthur wrapped his pelt around himself like a fur cape. He took his father's pack and shouldered it. "Papa? You look exhausted. Why don't you ride for a while? I'll hold the lead rope and make sure Yarrow behaves."

"I could do with a rest," Papa said.

"Go on," Gretchen said. "Ride. I have every intention of never sitting on another horse for as long as I live."

The word "live" sobered her. She still had a life, and Ruby did not. And what about her father? Did he still have a life, or had Stepmother ended it already?

She had to get home. She hoped she wouldn't be too late.

Thorburn mounted Yarrow and they started to walk south.

"Are you all right?" Arthur asked. "Did they hurt you in the prince's camp?"

"I'm fine," Gretchen said. The truth was she felt far from fine, but she didn't want to talk about it. It was bad enough to relive the scene again and again in her mind. To speak of it would make it even more real, more painful. "Can we be quiet for a while?"

"Certainly," Arthur said. He pulled the pack around and fished out a dented apple. He placed it in her hand. "We'll talk later, then. When you're ready."

"Thanks." She held the apple as they walked mile after mile in silence, squeezing it whenever tears threatened, bruising it until it was nothing but mush between her fingers.

A gentle rain pattered above their heads, dancing on leaves and coaxing a sweet summer scent into the air. Arthur took a deep breath, cleansing his lungs of whatever might have remained of the rancid fumes of war. Suddenly, although it seemed they'd been traveling for only a few hours, he began to recognize things: a boulder shaped like an ogre's head, the twisted, old apple tree atop the knoll, the patch of bluebells that never ceased blooming, even when snow fell.

He was home.

Sure enough, just ahead stood the little stone house where he'd been born. He blinked hard in disbelief.

"Is that your cottage?" Gretchen asked. "Already?"

"It is," Arthur replied.

"I shouldn't stay," Gretchen said. "But I'd almost give up a limb to sleep in a clean bed for ten or twenty hours."

"And to eat a proper dinner," Arthur added. "Fried fish and warm apple pie."

"Stop," Gretchen said. "You're killing me." She cringed, offended by her own choice of words, for herself and for Arthur. "Sorry."

"It's all right," Arthur said.

"No. Nothing is all right," Gretchen said.

The sorrow in her voice sent a pang through Arthur's chest. He didn't know how to answer her. So much *was* wrong. So much hurt. But as long as he was with her, he knew a little happiness. Of course, he couldn't tell her that. It would do neither of them any good.

They stopped near the front door. Yarrow shook his mane proudly.

"Are we home? Thank Ursa!" Papa said, sitting up straight on Yarrow's back. He yawned and dismounted simultaneously. "Didn't know a fellow could sleep so well atop a horse. Well, don't dawdle on the doorstep. I'm parched. We'll have a cup of tea before we see you off for good, lass. If Yarrow brought us home that quickly, he can get you to your ship before the sun sets."

"One cup of tea," Gretchen said.

Arthur's heart reverberated like he'd just won a great prize. For even five more minutes with her…

Thorburn headed straight to the hearth and jabbed at the dead coals with a poker. "I'll get the fire going and put the kettle on. Go change your clothes, son, and see what you can find for the girl to wear. A little soap and water wouldn't hurt, either."

"Come on," Arthur said. He led her through the sitting room and upstairs.

"It seems like a year since I was here last," Gretchen said when they stopped in the hall.

"I know." Arthur opened a closet door. He pulled out a wooden box and rifled through its contents. "Here. This was my favorite shirt before I outgrew it. And these trousers might fit you." His eyes pricked at the sight of the embroidery on the collar of the shirt. Mama had stitched his initials there in white thread. He stared at the letters, unable to move.

Gretchen took the clothes from his hands. "Thanks," she said quietly. "And Arthur? I'm sorry. If I hadn't come here…"

"I don't blame you. Mama only ever did what she wanted to do. That was how she lived her life." He cleared his throat and squared his shoulders, but a lump of grief remained lodged near his voice box. "You can change in my parents' room. See you downstairs when you're ready."

He closed the door of his room and leaned against it. He wondered if home would ever feel like home again.

Chapter Twenty-Five

26 June, 170 N.E.

Gretchen opened her eyes. Millicent hovered above her on humming wings. Thorburn stood beside the bed holding a tray of food and tea. She sat up and wiped drool off her cheek. Good heavens, she was still wearing the filthy green outfit Asphodel had given her. The last thing she remembered was sitting on the edge of the bed for a moment—and then she must have passed out cold.

Which hadn't gotten her any closer to home. Anxiety crept across her skin like hives. It was all she could do to keep herself from leaping out of the bed and rushing to find Yarrow so she could be on her way.

But Thorburn had risked and sacrificed much for her, and she wouldn't be rude to him when he'd gone to the trouble of making her breakfast. She'd already spent the night there; what harm would spending ten more minutes do?

"Good morning," Thorburn said without enthusiasm. He set the tray on her lap, and the scent of the cinnamon-sprinkled griddle cakes drifted up into her nose. "I tried to wake you when tea was ready last evening, but you were all but in a state of hibernation." She would have smiled if his tone had been different, but the old, jovial Thorburn was gone.

"I took your bed. Sorry."

"I slept well enough in the parlor. Now, eat up before it gets cold."

Arthur stood in the doorway. Gretchen's face heated with a blush as she realized how she must look: rumpled and grimy and drool-crusted, with hair like a torn-apart bird's nest. She chided herself for caring. Arthur had been a good friend, an exceptional friend, but it wasn't like he was her boyfriend or anything. He wasn't even exactly a boy. Well, he was—and he wasn't. Her face got hotter and she grabbed the fork.

"Will you be leaving directly after breakfast?" Thorburn asked. "Perhaps it would be best."

"I don't know," she said. The questions she'd been trying to avoid asking herself spilled out in a rush. "What if going back makes everything worse? Stepmother said not to come back without Ruby. If I show up alone, she'll probably kill my father out of spite. But if I don't go back soon, she'll *definitely* kill him. I'm so confused."

Millicent settled on her shoulder as if to offer comfort.

"That is a dilemma," Thorburn said flatly. "One I—"

Downstairs, someone pounded on the door.

"Who could that be?" Thorburn said. He slipped past Arthur and out of sight.

Arthur stepped into the room and closed the door softly. He put a finger to his lips to beg her silence. He was protecting her again, keeping her hidden from whoever had come to call.

"Elder Bern. Miss Cloverfield. I wasn't expecting you," Thorburn said in a voice loud enough to carry throughout the house. "Come in, come in."

Arthur tried to smile to reassure Gretchen. She'd stopped eating and held still as a frightened deer. He understood how she felt—and shared the sentiment. His knees trembled inside his trouser legs.

Today of all days, why did Elder Bern have to show up with Birna Cloverfield?

Arthur knew what would be expected of him. It was all part of the traditional betrothal process. The elders spent the month of May debating possible matches. In the weeks after the summer solstice, prospective couples were formally introduced and allowed to spend a few hours getting acquainted. Afterwards, an elder interviewed the young Bearfolk and decided if they were truly compatible. If all went as planned, contracts were signed. It was serious business. Bearfolk couples stayed together for life—for better or worse.

"Arthur?" Papa shouted up the stairs. "Come down, lad. We have important company."

"One minute, Papa," Arthur replied. His pulse sped as he moved close to Gretchen—for more reasons than one. His attraction to her affected his heart rate, but so did his dread of never seeing her again. "I might be gone for a while," he whispered. "But promise me you won't leave. I want to escort you to your ship. If I don't see you fly off, how will I ever know for certain you made it there—and weren't snatched by some faerie beast on the way?"

"Nice of you to offer, but I think I should sneak out now. For both of our sakes. What if that elder guy finds out you're hiding a human? Or worse: he finds out you're hiding the mighty Silverhair who won the war?"

"Get into the wardrobe if it makes you feel better." In spite of the dire situation, his heart lightened a little as he remembered their first encounter. It seemed almost comedic in hindsight, how he'd locked her in his wardrobe and hidden her from his parents.

"Arthur!" Papa shouted again. "Now, son!"

"Coming!" He implored her with a look. "Gretchen? Promise you'll stay?"

"All right. But I'm not waiting very long, I'll tell you that."

He pointed to the clean clothes on the end of the bed. "You could change while I'm gone."

"Nice way of telling me I stink," Gretchen said wryly.

Her faint smile made him fall in love with her all over again. He basked in it like it was the first spring sunshine after a hard winter. He didn't care that she wore more filth than fabric and smelled like an ill-kept barn; if he could have done anything at that moment with impunity, anything in the world, he would have kissed her.

She pointed to the door. "Stop staring and go, would you?"

He summoned all the courage he could and went to face the callers.

Chapter Twenty-Six

The door clicked shut. Gretchen set the breakfast tray aside. Her usual appetite wasn't there this morning. A funny fluttering had taken over her stomach instead. And it seemed to be Arthur's fault.

The way he'd been looking at her just before he'd left the room. It had done something to her, sparked something. There had been a moment when she'd thought he was going to kiss her, and she'd kind of wanted him to.

A sweet and awful pang of longing squeezed her heart. She'd had a crush on the guy who sat in front of her in chemistry lab last fall—but this was a hundred times more intense. This was serious trouble.

Or it could have been, if Arthur had been human and she'd been staying in Britannia. Unfortunately—or maybe fortunately—neither of those things was going to happen.

Agitated and a little annoyed at her unruly emotions, she got up and changed into Arthur's old clothes. Great. They smelled like him. Just what she didn't need.

She took a comb from the dresser and attacked her hair.

She braided it tightly into one plait. She'd lost her hair bands, so she opened a drawer to look for something to secure the braid. Among mismatched loose buttons and straight pins, she found a scrap of ribbon. And a small sketch of a bear, childish and smudged, and signed with the letter A.

Feeling just a little guilty, she slipped the picture into her pocket.

Convivial, manly laughter drifted upstairs. The Bearfolk men seemed to be having a great time. Arthur had mentioned some betrothal thing they did, and the elder *had* brought a girl to the cottage, so… Yeah, she needed to get out of the way if marriage-arranging was going on. Promise or no promise.

It would be better this way. No awkward parting scene. No silly farewell speeches. A clean break and a new beginning for them all.

She eyed the window. It would be a squeeze, but she could fit through. When she opened the casement, she was glad to see thick vines clinging to the stone wall below. They'd do for a ladder, she hoped.

"Goodbye, Bearfolk," she said as she swung her legs over the windowsill.

Elder Bern was a stout, neatly dressed Bear-fellow with an impressive chest-length brownish-black beard. The deep crinkles around his eyes hinted that he was at least two hundred years old. His acorn brown eyes appraised Arthur as he held out his hand in greeting.

"Good day to you, Arthur," Bern said. He stepped to the side and made a sweeping gesture toward a pretty, brown-haired girl in a yellow dress. "You remember my niece, Birna Cloverfield, from a few youth outings, no doubt?"

"Yes," Arthur said. "Welcome."

Birna looked him up and down just as her uncle had, but with a sweeter smile. He remembered her all right, and not only because she had kind eyes and plump pink cheeks. He remembered her because she'd knocked his front tooth out when they were six and put an earthworm in his pie when they were ten. Her demure smile wouldn't fool him into thinking she was one hundred percent innocent.

"The elders think you two would be a good match," Papa said. "I'm inclined to agree."

"Well, let's not get ahead of ourselves, Thorburn," Elder Bern said. "There is a protocol to be followed. Where is your good wife, by the way?"

Thorburn reddened and stuttered. Arthur offered, "Mama is in the north right now." It was true, even if not entirely illuminating. The elders would hear the whole tale soon enough, and if Papa wasn't ready to speak of Mama's death, what was the harm in putting it off for a few days? When the news came, Mama would probably be named a hero for dying in the final battle of the Bearfolk's long war—something that could only elevate their family name and make Arthur even more desirable in the betrothal game.

"She'd regret missing this occasion," Papa managed to say. "But we must proceed, regardless."

"Of course. Before the traditional courtship walk, I must ask you, Thorburn, as required by our statutes, is your son, Arthur, well-versed in our Bearfolk ways and prepared to be a law-abiding husband to one wife for all his days to come?"

"His mother and I have done our best to raise him to be so," Papa said.

"Good. I have here a signed document stating that Birna is also eligible for marriage at this time. So, shall we have a cup of tea while the young people take their stroll?"

"I'll make a fresh pot," Papa said. He wasted no time in crossing the room and putting the kettle on the fire.

The elder held up his right hand and addressed Birna and Arthur. "The blessings of the Great She-Bear Ursa and all the Bearfolk, past, present, and future, be upon you both. May these hours bring clarity and peace to you, Arthur and Birna, and may your match be confirmed." When neither of them moved, Bern added, "Go on. Take your walk. Outside with you."

Arthur followed Birna through the door. He thought he heard hoof beats in the distance, but that wasn't likely. Perhaps it was one of the many faerie birds with mimicry skills.

"Sorry about your tooth," Birna said, stopping at the end of the garden path and turning to face Arthur.

"And the earthworm pie?"

"Not so much," she said with a laugh.

"As I suspected. It wasn't the worst thing I ever ate, anyway." Arthur pointed left. "There's a pond this direction."

They walked to a bench at the water's edge and sat down. A few insects skittered over the surface of the water, and a single duck glided past.

"I'm not one for subtlety," Birna said, "so I'll speak plainly. I like you, Arthur. I always have. But I heard a disturbing rumor yesterday. My cousin told me you'd been seen with a human girl in the wood."

"It's true," Arthur said. "We were helping the girl find her sister, who had been lured here from the North American colony by Prince Barrett."

Birna cocked her head to the side. "You're red as a strawberry, Arthur. What aren't you telling me? Are you in love with her or something?"

Arthur stared at the duck. He couldn't lie and deny his feelings for Gretchen. It simply wasn't possible.

"I'll take that as a yes. Upon my word, Arthur! Surely you know better than that."

He nodded, keeping his gaze on the duck. "Knowing something in your head sometimes has no effect on your heart."

"But you sent her back to her colony, did you not?"

He met Birna's gaze and regretted it. The disappointment in her light brown eyes made him feel like the worst scoundrel in history. He looked back at the pond and said, "Not yet. She was preparing to leave when you and Elder Bern arrived."

"She's in your house? This is madness. You could be shunned, Arthur. Thrown out of the tribe forever."

"I know. I know. It was a matter of honor, to begin with. She was lost and it was the solstice and—"

Birna raised a hand to stop him. "Look, I don't want to talk about this anymore. It's crude and demeaning. I believe you when you say you were trying to be honorable. You've been honorable your whole life, and that's one of the reasons I've wanted to marry you since the day I knocked the tooth out of your head."

He hadn't imagined he could feel worse, but now he did. Another stone of guilt weighed down his already heavy heart. "Birna, I don't deserve—"

"No, you probably don't. But we're going back into your parents' kitchen and we're going to ask Uncle Bern to put us on the list of fall betrothals. Because that, Arthur, is the honorable and right thing for us to do. We're Bearfolk, and this is how we live our lives: keeping our religious traditions and obeying our laws, and finding joy in the company of our own kind."

"You're right," Arthur said. Gretchen was leaving, and he had to move on. Logic told him it would be silly to pine over her and cast aside the good future he could have with his tribe and a devoted Bear-wife. "I never wanted anything but a good Bearfolk life until… Well, I suppose I forgot what it meant to me. What it still means to me."

He slid off the bench and knelt before Birna. If he was going to be betrothed, he'd do it properly, in the customary way. So, although his heart fervently forbade it, he obeyed his sense of duty and spoke the words his forefathers had spoken to their future brides. "Birna, will you do me the great honor of becoming my betrothed? Will you marry me at the Yuletide, when the winds of winter blow? Will you share my home and hearth through every season until our earthly days are done?"

"I will, Arthur," she replied.

"Thank you," he said, feeling split in two. Part of him was relieved to be back on the path of righteousness, and part of him felt like a fish that had purposefully thrown itself onto a riverbank, knowing it would soon perish for lack of oxygen.

Birna took his hand and held it tightly, a move both territorial and tender. "You can thank me by sending the girl back to her kind immediately, and then writing me romantic letters every day until we wed."

Hand in hand, they walked toward the cottage. Birna chattered about wedding clothes and new cottages. Arthur pretended to listen.

How long would it be, he wondered, before he stopped wishing the hand holding his was Gretchen's and not this Bear-girl's?

Remembering Gretchen's statement that she'd only wait a little while for his return, he increased his pace, tugging Birna along. She laughed as if it were the best day of her life. Arthur prayed she wouldn't look back in a year or two and consider it the day she made a terrible mistake by trusting him.

As they entered the kitchen, an idea struck Arthur like a bolt of lightning, numbing him from top to toe.

Chapter Twenty-Seven

Yarrow whinnied and slowed as the airskipper came into view. Gretchen sighed with relief and patted the horse's neck. "Good boy, Yarrow."

Millicent flew off her left shoulder and darted around the ship a few times as if eager for some exercise. Gretchen's sore thighs and backside were also ready for a change of position. She shifted a little in the saddle and took stock of her surroundings, wanting to make sure she wasn't about to dismount into a nest of pixies or worse.

A few vines spiraled up the ship's landing gear and spread around its sides, as if the faerie forest had adopted it as part of its ever-shifting landscape. A fat yellow bird peered down at Gretchen from the twiggy nest it had built on the airskipper's wing. A clump of silver-speckled mushrooms grew atop the cockpit dome. She'd have to do some cleaning up before she could leave—which would be fitting practice for resuming life with Stepmother. Ugh.

Hard to believe it had been less than a week since she'd landed the ship in Britannia. Faerie stuff worked fast, she thought. But that was a lesson she'd already learned. She'd seen what faerie influence had quickly done to Ruby. She'd felt the effects of the hedge pixies' magic and seen a seven-course meal appear in an instant. Arthur could change from a bear to a young man in a matter of minutes.

Arthur had captured her heart with one look.

Was faerie magic to blame for that? Did the enchanted island want humans to stay so badly that it pulled whatever tricks it could to keep them there? Or were her feelings genuine? She'd soon find out, once she got the airskipper off the ground. If she was lucky, her longing for Arthur would evaporate like faerie dewdrops as she flew away, and she'd forget everything about him she now missed: his eager kindness, his dark eyes, the way his voice sounded as he whispered to her in the woods.

She jumped from Yarrow's back to the mossy ground. The horse stared at her as if he were waiting for something. She didn't have any oats or hay to offer him, so she stroked his black and white nose and said, "Thanks again. Sorry I can't pay you back somehow. You can go home now, wherever that is."

Yarrow nodded his head and then trotted away, and finally, Gretchen was alone. Unless you counted the bird that was about to be evicted and whatever creatures watched her from the trees.

She started yanking the vines off the hull. They were stubborn, clinging to the ship with the tiny tendrils they'd sunk into every available nook and cranny. As she worked, misgivings multiplied in her mind. How could any of this end well for her and her father? All she could imagine was more heartache and death.

Before she'd left to find Ruby, she'd considered begging Stepmother to allow her to take an apprenticeship on one of Colony Three's farms in Old Georgia. Their food growing programs were expanding, and they needed young people. If she headed there now, maybe she could change her name, forge some new I.D., and have her father kidnapped and brought to live with her. Happily ever after, right?

Except Stepmother would certainly find them. She had connections everywhere, and a way of making sure people owed her whatever favor she might demand.

Gretchen stood on tiptoe and lifted the melon-sized nest off the airskipper's wing. "Sorry, Mrs. Bird," she said. She promptly relocated the nest to the branches of a nearby ash tree, but the distressed bird flew off squawking, leaving a trail of feathers and glitter.

Finally, Gretchen climbed up and scraped the mushrooms off the cockpit dome. Her heart pounded in anticipation as she pressed the button to open the dome. She was really doing it. She was going home.

Without Ruby.

To face whatever she'd have to face.

Millicent hovered before her at eye level. "I'm going to miss you, bug," Gretchen said. "Or are you coming along? There are plenty of nice moths in North America. You could make new friends."

The moth hummed sadly in reply. She brushed her wings against Gretchen's cheek and then zipped into the forest and out of sight.

"All right," Gretchen said with resignation. She hopped into the seat and punched a code into the screen. "Time to power up. I hope."

The engine sputtered and then settled into its usual hum. She didn't know whether to laugh or cry, and couldn't waste time on either. There was no predicting faerie magic, after all. It chose now to let her go—but if she lingered five more minutes, it might reconsider its generosity.

She activated the take-off sequence and fastened her safety harness.

"Arthur? Are you ill, lad?" Papa asked. "Answer the question."

"What was the question?" Arthur released Birna's hand and rubbed his forehead. Ever since the idea had come to him, he'd been dissecting it in his mind. He'd lost track of the conversation after Elder Bern and Papa had welcomed them back from the courtship walk. He'd lost track of time and place, and had even forgotten whose hand he was holding. The idea was so big, so extraordinary…

"Do you find the match acceptable, youngster?" Elder Bern asked. "I would have assumed the answer to be yes, since you returned hand in hand with my niece, but your pallor and distractedness do cause me concern."

"Arthur proposed, Uncle," Birna said with undisguised joy. "And I accepted. Perhaps he needs a drink? The day is rather warm."

Arthur nodded. He did need a drink. He might need strong medicine. To consider what he was considering was nothing short of stark raving madness.

No, he wasn't even considering it anymore. He'd decided. He was going to do it. It might cost him his life, but he was going to do it. Gretchen was worth it. He loved her enough to accept whatever consequences might fall upon him as a result.

He was going to give her his magical pelt.

The room swayed. Sick excitement made it hard for him to breathe. Birna pressed a pen into his hand and directed him to the document on the table. "Sign this while I fix you some water with honey and mint. Grandpa always gives me a dose when I'm feeling off-kilter."

The words on the paper blurred together. He scrawled his name above hers without considering what it might mean.

"I'm sorry," he said. "I need to go to my room now."

"By Ursa, he is ill," Elder Bern said. "Yes. You'd best take to your bed before you faint. The paperwork is in order. Nothing to keep you here now if you're feeling unwell."

Arthur crossed the kitchen and stepped into the parlor on jittery legs.

"Write to me soon," Birna called after him.

"I will," Arthur replied as he rushed up the steps.

He hurried into his bedroom and took out the pelt he'd put away hours before. Clutching it against his chest, he ran into his parents' room to tell Gretchen his plan.

His stomach dropped when he saw the empty bed. She was gone. The wide open window provided evidence of her mode of escape.

He had no time to waste. He had to catch her before she left Britannia. He grabbed one of Mama's old satchels and stuffed his pelt into it, slung the bag over his shoulder, and then squeezed out the window. He half-climbed, half-tumbled down the ivy-sided cottage and ran to the stable. Lucky for him, Elder Bern and Birna had ridden a pair of Marendall horses that day. There would be no wrong turns on the way to Gretchen's ship—if her ship was still to be found on the soil of Britannia.

He mounted the black horse. "To the human girl and her ship, please," he said, hoping desperately that the horse's magic could get him to Gretchen easily and fast.

The Marendall neighed and sprang into action. Arthur clung to the reins as the horse's speed blurred the scenery around him. *This must be what it's like to fly,* he thought. The wind whipped his hair back and stung his eyes. It was exhilarating and terrifying and wonderful.

The horse vaulted over a stream and galloped up a hill, then slowed and stopped.

A strange whirring sound filled the air. Arthur rubbed

his eyes, and as they focused, he saw the sleek shape of Gretchen's airskipper.

He threw himself off the horse and stumbled toward the ship. "Stop! Wait!" he shouted. He climbed up the ladder built into the side of the airskipper and pounded on the cockpit dome. Inside, Gretchen flinched with surprise. And then she smiled.

His heart turned somersaults and he smiled back.

The glass slid open. "What are you doing here?" Gretchen asked.

"I brought you something. A gift." He shoved the satchel into her arms.

She peeked into the bag. "Fur?"

Out of breath, he struggled to speak. "A Bearfolk pelt. I remembered something. An old story. If it's true, a human can put on a Bearfolk pelt and use it to change their appearance."

"I don't understand. How would looking like a bear help me?"

"You can choose what to look like. You can go home disguised as Ruby. Your stepmother won't be angry then, and your father will be safe. As long as you wear the pelt, no one will know you're not Ruby. I mean, if it works. It's an old story, and—"

The console beeped loudly, and a crackly voice spilled out. "Message for Gretchen Werner from Ivory Werner: You have twelve hours to return to Colony Two. Your father will not survive beyond that time, poor soul."

Gretchen's face paled. "Stepmother. Look, Arthur, I have to go."

"Wrap it around yourself and ask the magic to make you look like Ruby. Kneel down and think of nothing else, just give in. It will hurt. A lot, probably. And if it's like when I Change, you'll have to shift back within seventeen or eighteen hours and then sleep for a while before Changing again."

She reached up and touched his hand where it clung to

the edge of the cockpit. "Thank you. You've been the best friend I've ever had, even if this doesn't work. I'll miss you, Arthur."

He turned his hand and caught her fingers in his. Holding Gretchen's hand was nothing like holding Birna's. When he'd held Birna's hand, it felt safe. Holding Gretchen's hand was like touching some new and dangerous magic. Every nerve in his skin sparked to life and broadcast happiness throughout his body and soul.

Their eyes met, and he never wanted to move again.

He wanted to tell her he loved her. He wanted to say, "This isn't just any fur, it's my own pelt. It's all that I am. All that I have always loved—until I met you. And it is yours." Instead, he simply leaned down and kissed her fingertips.

"I have to go," she said, slipping her hand out of his grip and pressing a button. "Good bye, Arthur."

"I'll miss you, too," he said as the engine's droning grew to a roar. "Good luck."

He tried to memorize her face as the glass dome began to close. Was that a tear in the corner of her eye, sitting there like a rare and perfect jewel?

He jumped to the ground and joined the waiting horse a safe distance from the slowly ascending ship. He laid one hand against the horse's neck, feeling its steady pulse. "Thank you," he said to the horse and to the universe.

The ship cleared the treetops and darted into the clouds.

The realization of what he'd done fell on him like a blazing meteor. He'd given away his sacred pelt, and with it, his ability to Change.

Was he still Bearfolk, now that he'd never be a bear again?

He shook, and couldn't stop shaking. He climbed onto the horse and whispered, "Home."

And as he rode, he wept.

Chapter Twenty-Eight

The airskipper settled onto the neatly mowed grass beyond Stepmother's flower gardens in Earth Colony Two. Fireflies flashed near the ground and in the pine trees at the edge of the property, welcoming the slowly rising moon. The cockpit dome slid open with a whoosh, and Gretchen inhaled the humid summer evening air.

She'd debated with herself the whole way home. Should she really use Arthur's gift and pretend to be her dead step-sister to save her father? Would she be able to live a lie until Stepmother was no longer a threat—possibly decades? Did she have another choice?

Now, seeing the colony's dome-shaped buildings in the distance and knowing Father waited inside one of them, she knew what she had to do. She still didn't believe she was the Silverhair of Bearfolk legend, but she could be a hero for her father. She grabbed the bag containing the pelt and climbed down from the cockpit. She ran for the woods beyond the patch of lawn.

There were no security cameras in this little section of

the parklands, thank goodness. She could change into Ruby without being observed.

In the cover of the trees, she sat on the mossy earth and pulled out the fur. It was heavy and thick and seemed too large for the bag she'd removed it from. It warmed in her hands as if in response to her touch, sending tingles through her fingers. A familiar scent rose from the fur: musk and pine and boy.

Arthur's scent.

Her chest ached as she realized what he'd done. He'd given her his own pelt, not just some spare magical hunk of fur he'd found in a closet. This was what he used to take bear form, what clothed him when he celebrated special days with his kin. This was part of who he was, like his voice or his heartbeat, and she'd taken it from him with only the briefest of thanks.

Had he given up being a bear forever for her sake? Heaven above, she hoped not.

Maybe she could return it eventually, just in case he needed it. But first, she had to save her father. She'd have to put the pelt on and let it do its work. Arthur had said it would hurt, and she was no fan of pain. Fear drove her pulse into a frenzy and dried her mouth. She wrapped the fur around her body like a hooded cape, and whispered to its magic.

"Please make me look like Ruby," she said, "and be gentle with me."

She closed her eyes and waited.

The bear hide hugged her, first conforming to her shape and then tightening and compressing. The pain built slowly, like boiling grains of sand penetrating her skin one by one and then twenty, thirty, a hundred at a time, searing and burning, melting her into something she was not. Her bones shifted and reset with horrible crunching sounds; her features transformed like clay mangled and molded by an angry artist. She was all pain, head to toe, inside and out. She wished for death and cried lava tears.

And then it was over.

She lay naked in the moonlight, curled up like a baby, moaning softly. She opened her eyes. Sitting up, she noticed her new, smaller feet and daintier toes. Her legs were curved differently. Her belly was flat and her navel scarred from when Ruby had tried to pierce it. On her forearm was Ruby's butterfly-shaped birthmark. Ruby's black hair spilled over her shoulders in bountiful waves.

Dang, this was weird. And a little chilly. What was left of her clothes lay shredded underneath her. She'd have to make a run for the airskipper and get the emergency warming blanket from the first aid kit to wear like a sarong until she found real clothes. If she was very, very lucky, she could sneak in the back door of the house and down into the laundry room without being seen. If she was unlucky… Well, she'd have to come up with a story. "The faeries took all my clothes," maybe.

She might as well get used to making up stories. She was going to have to explain quite a few things soon: how she'd gotten free of the fae, what had happened to Gretchen, why there would never be an alliance with Prince Barrett's people…

A mosquito bit her shoulder and another nipped her lower back. Yep. Time for clothes. She stood, counted to three, and streaked toward the airskipper.

Arthur rolled over in bed again. He yanked the blanket up to his neck and stared at the wall. He'd been awake all night, alternately proud of his sacrifice and sick about what he'd done. Chasing after Gretchen and giving her his pelt seemed like a dream and shocking, stark reality at the same time.

Dawn would come soon, and with it, his time of reckoning. How in the world would he tell his grieving papa what he'd done? How would he tell Birna?

There would be no dancing around the truth. He'd have to come right out and say, "I gave my sacred pelt away, and I'll never be able to Change again." He couldn't even claim he was sorry, for that would be a lie. He wasn't at all sorry he'd helped Gretchen. He wished he could have done more for her. He loved her, and he wasn't going to stop.

He heaved himself over onto his back and examined the shadowy ceiling. It wouldn't be fair for him to marry when his heart would never be in it. If he ended his betrothal to Birna before news of it spread through the tribe, perhaps he could spare her some embarrassment. She'd still have time to be matched to another before fall.

He threw off his covers and grabbed a pencil and paper from his bedside table. The letter he would write would not be one of the romantic messages Birna had requested, but neither would he break off their engagement with a few cowardly strokes of his pencil. She deserved better than that. The mistake was his, not hers.

Dear Birna, he wrote, *please meet me at Drover's Bridge tomorrow evening. We need to talk.*

Chapter Twenty-Nine

27 June, 170 N.E.

Dressed in Ruby's favorite pink-and-yellow-striped trousers and a crisp white blouse, Gretchen knocked on the door of Stepmother's home office at precisely eight o'clock in the morning. By her estimation, she'd arrived in plenty of time to satisfy Stepmother's ultimatum to return Ruby and save Father's life.

"Yes?" Stepmother responded, conveying great irritation in that single word.

Gretchen straightened her spine and gathered her courage. She'd never been much of an actress, but here she was, playing a role she had to nail. "Mommy? I'm home," she said, like Ruby would have. Hearing her stepsister's voice come out of her mouth was unsettling and strange.

The automated door swished open and revealed Stepmother standing behind her huge, white desk. Her tailored red business suit hugged her trim figure, and her dark brown, bobbed hair waved in all the right places. Grinning with scarlet-painted lips, she held out her arms. "Darling! Come and kiss me! Your inept stepsister certainly took her time in bringing you home. I was starting to worry about you, pet."

Grimacing on the inside but smiling sweetly on the outside, Gretchen walked into Stepmother's perfumed embrace. Stepmother kissed both her cheeks before holding her at arms' length and looking her over. "Your hair needs trimming. And you've gained a pound or two, haven't you? Well, we'll have it off again in no time. Tell Cook you're fasting until tomorrow night, and remind her that Mrs. Graham is coming for tea at four. I'm sorry, pet. Gretchen ought to be doing the messaging, not you. You need your rest. It must have been quite an ordeal spending time in the wild with those savage faerie people. You must tell me simply everything. Come back at two. I'll squeeze you in before my workout with Hugo."

"Two," Gretchen said, more than a little bewildered by Stepmother's reaction to Ruby's return. She'd expected a lot of happy tears and detailed questions, not comments on her weight and a teeny slot in the appointment schedule.

"On your way out, be a dear and ask Inga to get Gretchen in here as soon as possible. That girl can't afford to sleep late. It will take her days to catch up on her work, and I have a new project for her to oversee."

"About Gretchen," Gretchen said slowly. "She didn't come back."

Stepmother plopped in her chair and rolled her eyes. "You have got to be kidding me. Of all the irresponsible, selfish tricks! Found a faerie boyfriend of her own, did she? I should have expected it. She's always lacked judgment and sense. Good grief. It will take me a month to train a replacement."

"It wasn't like that. She—"

Stepmother held up a hand. "Stop. Save it for the appointment, pet. I'm too busy to hear Gretchen's tale of woe at the moment."

"I'll go, then," Gretchen said. She felt like a small child who'd just been shoved and kicked and called every bad name possible. On her birthday.

"Good. And no snacking, Ruby. You're already far too puffy." She gestured for her daughter to leave and returned her attention to her work-screen.

"One quick question before I leave, Mommy," Gretchen said, dread chilling her blood. If Stepmother had done anything to hurt Father, or if Father was dead, the Ruby charade was going to end abruptly and spectacularly. "Um, Gretchen asked me to look after her father. Is he—all right?"

"Go and visit the old fool if you like," Stepmother said. "He's locked in his suite, as usual. Now, I have calls to make, so scurry along."

Outside Stepmother's office, Gretchen shed tears of relief. If Father was okay, she would be, too. She took off toward his suite, Ruby's wedge heels clobbering the shiny floor as she ran.

Birna stomped her foot on the stone bridge like a child having a tantrum. A blue salamander scurried away in terror and a pair of sparrows took to the sky.

"No, Arthur. This is unacceptable," she said. "We are going to be married. We'll just have to find you another pelt. Or get yours back."

Arthur gripped the waist-high edge of the bridge with both hands. He'd thought Birna would cry or hit him when he broke off their betrothal. Instead, she seemed determined to find a way to go forward with the wedding plans. He shook his head and said, "I checked the *Annals of the Bearfolk* and all the lore books. Once a pelt is given away, its magic will never return to its original owner. And you know full well I can't just get another pelt. You're born with one, and if it's lost or damaged or given away, you're done Changing."

She paced the width of the bridge, nibbling her fingernails. "I have an idea," she said. "There's a wise woman, a Bearfolk witch, living up in the old Scottish highlands. Perhaps she can help. We could go there now, together, and seek her counsel. I reckon she could marry us, too. My grandparents eloped like that. The elders didn't like it, but they allowed it. And didn't Audley and Ebba Ashwood—"

"Birna." Arthur turned to face her. He laid his hands on her shoulders and said softly, "Please stop. If anyone's going away, it will be me. Alone."

She swiped his hands off and glared at him like an irate bramble pixie. Arthur took a wary step backward.

"Just say it, Arthur. Say it out loud. Tell me you still love the human girl. Tell me you ruined your life on purpose for her and that you'll never love anyone else and all that drivel. And I will tell you something: I was wrong about you. You don't possess a stitch of honor. You don't deserve to be Bearfolk. And you definitely don't deserve to marry me." She rushed off the bridge and mounted her waiting Marendall horse.

Arthur ran after her. "Please, Birna," he said. "Forgive me. You'll be happier with someone else."

"You're wrong about a lot of things, Arthur Woodley, but especially me. You know nothing about me—and nothing about what would make me happy." She pressed her heels against the horse's sides and sped away, leaving a cloud of gray dust behind her.

He stood still, choking on the dust. For all her bitter words, he knew he'd broken her heart. For that, he was sorry. He knew all too well what losing someone you loved felt like.

Papa stepped out of the shadows. His expression was grim, as it had been habitually since Mama's death. He shook his head woefully and said, "Ah, lad. You've made a grand mess of things."

"How long were you—?"

"Long enough to hear you've given up your pelt and your betrothal. I won't bother lecturing you, as it's too late for it to make any difference. You'd best hurry home and gather some clothes and food, and I'll take you to your great uncle's old place west of here in the Deepwood. You don't want to be easily found when Birna's family hears the news. Her brothers could make a full-grown giant run home to his mama."

"Will you shun me, too? Do you hate me, Papa?"

With tears in his eyes, Papa gripped Arthur's shoulders with his big hands. "I could never hate you. You're my sun and moon, lad. If you love Gretchen, well, I can't lie and say I'm happy about it. It's cost you so much, and can't come to a good end. You've given away your pelt, but you're still faerie-blooded. You can't live away from Britannia's magic for long. A few days, at best. And the girl—well, what kind of life would she have were she to settle here? Always hunted by some creature with a fondness for human blood, always in danger of being kidnapped. No, lad. I don't see much hope for you as a couple."

Papa gave Arthur's shoulders a squeeze before letting go. "Run along home. I'll catch up shortly. We'll talk later, after you're settled in the Deepwood. Why, I might join you there myself, after a time. The cottage will be too big for me with your mother gone, and without you."

"I'd like that, Papa." Arthur kissed his father's bristly cheek and then headed to the cottage where he'd been raised, the place that would soon cease to be his home. So many feelings tumbled through him as he wove his way through the trees: relief that Papa still accepted him, remorse for hurting Birna, grief over the loss of Mama, and sorrow because she'd murdered Ruby, a bittersweet longing to see Gretchen again, soul-deep anguish at the loss of his pelt and tribe. But he kept moving, and he would keep moving. For, unlike Papa, he believed that someday everything would come to a good end, and that somehow, in spite of a hundred impossible-to-conquer obstacles, he and Gretchen would be together again, and happy.

Chapter Thirty

Gretchen's father's bathrobe-covered back was to the door as he gazed out on the sunlit gardens he'd lovingly tended before he'd fallen ill. His shoulders were more hunched and his hair looked thinner than Gretchen remembered. Had her father's health declined at an increased rate in the handful of days she'd been gone? A lump of sadness gathered behind her breastbone.

"Father," she said with Ruby's voice.

He turned his hover-chair and smiled. "Hello there, Ruby. You look pretty as a picture today."

Gretchen hurried to his side and hugged him. He smelled like lavender soap and mint toothpaste, as he always had, even aboard the orbiter—although the scents had been artificially made and fainter then.

"I've missed you," she said. She sat beside him on the old blue chair he used to favor and bit the inside of her cheek to keep from crying.

"You're welcome to stop by anytime, Ruby." He pointed to a plate of cookies. "Help yourself, dear."

Gretchen took a cookie and held it in her hand. It was

killing her, letting him think she was Ruby. She needed to tell him everything that had happened, from the airskipper trip over the ocean, to seeing the amazing flowers and trees of Britannia; from being poisoned by pixies to the tragedy of losing Ruby on the battlefield. But she could tell him none of it. If he was as easily befuddled as he'd been when she left, he might accidentally rat her out to Stepmother.

Father nibbled a cookie. Crumbs rained onto his robe and lap. He used to be so picky about keeping his clothes tidy, but now he seemed not to notice the mess he made. "Tell me. Have you seen my Gretchen lately?"

"She's fine," Gretchen said. No way would she distress him by saying Gretchen was dead. Heavens, she hoped Stepmother wouldn't tell him that, either. He was so frail; such a shock might kill him.

"She promised to take me out to the gardens. The yellow roses are blooming, you know. My favorites. I can just make them out from here, to the left of the gazebo." He pointed a skinny, wobbly finger toward the window.

"I have to go to work in a few minutes, but I can take you this afternoon," Gretchen said. "If you're feeling up to it." She wasn't looking forward to spending the day shut up in the government offices drawing uniforms, but if she was going to pass as Ruby, she had no choice but to put in a few hours at Ruby's desk.

"Good. You come back then. I think I'll call my nurse and have her help me into bed for a little nap. I never sleep well at night, you know. I hear things. Voices. Songs, sometimes. Do you think the faerie folk have invaded the colony?"

"No, I don't. I think your medicine plays with your imagination."

"You never know. They're wily, the faeries. Tricky as anything."

"I know, Father," Gretchen said, wishing she could tell

him how very right he was. She stood and kissed the top of his wispy white hair. "Sweet dreams. I'll be back later."

"Au revoir, little Ruby. If you see Gretchen, give her my love."

How was she going to be able to stand this? It was torture. She swallowed back a sob and said, "I promise I will."

The automatic door whooshed shut behind her. Not for the first time, she wondered why neither treatment nor cure had been found for Father's illness. With all the advances in brain science and genetics and medicine, and with Stepmother's connections, it didn't make sense.

What did make sense, unfortunately, was the idea that Stepmother had caused him to be sick in order to keep him subdued. She had his influential name and his fortune. Did she really need his opinions, or his presence at meetings and parties where she flirted and connived her way into deals both political and financial?

"Ruby" was going to start keeping a close watch on Gretchen's ailing father. Since Ruby was rarely concerned with anything other than clothes, shoes, and boys, no one would suspect her of looking for evidence of treachery.

Her wrist comm chimed to alert her that she—Ruby— was due at work in ten minutes. Darn it all, she was going to change out of the too-high, wedge-heeled shoes before leaving for the office. She was willing to do a lot to impersonate her stepsister, but she was drawing the line at wearing uncomfortable footwear. She'd start a new trend today, as the real Ruby was wont to do. By noon, flat shoes would be officially "in." The six employees of the colony's shoe manufacturing company had no clue what was about to hit them.

The cabin in the Deepwood wasn't so bad—once Arthur evicted the mice and the brood of plate-sized, golden web-spinning spiders, and swept out a decade's worth of dust and droppings. He threw open the shutters to let the place breathe.

He let himself breathe. It felt like he'd been holding his breath ever since he'd figured out Mama was leading them to the battlefield. Now, as his lungs filled, he acknowledged the emptiness inside him. And he cherished it like a holy relic, for it was evidence that Gretchen was real, and that he'd loved her.

He wasn't going to cry again. Ursa above, how could he still have tears left after the gallons he'd shed since Gretchen left? He took his sketchbook and pencil out of one of his bags and headed outside. The rest of the cleaning could wait. He had all the time in the world. Truly, he didn't even have to clean if he didn't want to, at least not until Papa came to visit. The spiders, who were trying to sneak back through the open window, weren't going to complain about the dust.

Outside the cabin, he found a chair built from stones, an heirloom from a relative he'd never known. He brushed a few dead leaves off the seat and then tried it out. It was more comfortable than it appeared, but not somewhere he could sit all day. Some things were like that; fine for a brief time, but no longer.

He started to sketch without thinking, allowing the pencil to slide across the page where it might. An image from his childhood took shape on the page, a Yuletide dance attended by bright-eyed Bearfolk wearing crowns of ivy. They capered and spun on the paper, sharp teeth glinting in bear grins.

Something landed on his shoulder, light as a whisper. He lifted a hand to brush it off, but stopped as he recognized the humming of its small wings.

"Millicent," he said fondly. "I didn't expect to see you again."

She remained on his shoulder as he filled page after page, a silent yet welcome companion. Hours passed, and the birds and insects changed their songs as dusk fell over the wood.

"I hope you'll stay," Arthur said to the moth as he walked back to the cabin and she hovered overhead. She dipped down and rose up as if drawing a nod with her body. "Good. Welcome to our new home, then. I hope you don't mind a bit of dust, and a spider or two."

He stepped inside and set his sketchbook on the table. The last picture he'd drawn before his exile stared up at him: Gretchen's face wearing the expression she'd worn when they'd parted. A look that was wistful and questioning and altogether beautiful. Millicent perched on the paper's edge and seemed to examine it with her black eyes.

"I miss her, too," he said, voice cracking. "But at least we have each other, you and me."

CHAPTER THIRTY-ONE

The old-fashioned mantel clock in Stepmother's office had bonged twice ages ago. Pretty as it was, Gretchen hated that clock. Stepmother had commissioned it from the colony's artisans as a gift to herself when she'd won her last election. Obviously, it served as a decorative piece only, because esteemed parliament member Ivory Werner was late for the two o'clock appointment she'd made with Gretchen-disguised-as-Ruby. Apparently, even favored daughter Ruby wasn't exempt from the woman's arrogant rudeness.

Gretchen sank into a leather chair and fidgeted with the center front button of Ruby's pristine white blouse. While most people in the colony wore uniforms, those in certain jobs were permitted to wear whatever they wished. Ruby had secured that honor by working in the government's design department—and by being political superstar Ivory Werner's flesh and blood. At least Ruby's outfits weren't as itchy and annoying as the special coveralls Gretchen had been forced to wear on her jaunt to Britannia.

A tiny whiff of Ruby's signature scent wafted up from

the blouse. Gretchen gripped the chair's armrests as if to hold herself in place as a wave of grief swept over her. This wasn't the time or place for losing control of her emotions. All her energy needed to go to imitating Ruby with flawless accuracy.

The clock bonged again, declaring that two-thirty had arrived.

Finally, like an incoming storm dressed in scarlet silk business attire, Stepmother flew into the room. She spoke loudly to someone over her comm as she tossed her handbag onto the desk and flashed Gretchen a "wait one minute" finger.

Gretchen tapped her foot nervously a few times and then checked herself. Ruby was a nail-biter, not a toe-tapper. How many little mistakes could she make before someone accused her of not being the real Ruby? Then again, why would anyone expect someone who looked one hundred percent like Ruby to be anyone else?

"So, you're back," Stepmother said as she sat down behind the desk. "Did Prince Barrett agree to our terms? Please tell me you got it in writing. A contract signed in blood, as their barbaric faerie custom requires?"

"No," Gretchen said. "I'm sorry. There was a war and a lot of confusion. The prince got angry and sent me away. I was lucky to escape with my life, Mommy. If Gretchen hadn't—"

Stepmother swore. "I gave you one job, Ruby. One little job. All you had to do was get him to agree to the alliance. He was so smitten with you. Unless you're even dumber than I imagined, I cannot fathom how you could have made a mess of things."

Gretchen felt her face heat as anger surged through her. Good thing Ruby had a penchant for fits of temper, because one was about to happen on her behalf. "He's a faerie prince, that's how things got messy. Did you know he was going to use his magic on me and force me to marry him? Was that part of your grand plan?"

"Don't act like you weren't in love with him before you left the colony. You can't blame me for everything. Anyway, your faerie wedding must have been a spectacle. I don't suppose you captured any images on your comm."

"I hardly remember it, due to the faerie brainwashing that was going on," Gretchen said with a Ruby-appropriate yet genuine scowl.

"Good grief, you're as dramatic as ever. Well, what's done is done, thanks to your bumbling. My team will simply have to devise a different vote-winning strategy."

"Do you not even care what happened to Gretchen?"

"Since when do you care about common, ill-mannered Gretchen? She served her purpose and got you home. Need we have a parade in her honor? Honestly, Ruby, I think you have some sort of faerie magic hangover. You're behaving terribly. If anyone should be peevish, it's me. You knew how much I needed that alliance to help me become prime minister, and you let me down completely."

Gretchen stood, hands in tight fists at her sides, offended and angry for both herself and Ruby. She regretted her past jealousy of Ruby's relationship with Stepmother. At least Gretchen had been able to rely on the fact that Stepmother would always treat her like dirt. It must have been ten times worse for Ruby, not knowing from minute to minute whether the woman was going to shower her with gifts and affection or call her an idiot and smack her.

"Leaving already, pet? I thought we'd discuss some ideas for a dress I want you to make for me."

"I'm going back to work. Send them by comm." Gretchen turned her back on the woman and strode out of the room with her blood boiling. She didn't regret pretending to be Ruby to save Father, but she hadn't reckoned on the escalating emotional cost of living under Stepmother's thumb.

For a fleeting moment, she thought she caught Arthur's scent as she jogged down the stairs that led to the foyer. Maybe she had. It was his pelt molding her into Ruby's shape, his magic working in her cells. The idea, strangely, made her feel not quite so alone.

And made her miss him more than ever.

⁓

2 July, 170 N.E.

Outside the cabin door, Arthur found a wicker basket of blackberries and a brown jug filled with mint tea.

This was the third morning he'd found gifts on his doorstep. At first, he'd thought some friendly brownie had stopped by in the night and left the offerings of food and small necessities. Now, the strand of brown hair and a faint but familiar aroma clinging to the basket gave him a different, more disturbing idea.

He had a strong suspicion that the mysterious visitor was a Bear-girl called Birna.

He shouted her name and squinted toward the shadowy wood. Better to face her now and find out her intentions than to spend time wondering what game she was playing. Were the things she left tokens of forgiveness or presents from a Bear-girl still obsessed with marrying a peltless young man? Was the food laced with poison or meant to incite affection?

She did not answer his call.

Perhaps he'd catch her next time. If not, he'd leave her a note—although he hadn't the slightest idea what he should write to someone who might be mad or bent on revenge.

Millicent buzzed past him, beckoning him to follow her to the spring to wash up and fill his water bucket, according to their morning routine. He felt his pocket to make sure his knife was still there, and then trailed after the moth.

Ursa above, he hoped Papa would arrive soon. He'd feel safer in his father's company, and as much as he appreciated having Millicent around, she wasn't good at conversation. He needed someone to talk with about the weather, or fishing, or odd dreams, or *anything*—because he had to stop thinking about Gretchen all the time, or else he'd probably end up just as mad as he suspected Birna was.

Chapter Thirty-Two

27 July, 170 N.E.

It came as no shock to Gretchen when she was called into her boss's office exactly a month after she returned from Britannia. The enchanted bearskin made her look like Ruby, but it lent her none of Ruby's artistic flair. The vilest prison inmate didn't deserve to wear the abominations she'd designed.

Toby Alastair sat behind his desk looking like a handsome actor playing the role of a thirty-year-old government agency supervisor. His navy blue suit, neat blond hair, and dazzling white teeth were without fault. Gretchen understood why Ruby had been smitten with him before Barrett had gotten hold of her. He was one of those people whose presence made you weak in the knees whether you liked it or not—and he didn't even have faerie magic working for him.

"Hey, Rubes," he said, flashing a beguiling smile. "Sit. Tell me what's up. Did something happen to you while you were on leave? You hit your head, tried hallucinogenic mushrooms or something? Because, I mean, look at this." He slid one of

Gretchen's recent drawings across the desk. The messy, child-ish sketch of a security guard's uniform made her cringe. "My grandma could do better than this. Frankly, Rubes, I'm worried about you." His forehead creased appropriately, and his blue eyes locked onto hers.

"Um. Sorry. Yeah. I… Well, you know I was in Faerie Britannia. And I ate the faeries' food, so, yeah, maybe it warped my brain or something." Choosing Ruby-like words and phrases was still a chore, even after weeks of impersonating her. She forced her eyes to tear up by imagining dead puppies. "I'm really sorry, Toby. I'm trying, but it's so hard. Everything's so hard since I got back."

Toby stood and walked around the desk. He pulled Gretchen into his cologne-scented embrace and patted her back. "Aw, don't cry, Rubes. Look, I'll give you another week to get it together. If not, we'll just have to find you another position."

Gretchen stepped out of his arms and put on a grateful, syrupy smile. "Really, Toby? You're just the best."

He brushed a tear off her cheek with his fingertips. His touch made her shiver. Honestly, what was with this guy? Did he bathe in pheromones each morning?

Toby leaned back against the edge of the desk, crossed his arms over his chest, and made a managerial face. "One week, Rubes. It's business, nothing personal, you understand. I mean, I like you a lot, but I have a boss to answer to, too."

"I understand totally."

"Hey, by the way, I hear your mom's planning the party to end all parties. If you could score me an invite—or if you need a date…?"

Good heavens, she thought, *he's not asking me out, is he? No way am I falling into that trap. He's already dated and dumped almost every female between eighteen and thirty-five in the colony. Ruby's job isn't worth ending up on that sad list.* She blinked in a

Ruby-like fashion and said, "I'll see what I can do. So, I guess I should get back to work."

After a hasty goodbye, Gretchen scurried out of Toby's office. As she made her way back to the design studio, she wondered what sort of party Stepmother was planning—and then thanked her lucky stars that as Ruby, this time she wouldn't be put in charge of arranging the food, drinks, décor, staff, band, and who-knew-what-else.

Her wrist comm beeped as if on cue, requesting her presence in Stepmother's office as soon as possible. She had a very bad feeling that she was about to inherit Gretchen's job as Stepmother's event coordinator after all. As much as she disliked sitting in class all day, the idea of returning to school in September—as she would have if she'd kept her identity as Gretchen—was starting to seriously appeal to her.

Too bad she'd be stuck living Ruby's post-graduation life for the foreseeable future.

The knock on the door made Arthur fumble his pencil and startled Papa awake. A heavy black line marred Arthur's otherwise flawless drawing of a Marendall stallion prancing in a field of poppies. There'd be no erasing such a mistake.

"What was that?" Papa asked as he sat up straighter in his armchair beside the unlit fireplace.

The knock came again. Arthur stuck his pencil behind his ear and tucked his sketchbook under his arm as he crossed the room to investigate.

"Who's there?" he asked through the door, hoping the visitor wasn't Birna. In spite of several polite notes asking the Bear-girl to end her clandestine visits, she continued to leave gifts on the doorstep almost daily.

"It's Van Oakmoss," a deep voice replied. "Looking for Thorburn Woodley."

Arthur opened the door. Bearfolk were known for their height, but Van Oakmoss stood a foot taller than anyone Arthur had ever met. A farmer by trade, he wore a brown shirt with patched elbows and a pair of blue homespun trousers. A shock of white ran through the center of his long beard, but his brown eyes had a youthful glint.

"Come in, old friend," Thorburn said as he left the hearthside. "And tell us what brings you to the Deepwood. I didn't think anyone knew we were living here, truth be told."

Van stooped in order to pass through the doorway. "That's where you're wrong, Thorburn. I'm afraid there have been many rumors flitting about, tales of you and your lad, and even some of your wife. May I?" He pulled a chair out from the table and sat.

Arthur sat across from him, while Thorburn brought a stool from the corner and placed it beside Van. Anxiety chilled Arthur in spite of the stuffy August air inside the cabin. He wanted to know what the Bearfolk had been saying about him and his family—almost as much as he didn't want to know.

"I didn't come to gather gossip, mind," Van said, picking up a crumb from the tabletop and casting it to the floor. "Only out of concern, seeing as we've been friends since we were lads, Thorburn. And I swear I won't tell a soul we spoke, unless you ask me to. But it seemed to me you might need a friend, if half of what I've heard is true."

"Much appreciated," Thorburn said.

"I'll get you some cool water." Arthur got up and fetched a pitcher and cup. Unsteady with nervousness, he fumbled and almost dropped the cup on Van's shoulder.

"Where to begin," Van said as he took the cup from Arthur's shaky hand. "Well, first off, there's the story that your Lusela was the one who found the Silverhair and brought her into battle so the Bearfolk would win the war. 'Tis said she died there, your good wife, a noble death on the bloodstained ground, for the glory of our kind."

Thorburn scratched his beard thoughtfully. "There's truth and untruth in that tale," he said. "Lusela did die on the battlefield on the last day of the war. The rest... Well, I'm not certain about the girl being the Silverhair of legend. Lusela had her ideas, but I—"

"I'm inclined to think your wife was right," Van said with a faint smile. "There were witnesses. I've spoken to at least four who were there and saw the human girl on the field, her gold and silver hair shining as she commanded a Marendall stallion. Just the way my granny used to tell the tale."

"Well, then," Thorburn said. "You don't need my version of events, I reckon."

Van held his cup out so Arthur could refill it. "Do you know what became of the girl? Grimes Hollybush swears he saw you lead her off the field."

Thorburn nodded. "That I did. She was worn out and I felt it my duty to help her avoid being killed in a war that wasn't hers. But she's gone now. Went home to her kind, as far as I know."

"Ursa above! How I would have loved to see her, the Silverhair, in the flesh. I was hoping she'd be here with you. We wanted to have a feast in her honor and give her the old queens' crown, we did."

"She would have hated that," Arthur said under his breath as he sat down across from Papa. Gretchen had refused to believe in the legend, and Mama's belief in it had proven deadly.

Van leaned toward Arthur. "What did you say, lad?"

"Never mind him," Thorburn said, directing a cross look at Arthur. "He'd speak up if he had something important to say. What other news do you bring to the Deepwood?"

The big man drained his cup and set it aside. "I heard that your Arthur and wee Birna Cloverfield are on the betrothals roster for the fall. I'd congratulate you, but… Well, she's been acting strangely. She's always been odd, that one, but now she's taken to wandering off. Talking to herself. Pilfering stuff from her mother's pantry and spending entire nights out of doors. Her parents are at their wits' end, and the elders are thinking of declaring her insane and sending her to the madhouse up north." He looked at Arthur with sympathy. "I am sorry to tell you this, lad. A broken betrothal is a hard thing to endure, particularly if you care for the girl. But you're young, Arthur. Perhaps next fall…"

So Birna hadn't yet told her parents or the elders what he'd done. She'd protected his honor—but at what cost? Arthur's chair scraped the floor as he pushed back from the table. He wandered to the window with his chest aching. Had he driven Birna mad with his rejection, or was she already unwell before the betrothal? If he'd sent her over the edge, he regretted it deeply.

"Don't blame yourself, lad," Van said. "Her granny and aunt are both in the madhouse for life. Might be best you avoided being wed to her for the rest of your days."

"That's sad news indeed," Thorburn said. "Poor lass."

"Of course, there are those who reckon she's sane as the day is long, and that she's just thrown her morals to the four winds so as she can run off nights to meet Arthur alone in the forest. Since he moved away so sudden-like…"

"Great Ursa," Papa swore. "Does no one recall anymore that gossiping is expressly forbidden by our holy book?"

"Would that they'd remember." Van shook his head. "Aye, but there are as many tales as old biddies to spin them. June Clouden's been saying that Arthur fell in love with the Silver-hair and betrayed Birna and the Bearfolk with an unconsecrated marriage, breaking Birna's heart and shattering her mind.

Hester Whitewater told my wife she expected that Arthur was a student of dark magic who'd accidentally cursed Birna while practicing spells in her presence. Bluebell Juniper told that same story in reverse. But most folks say you and Arthur simply left to grieve Lusela in peace, and that you'll be back when you're proper ready."

Arthur gripped the windowsill with both hands. The conversation between Van and Papa lost all clarity as he stared out at the trees. All the Bearfolk knew June Clouden had a talent for telling the future. Her theory had contained much truth indeed. Arthur would have made it all true if he could have, "unconsecrated marriage" to Gretchen and all. What might that have been like? He imagined standing face to face with her in a grove of towering oak trees, her hands gripped by his as they swore eternal oaths under the moon and sealed them with a kiss.

"Arthur?" Papa's voice pierced his daydream. "Are you unwell? I told you not to eat that leftover trout pie."

"The pie was fine," Arthur said. He turned to face Papa and Van. "But I think I could use some fresh air."

"Go on, lad. Your old dad and I will sit here and talk about days gone by," Van said kindly.

Arthur stepped outside, but not soon enough to miss hearing Van say, "Poor lad. Heart's broken bad, eh? What a shame."

In the tall bushes ahead of Arthur, something stirred. A flash of dark blue and long, loose, brown hair flying.

"Birna!" he called. "Come and talk to me!" If only she'd come back, perhaps Van could take her home—where she'd be safe from wild things and herself. He stood still as stone and waited, but she did not return.

Arthur grabbed a bucket and headed toward the spring, giving himself a task to fill the time. A fat spider, big as his head, hissed at him as he passed the golden web it had crafted between two trees, as if he was going to force it to relocate again. "You're fine," Arthur said, a little sorry he'd made the spider leave the cabin in the first place. What good had it done, really? Papa would mourn Mama wherever he lived, and if both Birna and Van had found them without much trouble, so could anyone else who wished to punish Arthur for whatever they thought he'd done.

Perhaps they should just go back to their familiar, snug cottage and await Arthur's inevitable condemnation by the elders for giving away his pelt and ruining Birna's life. Let them shun him for real instead of acting out his own sort of shunning, making sure everyone knew that Papa had nothing to do with his choices.

Arthur stopped where a natural fountain spurted from the hillside. He stared into the dark pool below it as he continued to ponder a post-judgment future. Papa could return to his life and work, and Arthur could travel far, far away and live alone, or among other fae outcasts. Hadn't Mama told him a story once or twice about an island off the coast where toothless pixies, hornless unicorns, Marendall horses with no sense of direction, and other oddities dwelled together?

It might be the best place in the world for a Bear-boy who'd irrevocably given both his pelt and his heart to a human.

Chapter Thirty-Three

1 September, 170 N.E.

Gretchen had read somewhere that a person could get used to anything. She thought it was mostly true—and might become even truer given enough time.

She'd gotten almost used to walking and talking like Ruby and eating all the fancy green salads Cook piled on her plate. She'd gotten almost used to sleeping on Ruby's squishy mattress and wearing her fussy clothes. She'd become nearly accustomed to laughing with Ruby's co-workers about stuff she didn't find amusing, and she'd actually started to like watching old romantic comedies with Ruby's friends on Friday nights.

Most surprising of all, she'd almost learned to tolerate the intense pain of shifting forms every night and morning. Not that she liked it.

Her stomach grumbled for breakfast. Wearing her own skin but Ruby's hand-embroidered cotton pajamas, Gretchen knelt beside the bed and pulled out the box in which she stowed Arthur's pelt when she wasn't wearing it. Without opening the lid, she smelled him: boy and bear, pine and wood smoke. This, she'd never get used to. It unsettled her daily, this lingering scent that brought with it the memory of him carrying her away from battle on his strong back, her fingers gripping his fur—this fur.

Always followed by the heart-rending memory of the look on his too-human face when they'd parted.

Although the scent-memory was a powerful foe, she tried to think of something else. Indulging in Arthur-themed daydreams was pointless. She had a life to live here and now. Two lives.

Living her Ruby life meant she was going to have to ask someone to Stepmother's ball. And heck if she didn't have options. In addition to her boss, Toby, at least eight other guys had approached her alluding to it. Bouquets from a few of them crowded the top of her dresser, and a huge box of handmade candy from one eager suitor laid open on her desk, reduced to a few unchewable nougats and a mass of paper wrappers. If she had to pick a date according to the greatness factor of the gift, she'd be hard pressed to choose between the guy who'd brought the rare lilies and the candy maker. Ruby, however, would have based her choice on looks and charm, thus eliminating both of Gretchen's preferred competitors.

Her wrist comm chimed on the nearby nightstand. It was time to change into Ruby.

With a deep sigh, she lugged the weighty pelt out of the box and draped it over her head and shoulders. The magic prickled her skin before she spoke to it, as if it knew and accepted her now. As if it had always belonged to her and had forgotten Arthur's voice and shape.

She shivered as the pain shoved its way through her in a rush, and she sobbed as she gave herself over to her stepsister's form once again.

Arthur set his pack on the kitchen table. A wisp of dust rose up from Mama's favorite tablecloth, which would have given Mama a fit if she'd been there to see it. But she'd been gone for over two months, and the cottage had sat empty while he and Papa were hiding in the Deepwood. Dust, like time, did not hold back for anyone.

Millicent hovered over the vase of dead flowers, buzzing her displeasure.

"I'll get new ones later," Arthur said. "You can help me choose them after supper."

From the parlor came Papa's usual settling-into-a-chair groan. He'd never made that sound before Mama died. Her death had changed him almost as much as shifting from human to bear did. New wrinkles creased his face, and his hair had grayed. He'd become slovenly, sleepy, and joyless. When Arthur had suggested moving back to the cottage, he'd merely shrugged and continued to stare at the fire.

Arthur crouched beside the fireplace and arranged a pile of kindling. He'd make tea and Papa's favorite griddle cakes, and then perhaps he'd read one of the stories from the Bearfolk annals aloud. It would be like days gone by, when they were happy but didn't recognize it.

He clapped two firestones together and a spark leapt out from them and ignited the twigs. The fire crackled and blossomed. Arthur sat back on his haunches and watched the flames dance as he wondered what would happen to Papa once the elders sent him away. Perhaps Widow Thornberry would look after Papa, or he could move in with one of his brothers who lived near the sea. Arthur made a mental note to visit Widow Thornberry in the morning. It would be best to have things in order as soon as possible.

The equinox was not far off, and betrothal or no betrothal, Arthur would face judgment for giving away his sacred pelt.

He felt older than Papa looked. He was tired of missing Mama and Gretchen, tired of feeling guilty for breaking Bearfolk law, and tired of dreading the inevitable physical and emotional pain that would visit when the autumnal Change beckoned and he could not yield to its call.

Let my day of reckoning come quickly, Arthur thought. *Let it fall on me in full.*

At least then his future would be laid out plainly before him. He could stop worrying and speculating once the elders gave their verdict. Banishment had that in its favor if nothing else.

Chapter Thirty-Four

9 September, 170 N.E.

Although Gretchen daily mourned the senseless loss of her stepsister, she somehow forgot Ruby's birthday. Unfortunately, a lot of other people had remembered it—and had shown up to scream "surprise!" as she set foot in Stepmother's conservatory expecting a one-on-one meeting.

Stepmother rushed forward and embraced her. "Happy birthday, pet. Nineteen! Hard to believe, seeing as I'm only twenty-nine myself."

"Ha ha, Mommy." Gretchen put on a smile and hoped her cheeks weren't as cherry red as Stepmother's sequined, form-fitting gown. "Really, you shouldn't have gone to all this trouble."

"Trouble? You know I love parties, pet. Almost as much as you do. Now, mingle and have a good time. That adorable Toby Alastair is here, and that Greg Kent you liked back in school."

"Thanks, Mommy," Gretchen said. She made a beeline for the punch bowl. Ruby's favorite dance music blasted from unseen speakers and made Gretchen cringe inside. She and Ruby had never liked the same music. She wondered if she, as Ruby, could get away with announcing a sudden change of heart about something like that. It might be worth a try.

"Hey! Nice outfit," Toby said, sidling up next to her as she scooped orange punch into a cut glass cup.

"It's what I had on all day at work," Gretchen said, sounding a bit too Gretchen-like. She giggled and added for Ruby's sake, "Silly boy."

"Well, it looks better in this light. So, happy birthday." He shoved a small box into her free hand. "I designed it myself, just for you."

She set her cup down and opened the box. A gold bracelet set with rubies sparkled on a bed of green velvet. "It's beautiful. And too much, Toby. You're my boss, and I can't—"

He flashed an iridescent smile. "Stop. You love it, just admit it." He took the bracelet out of the box and slipped it onto her wrist.

"Well…" It was a bit flashier than the jewelry Gretchen usually wore, but he was right. She loved it. She'd never owned anything so opulent. It was hard not to stare at it.

"And hey, maybe I don't want to be just your boss. Have you decided who you're going to the ball with? Because that's what I'd wish for if it was my birthday." His charisma hit her full blast. Darn it all.

"I—um—haven't decided. You know it's complicated, with my mother's position and all. I have to ask for her approval beforehand."

"Come on, Rubes. I know she likes me." He gave Stepmother a little wave across the room, and the woman beamed like a besotted teenager.

"I'll let you know soon, okay? Now, if you'll excuse me, I'd like to go change into something party worthy. And do *not* offer to help or I'll dunk your head in the punch bowl so fast you won't believe it."

He laughed and took a dramatic step back. "Whoa. You're different tonight, Rubes. Spunky. I have to say I like it."

"I'm nineteen now. Older and wiser. See you later, Toby." She wove her way through the crowd, past the four-tiered cake and the elaborate buffet, and hurried upstairs to Ruby's room.

The door slid shut and she commanded it to lock. She threw open the closet doors and pulled out an iridescent blue-black gown. Stepmother had given it to Ruby for Christmas, and Ruby had never worn it—mostly because of the color.

Ruby had hated blue. Shoot, Gretchen wished Ruby was around to still hate blue. And to dance until dawn to her favorite, awful music, and to flirt with every guy in the room, and to laugh with that ridiculous, bubbly, contagious laugh of hers.

"Sorry, Ruby," Gretchen said as she stepped into the sparkling dress in her stepsister's stead. A pang of grief made her stomach sink. They might not have been close, but they'd been sisters—DNA notwithstanding.

The floor shook as another tune blasted downstairs. It was going to be a long night, but not for her. She'd have to take off the pelt before midnight. One time, she'd unintentionally left it on longer than eighteen hours, and she'd felt like her skin was about to melt off her body as the magic rebelled. She wasn't about to endure that again.

"Ruby?" Stepmother called from the hallway. "Your guests are waiting for you to blow out your candles. I hope you've put on something nice."

"Coming, Mommy." Gretchen reached for a pair of twinkly, gold, too-high heels but changed her mind. Everyone knew Ruby preferred to dance barefoot. Gretchen would honor her memory by doing the same—gratefully.

Arthur sat on the doorstep in the moonlight, listening to the shrill nighttime songs of the insects. He made a decision. Tomorrow night, he would go to the elders' council meeting and tell them everything. The idea didn't scare him anymore. Perhaps grief had numbed his emotions, which didn't seem so terrible a thing. At least he wouldn't have to cry himself to sleep like Papa did every night.

The nearby bushes rustled. He knew, as surely as he knew his own name, who had stirred the branches.

"Go home, Birna," he said in a bored voice. "You're wasting your time."

Something flew out of the bushes and landed at his feet. He reached down and grabbed it. He squinted at the rectangle of cream-colored cloth in the hazy moonlight, easily recognizing it as a traditional Bearfolk-man's wedding scarf decorated with an intricate pattern of vines, berries, and his initials entwined with Birna's.

He stood and flung it back into the shrubbery.

"It's over, Birna. Do you hear me? I wish you the best, but it's over between us."

He turned, went inside, and locked the door behind him.

Chapter Thirty-Five

At eleven o'clock, Ruby's party ended with the formal announcement that the birthday girl had a headache. The guests filed out slowly, kissing Gretchen's cheeks and inviting her for future dinners or drinks. Gretchen suspected someone had added something stronger than fruit juice to the punch bowl, for one young man loudly proposed marriage as he left, another whispered his comm number into her ear like it was the world's biggest secret, and one of her fellow designers stumbled head-first into the fountain in the foyer.

The swish of the bedroom door shutting behind her was music to her ears. "Lock door," she said as she pulled the tight blue dress off and tossed it onto the bed. She took a nightgown from her dresser and carried it to the place where she always knelt to change.

Heavens above, she was tired.

"Let's get this done quickly and painlessly," she whispered to the enchantment enveloping her. "Please?"

The pain came with the magic, separating bearskin from human flesh like an invisible, dull blade, and wrenching Ruby's features back into Gretchen's. She heard herself moan, whimper, and finally sigh as the shift concluded. She lay still on the floor beside Arthur's pelt and stared at the ceiling, relieved to be wholly Gretchen once more.

"Whoa. What the frick was that?" a familiar, masculine voice said.

She scrambled to cover herself with her nightgown and stood up. "Toby?"

He swore eloquently. "I must be really drunk because you look like Gretchen, but she's dead. But also, I'm pretty sure I just watched Ruby morph."

"Yeah, you're drunk," Gretchen said emphatically. She pointed toward the door. "Go home and sleep it off."

"Lights up," he said, and the room brightened.

"Hey! So not necessary!"

"Oh my freaking Uncle Jethro," Toby said, approaching her with wide eyes and a bemused smirk. "You *are* Gretchen. What's that fur you had? Is it some kind of magic thing?"

"It's just a fur coat. A birthday gift. You're hallucinating. Someone must have slipped something into your drink. I'll call a driver for you. You'll feel better in the morning."

"I feel pretty sober right now, to tell you the truth. Anybody else know what you've been up to?" He eyed her like she was something between an alien species and an exotic dinner.

"Please, Toby. Just go home and forget about all this. I'll get you into the ball. I promise."

"You'll do better than that. I want a promotion, and I want you to date me—as Ruby—for as long as I say. I want to show up in all the newsfeeds on the arm of the future prime minister's hot, mischievous daughter. And I could use some cash, too, while you're granting wishes."

"Fine. But you have to swear to keep this a secret. I mean

it, Toby. I'm only doing this to help my father. If Stepmother finds out, she'll kill him—and me."

"Deal. Now, switch back to Ruby. Since we're dating, a good night kiss seems totally reasonable." He stumbled forward drunkenly, and Gretchen stepped backward to avoid him.

"Not a chance. I can't change back until morning. You might as well leave."

"Fine. You're not my type looking like *that*, so, yeah. But I'll be back tomorrow for my big first date with Ruby."

"Try not to be seen on your way out, would you?"

"Right. What would the servants say?" He winked and waved his hand over the sensor to open the door.

As soon as the door slid shut behind Toby, Gretchen slumped onto the floor. She gathered the mass of still-warm fur to her chest and hugged it tightly, trying to exact comfort from the thing that might have brought her ruin.

After hours of tossing and turning, Arthur gave up on trying to sleep.

He lit the lamp on his bedside table and picked up the third volume of the *Annals of the Bearfolk*. He adjusted his pillows and opened to the last page he'd read, the final paragraphs of the tale of the ancient warrior Queen Arcadia, who in her great wisdom had first commanded the laws of the Bearfolk to be written down on scrolls.

His eyes lost focus as he remembered Mama teaching him the laws when he was four years old. She'd recited them as they weeded the garden together, reviewed them at bedtime, and made him repeat them at least a hundred times before he got them right. And then came the unforgettable day when she'd brought him before the elders. He'd spoken the sacred words with conviction and accuracy, gaining admission to their most elite primary school.

He'd loved that school—especially the classes on history and ritual. His teachers had predicted he'd make a fine elder after he'd had another century to mature, and he'd intended to prove them right by living a righteous life. He'd relished every holy day, offered all the proper sacrifices, and obeyed his parents (most of the time). He'd studied the many annals and thick volumes of theology, memorizing all that he could. Yes, he had loved everything about being a faithful son of the Bearfolk, and he'd been good at it.

Until Gretchen had arrived, and his heart had informed him that it was more honorable to help the helpless than to selfishly stick to the rules. Now that she was gone, the old rules called to him again. The old stories soothed the sore places in his soul a little.

He turned the page. The next story, "The Wedding of Berengari and Mahon," began with an illustration of the legendary royal couple dressed in traditional finery. The sight of the wedding clothes reminded him of Birna and the scarf she'd tossed at him. He shut the book and set it aside. He'd hoped to read himself to sleep, not to stir up his worries.

Sinking down under the covers, he closed his eyes. An image of Birna wearing Berengari's beribboned skirts and starry veil haunted his mind. Poor, mad Birna in the garb of a queen, making holy matrimonial vows in front of her elder uncle, her high-ranking parents, and all the Bearfolk of the region.

A new thought struck him, and he sat up, breath quickening.

Birna's family was eminent, and probably desperate to downplay the rumors of her madness. If he married her as if nothing was wrong, would her family be willing to petition the elders to grant him forgiveness for giving away his pelt?

Might they urge the council to allow him to remain part of the tribe—procuring for him the right to attend gatherings and celebrations without fur?

After all, Bearfolk blood still ran through his veins. Surely the loss of his pelt did not completely negate his heritage.

Ideas multiplied in his head. Now that he was so close to losing everything he held dear, he sought loopholes in the Bearfolk laws he'd always revered. He looked for gray areas in what he'd formerly seen as black and white rules.

He could never be with Gretchen, so why not marry Birna if it meant he could stay with Papa and their tribe? Many Bearfolk marriages turned out to be business arrangements, for economy and breeding but not love. There was no shame in that. And who knew? Maybe marriage would bring Birna peace and settle her mind a bit.

He extinguished the lamp, his decision made. Instead of visiting the elders and offering his confession, he'd call on Birna's family and plead his case.

Sometime near dawn, he fell asleep and dreamed of dancing in the sacred glade upon the equinox, his human feet skipping to the music alongside the many paws of his beloved kinfolk.

Chapter Thirty-Six

14 September, 170 N.E.

Stepmother and Toby kept Gretchen so busy with party-plan-ning, work, and dates that she barely had time to breathe. With the bearskin restricting her schedule as well, sometimes days went by between visits to her father—which saddened her *and* put a damper on her search for the true source of his illness.

Somewhere in the house, an old-fashioned clock chimed the hour as she hurried toward Father's suite. She picked up her pace. She'd only have a few minutes to spend with Father before Toby came to take her out for dinner. For the fourth blasted night in a row.

Stars in heaven, she wished her boss hadn't snuck in her room the night of Ruby's birthday. Dating him as Ruby was beyond creepy. His innate charm no longer worked on her. She hated holding his soft, squishy hand and hearing him spout romantic nonsense to Ruby. It was like he really believed Gretchen *was* Ruby when she was disguised as her.

Last night, she'd dodged his attempt at a kiss. Tonight, she might not be so lucky. Ugh.

Gretchen waited for the door to Father's room to slide open. The lights in the suite were turned down low, and his hired companion/nurse, Kiki, wasn't sitting in her usual chair. Father lay still in bed. His face matched his white sheets.

"Father?" She touched his pajama-clad shoulder lightly, hoping to awaken him without scaring him. When that didn't work, she raised her voice and patted him more forcefully.

"Good luck getting a response from him. He's been asleep all day," Kiki said from behind Gretchen, startling her. Kiki was too like a spider, with her gangly limbs and uncanny ability to sneak up on people. "Slept through yesterday, too. Dr. Barnes says he probably won't last much longer."

"No," Gretchen said. She turned her face toward Ruby's childhood friend. "That can't be right. He seemed better last time I was here."

Kiki shook her head and took a sip of tea from an oversized mug before responding. "Dr. Barnes is one of the best doctors in the colony, Ruby. I think he knows a little more about medicine than you do. Anyway, what do you care? When we were in school, you always said you hated your stepdad's guts."

"Maybe I've changed. People do change. Maybe I realized I was a brat to him growing up, even though he was always nice to me. Maybe it makes me sad that I'm the only daughter he has left." Gretchen slipped her hand into her father's. The unnatural coolness of his palm caused her hopes to sink lower.

Kiki shrugged, apparently unconvinced, but Gretchen knew pursuing an argument with Nurse Kiki would be almost as stupid as delving into details of the friendship Kiki and Ruby had shared growing up. Kiki knew Ruby in a way Gretchen never had, and Gretchen didn't want to stir up memories she'd have to fake. She needed to keep the focus on Father's health.

"Have any other doctors come to see him? Has he been medi-scanned recently?"

"Not in the six months I've worked here. Yeah, it does seem odd they never bring in the medi-scanners. They've updated the systems three times this year, and you wouldn't believe the stuff the scans pick up now." Kiki set her tea on Father's bedside table and sat down in her usual chair. "No offense, but I get the impression your mom might not be all that sad to see him go."

"Sometimes I wonder that myself," Gretchen said sadly.

"Exactly why I'm never getting married. Ninety-eight percent of the time, it starts out all great, but after a few years it's nothing but bitterness and backstabbing."

"You may be right." Gretchen gazed at her father for a moment, considering the best way to get what she needed from Ruby's friend: namely, a clandestine appointment with a medi-scan machine. She put on her version of Ruby's "let's make mischief" face and pulled Kiki close enough to whisper in her ear—just in case the room was under surveillance. "So, Kiki… Could you maybe get a hold of a medi-scanner for a few hours? Secretly?"

Kiki whispered back, "What's in it for me? I could get fired for this, you know." She pulled Gretchen to the window and they continued their quiet conversation facing the lawns.

"How about a ticket to the ball and whatever dress you want from my closet?"

Kiki grinned. "Can I bring a date? It would help me get the scanner. The scanner tech guy I know is into parties, and he's hotter than Gunther Wilkes from our eleventh grade linguistics class. In a nerdy sort of way."

"Gunther was something to behold," Gretchen said, although she couldn't remember him to save her life. "When can the scanner guy get here?"

"Slow down, space cowgirl. I'll have to talk to Hank first and see if he's up for it."

Father moaned softly in his sleep. The sound made Gretchen's heart flutter with fear. "Okay. Just try to make it soon, please. I'll throw in a pair of shoes if you can get him here before tomorrow."

"You're giving away shoes, girl? You *are* serious," Kiki said. "I like this new undercover superhero Ruby. Still a tricky number, but with bonus determination."

Gretchen couldn't help smiling at the compliment Ruby would have so relished. "Like I said, people change."

Birna's family lived farther away than Arthur had imagined. He'd set out from home in early afternoon, and now, as his feet begged for mercy, twilight was tinting the countryside's rolling hills with its dark brush. He was pretty sure he'd been led astray by a couple of enchanted paths during his journey. If only he'd ridden a Marendall horse instead of walking, he might have been homeward bound now instead of still on his way to confront Birna's parents.

He shivered with dread at the thought he might be stuck staying overnight with the Cloverfield family. If things went badly, it might be safer to sleep in the hedgerows.

"You lost, lad?" an old Bear-woman asked from under a drooping pear tree. Her wide apron pocket sagged with the weight of her harvest. Her eyes were a stunning bright blue, a shade rarely seen among the Bearfolk.

"I'm looking for the Cloverfields' house," Arthur replied.

The woman pointed with her crooked forefinger. "Just over there it is. Place with the green shutters. You kin?"

"Just visiting. Thank you for your help, ma'am."

The woman tossed a pear into his hands. "'The old shall

help the young, grant them sustenance, and show unto them a goodly path,' so says our holy book."

"Second epistle of King Orso," Arthur said. "Chapter eight, verse seventeen." He'd memorized the entire chapter when he was nine years old, and he hadn't forgotten one precious word of it.

"Get on with you, clever boots," the grinning woman said with a wave of dismissal.

On the Cloverfields' doorstep, Arthur took a deep breath and tried to stop his knees from trembling. He knocked twice and waited. Maybe they were out. Maybe it was a sign he shouldn't go through with his plan. What had he been thinking?

He took a step backward, ready to make a run for home, and then the door opened.

"Who's calling?" a young Bear-girl asked with the air of an annoyed princess. She was a smaller, daintier version of Birna, six or seven years old, with two nut-brown braids hanging over her shoulders. Her white pinafore was smeared with jam. "Mama said we're not buying any more apples from wandering elves this year because the cellar's already crammed full. Are you selling apples?"

He held back a laugh. "Do I look like an elf?"

"A little."

"Well, I'm not. I'm Bearfolk like you, and I've come to see your parents."

A woman's voice came from within the house. "Wilda, who in the world are you talking to?"

"I have no idea," the girl answered. "But he's asking for you, and he doesn't have apples."

"It's Arthur," he called through the doorway. "Arthur Woodley."

"Ursa bless us," the woman said, rushing to take Arthur's hands. She was younger than Arthur's mother had been, perhaps by fifty years or more. Only a few strands of gray ran through her braided crown of dark hair, and her skin crinkled just a little around her dark eyes. She wore a wine-red dress with a high collar and ankle-length hem. "Welcome, Arthur. Come in this instant, dear. Wilda, fetch your father and send him to the sitting room. And where is your sister?" Her voice quivered with anxiety.

"How should I know, the way she wanders off?" Wilda said impishly.

"Dear me," the woman said as she led Arthur through the entryway and into a high-ceilinged parlor. "I hope you'll forgive Wilda's cheekiness. She's really a good girl most of the time. Here we are. Do sit down."

Arthur chose a wing chair and his hostess perched on the edge of a sofa across from him, looking like a nervous bird.

Hands in her lap, she fussed with the buttons on her cuff. "You may call me Jessamine. We've met before, at a Yuletide dance when you were younger than our Wilda. But I don't imagine you remember."

A towering figure of a man entered the room, the top of his head barely clearing the doorway. His broad shoulders and swaggering gait implied authority and strength, but his wide, affable smile suggested that he was as kind as he was large.

These were not the parents Arthur had expected to meet. He'd thought they'd be much older and far more threatening.

"Arthur Woodley," Birna's father said, shaking his hand firmly. "We're blessed to have you in our home. I'm Bradley Cloverfield, and you've met my good wife Jessamine." His smile faded as he sat beside his wife. "I hope you've not come bearing bad news. We know there are rumors circulating…of an unpleasant nature. But a contract is a contract, is it not?"

Arthur slid to the edge of his chair and tried to remember the speech he'd practiced in his head fifty times on his journey. "I don't wish to bring dishonor upon your household, sir," he said. "As I'm sure you don't wish to bring dishonor to my family."

"Please," Jessamine said, tears flooding her eyes. "We know our Birna has been a little strange of late, but we've found a wise woman who gave us herbs to help, and if you knew how much she loves you, Arthur. How she's talked of marrying you since she was knee-high to her father—"

"Hush, wife." Bradley wrapped a big hand around his wife's small, fretful ones. "Let the lad speak his piece."

"I don't want to break the betrothal contract," Arthur said. "I believe in our ways, and I want to do what's right. I'm willing to marry Birna—but first you should know the truth about me. About what I've done."

Relief lifted the corners of Bradley's mouth. "Ah, lad. A young Bear-fellow makes mistakes. Let the past rest. No need to confess your sins to anyone but Ursa above."

"I gave away my pelt," Arthur blurted. His heart beat so rapidly that he grew dizzy. "There's no getting it back. I can't shift. Not ever."

Jessamine gasped and covered her mouth. Bradley stood, and then sat again, face pale.

"Why would you do a thing like that?" Bradley asked, running his hands through his thick hair.

"To help someone I cared for. Birna didn't mention anything about the girl, I take it."

"No, she did not." Bradley stood and paced. His footsteps shook the floorboards. "By Ursa! It baffles the mind. And you think you can still marry my daughter, peltless and defiled as you are?"

"No disrespect, sir, but who else is going to marry her? She's been roaming the countryside at all hours unchaperoned, singing and talking nonsense to herself. Some say we've been living together unlawfully already—which is untrue, I swear. Nonetheless…"

Jessamine spoke up. "He's right, Bradley. We've both heard the gossip. Her reputation is in tatters. Ruined."

Bradley grunted.

Arthur looked up at the big man whose face was etched with bewilderment and sadness, and said with conviction, "I came here with a plan to help us all. If we go ahead with the announcement of the betrothal at the equinox, no one will dare accuse her of immorality. As you said, the young are prone to behave foolishly; therefore I think the elders will look the other way knowing we're legally set to marry in a few months. In return, I ask for your help."

Bradley glared at Arthur. "You want us to cover up your shameful crime? Your purposeful sin? Our daughter can't help being ill. But you! You chose to give away the very thing that made you one of us."

Jessamine reached out and tugged her husband's sleeve. "He will suffer the consequences of that choice for the rest of his life, Bradley. I think his inability to Change will mean little to Birna. She loves him. With his care and the herbs, she might even fully recover."

"I'm not asking you to be dishonest," Arthur said. "I'm asking you to use your influence with the elders to obtain a special decree of grace for me. All I want is to continue to live among the Bearfolk and to abide by our ways. In return, I'll be a faithful husband to Birna and do my best to make her happy." His voice cracked with emotion. He bowed his head and awaited a response.

Hasty footsteps brought Birna into the room. She knelt at Arthur's feet, grabbed his hands, and kissed them. "I knew you'd come," she said. "I prayed all night to Ursa and her son, and I knew you'd come. Oh, Arthur, I'm so sorry for how I've behaved. I'm so much better now that Sister Greenhill gave me her medicine. I don't care what went on with the human girl anymore. I love you, and all I want is to marry you."

"Birna," Bradley said, pulling her to her feet and turning her around to face him. "He can't Change. Do you really want to marry someone who can't celebrate the holy days with you? Someone who can't run through the forest beside you on all fours, clad in sacred fur?"

"I would marry him if he grew horns and wings and smelled like a bog troll, Papa. It's all I've wanted since I was a wee lass."

Bradley embraced his daughter and sighed. A tear rolled into his beard. "So be it, then. If the elders agree to the decree of grace, you can marry the boy come Yuletide."

"Thank you, Papa," Birna said, again and again.

Something like peace settled over Arthur. He leaned back in the chair as Birna embraced her happily weeping mother.

Everything was going to be fine for him after all.

If only he could be sure everything was fine for Gretchen.

Chapter Thirty-Seven

15 September, 170 N.E.

Gretchen had been forced to fake gag until she almost really threw up in order to get Toby to end their date early. She watched his mini-airskipper zip away before making a run for Father's suite. Kiki and her medi-scanner tech friend were due to meet her there in five minutes. If she got any more nervous, she might throw up after all.

At this hour of the evening, most of the servants had gone home, so she reached the suite without being seen. When the door slid open, she saw Kiki and Hank standing ready beside Father.

True to Kiki's word, Hank was nerdy but cute. He had a lot of unruly blond hair and a square jaw, and he wore a retro-style knit shirt printed with dinosaurs and a snug pair of blue jeans. The uniform police (if they had existed) would not have been pleased.

"Hey," Hank said. "You ready?" He held up a white, box-shaped instrument the size of her shoe. "I need to return this puppy before ten."

Gretchen nodded. "Please."

Kiki pointed to the ceiling. "I covered the security camera lenses with tape before Hank arrived, just to be safe."

"Thanks, Kiki," Gretchen said. "I owe you earrings to match that dress."

"You're right, you do."

Hank tapped a code into the touch screen on the medi-scanner. It tweeted like a sick bird and began to emit red light from its underside. "Right. Here we go. As long as he holds still, we'll be done in sixty seconds."

"That shouldn't be a problem," Kiki said. "He's pretty good at holding still these days."

Hank slowly waved the instrument over Gretchen's father's body, scanning him from head to toe. Little beeps and clicks sounded as he worked. Gretchen held her breath and watched Hank's face for hints about the results, but his blank expression gave away nothing.

"Done," Hank said. He touched the screen again. "Now it's examining the data, and three, two, one—wow." He cringed and held out the device for Gretchen to see. "Never saw anything like this before. So, who is it that wants your stepdad dead?"

Gretchen gasped. She knew the names of the plants listed on the tiny screen. Many of them had been used as medicines hundreds of years ago. When she was thirteen, she'd had a summer-long obsession with the herbal remedies of medieval England. She'd never expected it to come in handy.

She'd never expected to learn that her vile stepmother had used the herbs to poison Father into a state of illness that slowly progressed from absent-mindedness to death. She shivered with revulsion and clutched her threatening-to-puke stomach.

Blast, she'd been a bad daughter. She should have noticed the signs, found him other doctors, something…

Kiki leaned close and pointed to one of the readings. "That

probably explains the dementia." She moved her finger down. "And there's why he's been asleep all week. My word, Ruby. If we don't detox him tonight, he might not see tomorrow."

"Can you help me?"

"You should call the authorities," Hank said. "This is way criminal stuff."

"No. We can't. Stepmoth—I mean, Mother's up for nomination for prime minister. That's why she's having the ball, to announce it. She'd find out it was us, and she'd have us killed next. You don't know how she is."

"Then we'd better get to work on our own," Kiki said. "I'll go with Hank to return the gadget to the clinic, and I'll snatch a few meds while we're there. You up for an all-nighter, boyfriend?"

"Sounds delish," Hank said. "I mean, no offense, Ruby. I'm sorry about your stepdad."

"Just hurry," Gretchen said. "And if I'm not here when you get back, it's because Mother demanded my presence. Do whatever you have to do to help him, whether I'm here or not." She took a fob from her pocket and pointed to a door on the other side of the room. "Here. This gets you out the back. No cameras out that way." Stepmother's "secret" escape route, designed to allow her own devious comings and goings, had helped the real Ruby sneak out to meet boys a hundred times. Gretchen had never imagined she'd have to use it for anything.

"Aces," Hank said, taking the fob. He grabbed Kiki's hand and pulled her along. "See you later, Ruby."

"Don't worry, girl," Kiki said as she walked away. "There's a good chance we can save him."

"I hope so," Gretchen said.

Once Hank and Kiki were gone, she glanced at her wrist comm. She'd have to change forms soon, whether it was convenient or not. She moved to her father's side and kissed his clammy forehead.

"I'll be back soon," she said. "We're going to help you. I promise."

The door slid open. "What's going on in here?" Stepmother asked. She was holding a small packet in her hand—which Gretchen suspected contained doses of poison. She nonchalantly stuffed it into the pocket of her custom-made faux leather business jacket.

Gretchen's face burned. She adjusted the bed sheet and said, "Um. Hi, Mommy. I was just visiting. I promised Gretchen I would, before she—"

"Honestly, Ruby. Sometimes I think those faeries warped your mind. This man is none of your concern, and you certainly don't want to catch whatever malady he has. It baffles me that he's still alive, the tough old bird."

Gretchen opened her mouth to speak, but Stepmother interrupted her again. "There's nothing to discuss. Go to bed, pet. You look absolutely frightful. Your skin is all blotchy, and you need to look your best for the ball, you know."

"Yes, Mommy. Good night." She fast-walked out the door, her heart tripping with fear. What if Stepmother gave Father the fatal dose tonight? What if Kiki returned and Stepmother caught her sneaking in armed with antidotes?

She stopped in the hall and messaged Kiki a warning on her wrist comm. It was all she had time to do. The pelt had started to warn Gretchen that it was past time for her to shift, shooting spikes of agony through her muscles.

As she resumed her rush down the corridor, fatigue and worry overtook her. What if she failed to save her father like she'd failed to save Ruby? The thought that she'd taken away Arthur's most precious possession and used it in an exercise in futility made her want to weep.

Maybe Stepmother had always been right about her incompetence. Maybe everyone would be better off if she left the colony and started a little farm on her own, far away.

Cringing from the mounting pain, she stumbled into Ruby's bedroom and locked the door. It was as if the pelt's magic knew it could take charge then, for she didn't have time to kneel before the hidden bearskin started to wrest itself from her. A blinding symphony of agony consumed her senses and she collapsed onto the floor beside the bed. More quickly than ever before, Ruby's skin became hide and fur and then fell from Gretchen's body.

She shoved the bearskin away with her foot, trying not to look at it. Trying not to think about Arthur and how unworthy she was of his sacrifice.

Gretchen reached over to pull the quilt from the bed. She nestled within the plump blanket, shivering and feeling more helpless and alone than she had in a very long time.

16 September, 170 N.E.

The equinox was fast approaching.

In the late summer sunlight, Arthur worked in the orchards with his father, plucking apples from the trees and dropping them into baskets. The harvest was plentiful, the apples plump and sweet. They'd sell well at the autumn markets, and the profits would give Arthur and Papa a comfortable year ahead.

As Arthur adjusted his grip on the ladder he'd climbed, Millicent perched on a branch above his head, her colors bright as the fruit. Like a faithful dog, she never strayed far from Arthur. Small and wordless as she was, she felt like a friend to him.

A little breeze rattled the leaves as it passed through the rows of knobby trees, but it didn't obscure the sound of Papa's intermittent sniffling. He'd cried every day of the harvest, rain or shine, and Arthur knew he was remembering his wife. They'd planted this grove in the early days of their marriage, and tended the trees like row after row of children, year in and year out. Faerie trees, like faerie folk, lived long in most cases, and these trees had seen Papa and Mama through many seasons of life.

Arthur tried to imagine planting saplings with Birna. Her sizable dowry would enable them to plant an orchard of rare golden Avalon pear trees if they so chose. A few bushels brought to the faerie high king's court each fall, and they'd be almost as rich as the high king himself in less than a decade. Their children would lack for nothing.

But he couldn't picture Birna planting saplings at his side. No matter how he tried, he couldn't even imagine swearing holy vows to her in the light of the Yule bonfire. It was most unsettling.

An apple slipped from his grasp and bounced off the lower limbs of the tree before thumping onto the ground. He couldn't deny the effects of gravity, and he couldn't deny the reason why he was unable to think of Birna as his wife. His heart had left Britannia with his pelt. With Gretchen.

Papa tried to cover a sob with a few coughs. Arthur picked another apple, and then another. He told himself it didn't matter if he could imagine Birna as his bride; what was ordained by Ursa would happen. He'd do as he promised, and perhaps someday, Ursa would bless him with a new heart that could love Birna as she deserved. Until then, he would follow Papa's example. He'd keep breathing and working, eating and sleeping, a servant to Bearfolk law and the passing seasons.

"Hello!" Birna called from the orchard gate. "I've brought scones and honey."

Papa shouted in reply, "Just the thing we needed!"

Arthur climbed slowly down the ladder, heart as heavy

as the apple basket strapped to his hip, but he put on a smile for the girl who loved him.

Ursa, help me grow to love her soon, he prayed as he took off the basket and rested it against a tree. He waded through the knee-high grass to meet his future bride. *Help me, somehow, to become an honorable Bearfolk husband.*

"Come and sit," Birna said. She wore a new, sky-blue dress embroidered with heart-shaped leaves, and her face was radiant with happiness and health. She held up a scroll of parchment tied with a red ribbon. "I brought something extra special for you. Papa received it from the court of elders just this morning. Your decree of grace. You're one of us forever, Arthur."

"Huzzah!" Papa shouted as he hopped off the lowest rung of his ladder. "Praise Ursa!" He grabbed Arthur and twirled him about in a celebratory dance. Birna laughed and clapped, and Arthur laughed, too, genuinely. Papa's joy lifted his spirits and gave him hope.

"Bearfolk forever," Arthur said as he took the scroll from Birna's hand. He knew its existence was nothing short of a miracle, and he was as grateful as he could be.

Chapter Thirty-Eight

18 September, 170 N.E.

Gretchen hated the retro, white, twinkly lights more than she'd ever thought a person could hate twinkly lights. Of course it was Stepmother's fault. She'd insisted that the colony's largest hangar, where the ball was to be held in less than a week's time, would have thousands of tiny lights suspended from the high ceiling like strings of stars, and more twinkly lights dripping down the walls. As a result, Gretchen had spent hours after work each night untangling the things, and she feared she wasn't half done with them.

At least her busyness had gotten her out of a few dates with Toby. She'd had enough Toby to last her two lifetimes.

She picked at a knot with a pair of long-nosed tweezers, hoping her wrist comm would buzz soon. Kiki had been sending frequent messages about Father's health. Earlier that day, Kiki had reported that Father had finally woken up for half an hour and eaten a few spoonfuls of broth. He'd spoken hoarsely, but sensibly. The antidotes were definitely working. He might recover—*if* they could keep Stepmother from poisoning him further.

The plan was for Kiki to always be in the room when Stepmother stopped to visit. So far, she'd managed to do so, using excuses fraught with medical terminology Stepmother couldn't comprehend. The woman's enormous pride kept her from asking questions, and her fear of germs kept her visits brief—thwarting any plans she might have had to inject Father with her concoctions.

Now, if Gretchen could just find five minutes to spend with him… But there wasn't much chance of that. She had appointments with the florist, the caterer, the band leader, and the dressmaker, besides being constrained by her work schedule and the pelt's timetable. Ugh.

She tossed the string of lights aside and glanced at her wrist comm to check the time. It was later than she'd thought. Her Ruby-skin was getting itchy and hot, and her rumbling stomach reminded her she'd forgotten to eat dinner.

"Lex," she said to one of the high school girls she'd hired to help decorate, "I have to go. You and Leslie should go, too. Just finish the section you're working on and call it a night."

Lex looked worried. "But your mom said—"

"I'll deal with her. We're getting too tired to do a good job, anyway." Gretchen grabbed her handbag and design tablet and headed for the door. "See you tomorrow."

The instant she stepped outside, the late summer air embraced her. The path between the hangar and the air-bike lot was flanked by rose bushes, and their scent always brought to mind her real mother, although she wasn't sure why. Maybe her mother had worn rose perfume, or used rose-scented shampoo. Maybe she'd just smelled good naturally. She'd never thought to ask her father about it. If his full memory returned with Kiki's treatment, maybe she'd get the chance to ask him in a week or two.

"Hey, gorgeous," Toby said, startling her so that she gasped.

He leaned against a white metal lamp post beside the air-bike rack, wearing tight jeans, a silver shirt, and—was that *eyeliner*?

"Hi. I hope you didn't come all the way out here to see me. I don't have time to chat. I have stuff to do at home."

"Secret stuff? Fur-related stuff?"

"None of your business stuff, Toby. We'll talk tomorrow at lunch, okay?"

"Ruby," he said, drawing the name out in a sort of half-whine that was probably meant to be cute. "I miss you."

"Cut it out, Toby. You know who I am. And let's be clear, once the ball is over, we're over."

"Fine, but until then, we're together. I'll ride home with you. There's room for two on your bike."

"Two ten-year-olds maybe."

"Get on the bike and scoot forward. I'll let you steer. Unless you want me to tell the all-powerful Ivory Werner about your hoax?"

"I hate you, Toby."

"That's why I adore you, Rubes. That attitude. It makes me sweat."

"How appealing." She swung her leg over the bike, switched it on, and backed it out of the rack. Purring, it hovered a few inches above the ground. "Get on if you're getting on." Dang, she hoped he'd slide off the back and into a large mud puddle before she reached home.

He mounted the bike and pressed his chest against her back. Goosebumps of revulsion raised on her arms. How had she ever found him charming? She revved the engine and accelerated from zero to fifty miles per hour in a few seconds. His grip tightened and his breath tickled her neck. The sooner this ride was over, the better.

Five minutes later, she swerved onto Werner property. Heavens above, she needed to change. Her blood burned like liquid fire, and every inch of her body itched. It was weird how the magic chose different methods of torture each time. She scratched her ear and then her throat, but it only made things worse. She'd have to get rid of Toby fast, but how? He had all the sticking power of the world's biggest leech.

She slowed the bike. The garage built into the side of the mansion sensed her approach and opened its doors. She fit the bike into its rack and powered it down before awkwardly dismounting.

"See you at lunch," she said. "Bye."

He climbed off the bike and grabbed her arm. "Not so fast, Rubes. Let's walk a little. It's a nice night."

"You know I can't, Toby. Please just go home."

"You know what I'd like? I'd like to watch the magic. You know, the fur shedding thing where you morph from hot Ruby to boring Gretchen. It was dark last time, and I feel like I missed some of the show."

"Well, that's not going to happen."

He turned his arm and poked his wrist comm. "Should I call your mommy for you?"

"Please, Toby. This isn't a game. Don't you think I've lost enough without losing the rest of my dignity?" She covered her mouth with one hand as her stomach considered rejecting its contents.

"Wow, you look sick. Is it going to happen now? Like, can you not even stop it?"

"This isn't a joke. It hurts. And yeah, it makes me kind of sick sometimes. I'll get you money, a brand new airskipper, whatever. Just go."

"Fine," he said. "Let me borrow the bike so I don't have to walk all the way across the colony. The comm says it's going to rain in five minutes."

Now shaking uncontrollably, Gretchen struggled to enter

the security code into the air-bike's control screen. Once, twice, three times she messed it up before her knees buckled and her backside met the tiled floor.

"No," she said to the magic, although she desperately wanted to say yes. Her heart threatened to explode in her chest and her head throbbed. She was dying. Her vision went black. Her head smacked the ground. "Please," she whispered, half-conscious, and the magic took it as an invitation. It crashed over her in a sharp-edged wave, cleaving her into two: pelt and girl. Bearskin and Gretchen.

"Shiz," she heard Toby say in a faraway voice. "Oh my heck. What do I do?"

She opened her eyes as Toby tossed his jacket over her body. "Um—I'm really sorry," he said shakily. "I didn't think it would happen out here. And ew. I mean, not a pretty sight. Melting flesh and all that."

"Sorry to offend." She glanced up at him as she sat up. His eyeliner was smudged. He looked like a sad raccoon. "Are you crying?"

He whipped off his shirt and crouched beside her. "Here. Put this on, too. You look cold."

He'd definitely been crying. He stood and turned his back so she could put on the shirt. "I am really sorry, Gretchen. I shouldn't have messed with you. I didn't know it would happen out here." He sounded different, like a little boy instead of an arrogant fashion designer. "I know I'm a jerk."

"You should go," Gretchen said. As she stood, she heard a vehicle approaching with a low hum. Stepmother's vehicle. She'd be there in seconds, by the sound of it.

"Your mom?" Toby asked.

"Come on," Gretchen said, shoving the bearskin into his arms and throwing her leg over the bike. "She can't see me like this."

He mounted behind her and spoke into her ear as she backed out of the rack. "Head to my place. Building three in the east sector. Don't worry. I won't try anything ungentlemanly."

She used a voice command on the bike, giving the address and the desired speed. They'd take a less-traveled route to avoid crossing paths with Stepmother. "Hold on," she said as the bike accelerated. "This thing goes faster than you'd think."

"Bring it on, babe," Toby said, sounding like his usual self again.

～

19 September, 170 N.E.

Sometime between midnight and morning, Arthur looked up from the fireplace's orange embers to find his father watching him from the doorway that led into the bedroom.

"Trouble sleeping again, lad?" Papa asked. He tied the sash of his robe tighter and yawned as he crossed the room. "Mind a bit of company?"

Arthur shook his head. Papa brought a stool to the fireside and sat down. For a while, he said nothing as he stared into the flames. And then he scratched his beard and said, "You can tell me what's wrong, you know. It's been a hard year, this one, and it seems to be catching up with you."

"Yes," Arthur said. His throat felt too tight to speak further. Besides, he couldn't easily describe what was wrong. It was more a heaping pile of things rather than just one.

Papa met Arthur's gaze. "I do apologize if my grieving bothers you. I try to save it for when you're not around, but sometimes it hits me like a brick to the head. Or the heart, more like."

"I miss Mama, too," Arthur managed to say. "And I don't want you to pretend you're not mourning the loss of her. Please don't try."

They sat in silence, save for the crackling and popping of the fire, until Papa said, "I thought you'd be happy when your decree of grace came, but by my reckoning, you're gloomier than before. Are you afraid of what it will be like when the Change calls on the equinox and you have no pelt to wear? Is that it, lad? Or are you nervous about the formal betrothal ceremony? It's just a few words said by the elders and a dance with your girl."

Arthur used a metal poker to stir the embers. Sparks rose up the chimney. He rested the poker against the stone wall. He didn't want to tell the truth, for speaking it aloud would tarnish his newly cleaned slate. He'd been given grace to remain Bearfolk—yet his heart kept longing for what Bearfolk law forbade.

"Will you not tell me, then? Your old papa understands more than you think. I've seen more than a century of joys and sorrows, haven't I?"

"It doesn't matter," Arthur said. "I have everything I've wanted since I was a wee lad, except for Mama's presence. I'll do my duty, and all will be well. Like you said, it's been a hard year. Next year will be better, surely. Birna will come to live with us in December, and by next spring, our sadness will be a memory." The words were bitter and salty on his tongue, flavored by unshed tears.

"It's the human girl," Papa said, as if suddenly enlightened. "You still care for Gretchen."

Arthur bowed his head in shame. "I'm sorry, Papa. I've tried to stop thinking of her, to stop wondering how she is and what she's doing. Every time I think I'm done with all that, I see her in a dream or hear a laugh like hers in the village marketplace, and I go back to missing her all over again. Worse."

Papa swiped a tear from his cheek. "That's how it is for me, lad, missing your mother. And so I'm sorry for you. And for Birna. Have you told her?"

"She's known since the day her uncle brought her for our courtship walk. She says she doesn't care. She believes I'll come to love her if I do what's right and marry her."

"Do you believe that?"

"Sometimes."

"Ursa above, lad. The equinox is only a few days off. If you take vows at the betrothal ceremony, there's no undoing them. You'll be as good as wed in the eyes of the law. No way out but death or permanent exile. What do you plan to do?"

"I don't know."

"Well, I see why sleep eludes you now. I doubt I'll sleep myself until this muddle is behind us one way or another."

"I am sorry, Papa."

"Don't be sorry. Love is unpredictable, as untamable as lightning. Did I ever tell you how I fell in love with your mother? She was days away from being betrothed to the high elder's grandson. We met at Little Woolsey market, where she was selling lace she'd made. I made a pretense of buying some for my mother, and when I dropped the coins into her hand, our eyes met and we both knew she'd never marry anyone but me. It was quite a scandal. Tears, harsh words, threats, and a few blackened eyes ensued before all was settled. In the end, it was worth it. We were happy together—even though she was bossy and fond of a fight."

Papa stood and rested his hands on Arthur's shoulders. "I'm proud to call you my son, no matter what you decide. I'll ask you just one thing before I leave you to your thoughts. What would you do if there were no rules or restrictions? And would you be able to live with yourself for the next century or two if you did—or did not—do that thing?"

Papa kissed the top of his head and shuffled out of the kitchen.

Arthur tossed a small log onto the fire and watched it

burn until nothing remained but cinders. He knew, as he had known since the solstice, what he truly wanted. It was the exact opposite of what he'd wanted before Gretchen had ambushed his life. What he didn't know was if he could pay the high price it would cost—or if he'd be able to live with himself if his actions sent Birna back into the depths of madness.

Questions multiplied as the birds outside the cottage chirped at the rising sun. What if Gretchen didn't care for him? What if she did? Where would they live and work? What if she needed to stay in her stepmother's house pretending to be Ruby for the next thirty years? What if he was never allowed to see Papa again? What if he and Gretchen had children someday and they were born with fur or pointy snouts?

"Enough," he said aloud. He stood and went to pour himself a cup of water, no more sure of what he would do next than he had been when the night began.

Chapter Thirty-Nine

Stepmother's voice scolded Gretchen from her wrist comm. "Aren't you a little old for sleepover parties with your friends, Ruby? And how do you have time for silly, girlish nonsense when the ball is coming up so soon?" Gretchen rolled her eyes and muted the comm. No more messages till morning. Well, daylight. Technically, it was already morning. Three a.m., to be precise.

Toby pressed a mug of chamomile tea into her hand and sat on the opposite end of the puffy white sofa that took up a third of his black, white, and red living room. "You okay?" he asked.

She shrugged. "As okay as I'm going to be at this point."

He plopped his bare feet onto a furry red ottoman and relaxed into the sofa cushions as if he had no intention of going to bed. She'd thought he'd be one who valued his beauty sleep—but the last few hours had taught her that he wasn't as predictable as she'd believed. Here in his home, he still had a handsome face, but he'd dropped his usual rakish demeanor and polished charm. His blond hair flopped over his forehead, and the old t-shirt he'd put on was badly wrinkled.

"I have to apologize," he said sheepishly. "And not just for tonight. For how I've treated you ever since you came back to work, and especially for everything since the birthday party. I've been a real degenerate. A total cad."

"I won't argue with that," Gretchen said.

"Yeah, well, I know better. Somewhere along the line, I got carried away pretending to be somebody important. I let my job go to my head. 'Unpopular kid grows up into hot exec,' you know? Only to transform into a total butt." He smiled crookedly, genuinely.

"Funny what people will do to get other people to like them," Gretchen said. "We could write a manual together."

"An excellent idea. We'd sell millions of copies." He crossed his ankles on the ottoman. "So what's the deal with you and the masquerade? It's apparently not for fun."

"Long story," Gretchen said. She took a sip of tea and considered how to begin.

"I'm a pretty good listener, when I'm not being a butt. Just the highlights, maybe?"

She wrapped both hands around the warm mug. "Hmm. Okay. The short version is that Ruby went to Faerie Britannia and got enchanted into marrying a faerie prince. Stepmother sent me to bring her back, but Faerie Britannia—it's more dangerous and full of magic than you can imagine. I tried my best, but Ruby ended up getting murdered. Oh, and I forgot to mention that good old Ivory Werner told me not to come home without Ruby or she'd kill my father."

"Dang. She's colder than I thought."

"I'd made friends with this shape-shifting faerie guy, and he gave me the magic bearskin so I could come home and help Father. I think it probably ruined his life, though. It makes me sick thinking about it."

"He must have really cared about you."

"We'd been through a lot together in a short time. Bonded on the battlefield, or something like that. Still—yeah, I think you're right."

"Did you love him too?" he asked with a roguish gleam in his eye.

She tossed a small pillow at his chest. "Shut up, Toby."

"Sorry! Sorry." He put on a serious face. "But really. Did you?"

"I don't know. Maybe. It's all so much more complicated than that. Besides, it never would have worked."

"Tragic love. My fave."

She tossed another pillow at him. It bounced off his knee and landed on his lap. "You're still terrible, even minus the Prince Charming front."

"Sorry." He cleared his throat and hugged the recently thrown pillow. "Reforming isn't easy."

"Tell me about it after you become your stepsister twenty or thirty times. Do you mind if I get some sleep?" Gretchen said, stifling a yawn. "I have ball preparations to manage once the sun's up."

"Sure. Just one thing I want to say." He leaned forward, expression earnest. "Your stepmother's a bigger jerk than I am if she doesn't see what a great person you are, Gretchen. You risked your life for Ruby and your father, and you've suffered for it every day since. You're smart and kind and a better person than she'll ever be. If I were you, I'd stop wearing that fur and show her who you really are. Take your father to live in another colony and forget that witch."

"Thanks, Toby. I'll think about it."

He stood, grabbed a folded blanket from the back of a black velvet wing chair, and handed it to her. "I'm on your side, whatever happens. I mean it. Need anything else?"

"Just sleep, thanks."

"Right. Good night."

Gretchen stretched out her legs and spread the blanket over them as the lights dimmed. She closed her eyes and dreamed of walking beside Arthur in the enchanted woods, of taking his hand and feeling like herself, her true self. Not the girl who lived to please her stepmother or wore another's skin, but the girl she'd been born to be. Dream-world Gretchen felt strong and happy as she turned toward Arthur and took his face in her hands. Their faces moved closer together, and…

Her wrist comm's alarm buzzed her awake.

20 September, 170 N.E.

Arthur nibbled his fingernails to shreds. The equinox was in two days. Two days! Two days until he'd have to speak sacred vows and promise to wed Birna. Two days until the magic tortured him for the sin of giving away his pelt. If ever he'd hated Bearfolk rituals, it was now.

He walked through the apple orchard with Millicent flying beside him, checking the latest ripening trees for any remaining fruit. Rain sprinkled onto his head and shoulders, gently at first, and then it began to fall with a vengeance.

"Pocket?" he asked the moth, offering his open palm as a landing spot. She lighted, her tiny feet tickling his skin. He tucked her into the roomy pocket of his jacket and kept walking—although a sensible person would have gone home.

Rain soaked through his clothes and ran down his face like a hundred tears shed at once. He wasn't thinking anymore. What was the point? There was no real solution for his problem. He was going to have to marry Birna. He couldn't throw away his tribe and traditions for an infinitesimally tiny possibility that some miracle might happen to reunite him with Gretchen—who'd probably forgotten him by now, except when she had to put on his pelt.

He trudged across a stubbly field and through a muddy brook. He took a path into the woods, not giving a thought to bramble pixies or snapping-dragon flowers or anything else that enjoyed preying on unwary travelers.

The rain kept cascading from the sky and he kept walking. Sometimes the trees caught some of the downpour in their branches; at other times, his body bore its full assault. He slipped on wet moss and slick pine needles. His shoes squelched with every step.

Two days until the equinox, the voice in his head said as he trudged onward. *Two days.*

Ahead, almost shrouded in vines, stood an old shed. Perhaps a woodsman-elf had slept there long ago. Weary of walking, Arthur decided to wait out the storm inside—unless some unsavory creature already occupied the place.

He yanked hard to open the wooden door and ducked inside. Gasps greeted him.

He wiped water from his eyes and squinted into the dim corner. Two figures sat close together there, as wet as he was. Sweethearts holding hands and blushing at being discovered.

"Birna?" Arthur said, feeling as if he'd been whacked in the chest by a board. He reached out to touch the splintery wall, trying to steady himself. Birna was holding hands with a freckled-faced Bear-boy with shaggy hair and odd, brightly dyed clothes—which was simply impossible.

She scrambled to her feet. "Arthur? What are you…? We were caught in the storm and…"

"Two days," Arthur said. It was all he could say. And then he laughed. He felt insane, unhinged. Surely this was a dream. A hallucination.

Birna pulled the Bear-boy to his feet and close to her side. Her sodden yellow dress stuck to her body like another skin. The top two buttons were undone, revealing her pale neck and upper chest. "This is Swithin, the wise woman's son," she said.

"Were you planning to tell me about this?" Arthur asked.

"Of course I was. Arthur, please. Please don't hate me. We met when my parents took me to get herbs for my illness. We didn't even speak at first. But then he started to deliver the medicine to our house, and we became friends. Even up until last week, we were just friends."

"And now? You look rather cozy now."

"Don't be crass, Arthur. Nothing unseemly has happened. And you don't love me, anyway. You and I both know that."

"We want to be married," Swithin said. He spoke slowly, with an accent Arthur had only heard in the speech of the very oldest Bearfolk. "We beseech you to free her from the contract."

"Please, Arthur? You still have your decree of grace. No one can take that from you," Birna said. "I don't care if you let the blame fall on me for the break-up, either. It will make it easier for you to find another bride next year. If that's what you want."

More relieved than disappointed, Arthur stared at the pair of dripping, guilty faced, besotted Bearfolk. He wanted to laugh and cry at the same time.

"Say something, Arthur," Birna said. "Anything."

"Ursa's blessing on you," he said. He smiled so broadly his cheeks hurt. He was certain he looked like a madman, but he didn't care. "Go and tell your parents you've found your true husband."

He turned his back on them and stepped outside. Overhead, the dark clouds were sailing toward the coast. Sunlight streamed through the misty air, and the birds chirped in celebration of the storm's end. Now eased of his heart's heavy burden, he ran all the way home to share the news with Papa.

He was going to the colony to find Gretchen. Nothing could stop him.

Chapter Forty

21 September, 170 N.E.

Gretchen could hardly believe her eyes. Her father was sitting upright in bed in clean, striped pajamas, nibbling the corner of his toast. Kiki looked up from her knitting and grinned proudly.

"Ruby," Father said in a hoarse voice.

"Don't strain yourself," Kiki said in her official nurse tone. "Baby steps, remember?"

Father nodded. Gretchen came close and took his hand. "You look so much better, Father."

He squeezed her hand in reply, smiling.

"Can we talk?" Kiki said, gesturing to the little porch outside the French doors.

Gretchen followed Kiki out and waited to speak until the doors swished shut. "Is he cured?"

"Maybe eighty percent," Kiki said. "He's wobbly on his feet, and has some memory loss. But with time, and no more poisons, I predict a full recovery."

Gretchen had never been much of a hugger, but she grabbed Kiki and embraced her. "Thank you."

Kiki laughed as she stepped out of Gretchen's arms. "It's pretty amazing, right? But it might be a problem keeping old Ivory and her concoctions from getting to him. I've been here almost constantly, and my friend, Lee, subs for me when he can, but—"

"We need to get him out of here."

Kiki nodded. "As soon as possible. I don't think his body could survive another bout with the evil medieval medicine chest. He's already endured, what, like a solid year of that witch poisoning him?"

Guilt rolled through Gretchen in a nauseating wave. She should have noticed the oddness of Father's sickness sooner. From now on, she'd be a better daughter. "I'm applying for a job in Colony Three. If I get it, I'll take him with me and make sure he gets proper care."

"She'll never let you take him, Ruby. Not with the election coming up. I've heard her harping on the 'poor me, my husband's so sick' string so many times on the newsfeeds that I could puke. She needs those sympathy votes."

Gretchen lifted her chin defiantly. "I've been around long enough to know things that could get her thrown into prison for fifty years. I think she'll let him go if I threaten to tell her secrets to the police before the big election."

"Ruby! You sneaky little biscuit," Kiki said. "You'd do that to your mother? I mean, she totally deserves it, but this guy's not even your flesh and blood."

"He's a good man. He didn't deserve to be almost killed to get her a few stupid votes."

"Agreed." Kiki bit her lip and looked pensive for a moment. "My uncle works at a wilderness research outpost about an hour outside the colony. Almost nobody knows about it. I think we should arrange to sneak your stepdad to Uncle Fred's during the ball, while Ivory's occupied."

"That would give us more time to figure out what to do next."

"Yes, and give the poor guy more time to recover. I'll get in touch with Uncle Fred and get Lee on board to help us."

"How will I ever thank you, Kiki?"

"You already did. The dress, the shoes, the jewelry, the tickets to the ball…"

"It doesn't seem like enough."

"Friends don't keep score, Ruby. Anyway, it's been kind of fun, all this risky undercover stuff. I'll comm you about the details of the great escape tonight. See you at the ball, all dressed up and ready to dance?"

"Tomorrow night at six. If I don't drop from exhaustion before then."

"Can't wait," Kiki said, shimmying her hips with glee.

"I can't wait, either. Can't wait until it's over, and I can take a nap."

"Ruby Werner! You used to be the party queen. I'm shocked! Better start sucking down the energy drinks now. It's going to be a magical night."

"The equinox," Gretchen said, suddenly remembering a Bear-boy who had no magic pelt for his special celebration.

"Equi-what?" Kiki pressed the button to open the doors. "Never mind."

Poor Arthur, she thought. Whatever he'd have to suffer on the night of the equinox would surely be worse than anything she'd have to face during Stepmother's ball.

"I need to borrow your griffin, please," Arthur said, bowing low before Grilsa. The potent fragrance of her flower gardens combined with his nervousness and rendered him quite dizzy.

He almost couldn't believe he'd found Grilsa's house in the first place. He owed Millicent much for her service as a reliable route-finder.

The bronze-skinned faerie laughed and replied, "A strange greeting you give me, Arthur Woodley. Come to my table, and we shall discuss your request."

Arthur followed Grilsa into her house, his muscles tense with anxiety. It had taken almost a full day for him to reach her, and now the equinox was less than a day away. If the magic incapacitated him as punishment for not Changing, he'd be delayed another day or more. He had this nagging feeling that Gretchen needed him desperately, that he had no time to waste—and no way to know if his intuition was correct.

With soundless footsteps, one of the brownie housemaids brought tea and pastries to the dining room table as he pulled out a chair to sit. Millicent landed on his shoulder and folded her wings against her body.

Grilsa poured the tea and passed the plate of colorful little cakes. "Speak when you are ready," she said kindly. "And know that I shall keep any secrets you share, upon my honor."

He told the tale as quickly as he could, confessing his heart's truth. When he was done, Grilsa wiped a crystalline tear from her cheek and said, "I shall grant your request, Arthur Woodley. Your heart is pure and your intentions are admirable. You may borrow Enfys, my swiftest and most resilient griffin. If I feed her Avalon pears drenched in the honey of Snowdonian singing bees, she'll be able to carry you to North America in half a day's time. She is as good as a Marendall mare when it comes to navigating, and far less skittish in unfamiliar circumstances."

"What will you accept as payment?" Arthur asked.

"The payment I require is this: bring young Gretchen here when you return Enfys to my stables. I desire to see the girl again, and to hear of all that she has learned and endured since last we met. And if ever you and she decide to marry, you must promise to allow me to perform the ceremony here. My gardens bloom best when true love treads their paths."

"I promise to bring her," Arthur said. "If she agrees to come, that is."

Grilsa smiled and stood. She offered her arm to Arthur. "Time is not something one should waste when courageous acts await. I'll take you to Enfys now."

Arthur took her arm. Grilsa was so steeped in magic that his skin tingled and warmed where it met hers, even though the fabric of his shirt and jacket prevented their flesh from actually touching. Good thing she was on his side. With such power, she could likely reduce him to a mud puddle with a glance if she so chose.

They walked outside, through an herb garden, and down a pebbled path to a fenced meadow. Arthur's breath caught when he saw the pair of majestic griffins reclining in the grass like lazy pet cats. They were the size of large work horses. Their eagle-like heads and wings were white-feathered, and their muscular bodies and tufted tails resembled those of lions. "They're magnificent," Arthur said.

"Twenty years it took to tame them, but now they're loyal to me and one another until death." She raised her hand and gestured. "Come, Enfys. This is Arthur, and he shall be your master for three days and nights, and you shall obey and protect him as you would me."

Enfys approached and bowed her head.

"Scratch her head and speak to her," Grilsa said. "Let her become acquainted with your scent and voice while I fetch the pears and honey."

The griffin made a low purring sound in her throat as Arthur caressed her soft, curved forehead. "Enfys," he said.

"We're going on an adventure together. I hope you like flying over water, because the notion makes me a bit queasy. It will be worth it, though. At least I hope so."

He tried to imagine Gretchen's reaction to seeing a griffin land at her front door with him astride it. He wanted to think he'd look heroic, but he'd likely look tired, windblown, and maybe a bit green. But no matter how he looked to her, he knew for certain that she'd look beautiful to him.

His heart pounded hard as he realized that only a handful of hours and one large ocean now separated him from the girl he loved.

Chapter Forty-One

22 September, 170 N.E.

Gretchen groaned when she saw the reflection in Ruby's old-fashioned cheval mirror. Ruby's pretty face looked back at her, lovely as always (in spite of the scowl), and her dark hair had been professionally arranged into an elegant chignon—but the dress she'd been forced to squeeze into was just *ugh*.

Stepmother had chosen the bright pink satin gown and insisted that the dressmaker embellish it with enough rhinestones and ruffles to choke a hippo. The thing looked like a cherry cupcake had exploded in a fake diamond factory. The matching shoes were equally horrifying and painfully pointy. She'd put up with the torture-by-fashion for a few hours, and consider it her final act of submission to Ivory Werner. By morning, if all went as planned, she'd be a free woman, hidden away with her father at Kiki's uncle's place.

"Knock knock," Toby said from the doorway of Ruby's suite. "Your date has arrived. Holy strawberry milkshake tornado! What happened here? Who made that abomination?"

Gretchen spun to face Toby. He looked model perfect in his all-black evening suit. *The nerve.* The newsfeed commentators were going to have fun with this. Best-dressed guy escorts worst-dressed girl *ever.*

"Stepmother's new pet designer made it. Lester something-French. It's as bad as I think, isn't it?"

"Worse. Sorry." He swung a blue garment bag around from behind his back. "Fortunately, I came prepared to save the day." He hung the bag from a hook on the wall and unzipped it to reveal a deep purple ball gown sprinkled with tiny specks of silver, like the sky just as night takes hold. It was everything she would have put into a dress if she hadn't been utter rubbish at designing. Toby smiled as she stood gawking. "Happy birthday, by the way."

She rushed to run her fingers over the twinkling satin bodice and tulle skirt. "In all the chaos, I forgot it was my birthday. How did you know?"

"I hacked into your bio-profile, of course. After I hacked into Ruby's to get the dress measurements. When I overheard Rose whining about the nightmare gown she'd been hired to work on for you—I mean Ruby—I figured I could come up with something more Gretchen-like. That new fabric-creating equipment works like a charm. It cut everything perfectly, too, but I tackled the sewing myself."

"You did? You must have stayed up all night."

"Yeah, the dark circles under my eyes are not a fashion statement this time. But we can chat later. Go and get changed. The newsfeeds say half the guests arrived early, so your step-monster is probably about to stroke out."

Gretchen kicked off the hideous neon shoes, grabbed the top of the hanger, and carried the heavy gown into the walk-in closet. "Just so you know," she said as she wriggled free of the pink nightmare dress, "I'm going to hug you later, after it doesn't matter if you're wrinkled."

"A wise decision," Toby replied. "I agree to submit in a gentlemanly manner."

Gretchen's mini wrist comm, made to look like a diamond bracelet, buzzed. Stepmother's voice spilled out of it like a putrid flood. "Ruby, get over to the venue immediately. You should have been here hours ago. I can't believe—"

"Mute all calls," Gretchen said. She wasn't going to let the woman ruin what might be the only great part of the night. She'd never been much for clothes, but this gown! Perfection. She was pretty sure she'd still be thinking about it when she was a hundred.

"Zip me?" she said as she stepped out of the closet.

Toby did as she asked, and then spun her around. "Dang, Gretch. I think I'm going to cry."

"Is that good or bad?"

He pulled her to the mirror. "Look."

"Rot. Now I'm going to cry." Gretchen stared at the image of her beautiful stepsister. As happy as she was with the gown, seeing Ruby ready for the ball made her heart clench with grief. "Ruby would have loved this," she said.

Toby smiled sympathetically. "No tears. I don't think that fabric would react well to salt water." He wiped her cheeks with the pads of his thumbs. You'll just have to enjoy the night for her. And for yourself. Come on. You've got this. Also, once you see my dance moves, you'll be too busy worshiping me to remember any of your troubles."

"Heaven help us all," Gretchen said. "Wait. I don't have shoes."

"Hold on. They must still be in the bag." He darted into the closet and returned with a pair of almost transparent pumps. Whatever they were made out of glimmered like glass encasing tiny fireflies. He held them up like a trophy. "Now these. These cost me way more than I care to mention. Totally worth it for the look on your face, however."

He set the shoes on the floor and she slipped her feet into them.

"And to think I hated you until a few days ago," she said.

"Miracles do happen."

"Let's hope there's more to come. Stepmother's perturbed with me already, and the party hasn't even started."

"Forget her. Let's have some fun for once. You deserve it."

They hurried downstairs to the waiting hover-limo.

Arthur clung to the griffin with his hands and legs. The salty scent of the ocean filled his nose, and far below, he could see endless, ever-shifting, dark waters. He'd ceased to be afraid. Now, a steady peace filled his heart. Whether he lived or died, he'd tried his best to do what he believed was right.

His head ached, and his skin felt raw. Even above the Atlantic, he felt the call to Change. Perhaps he should have waited until the equinox had passed, but he'd hoped that leaving Britannia would lessen the magic's effects and blunt the punishment he'd earned.

"Please," he begged the magic. "Have mercy on me this one time."

The griffin squawked and dipped through a thin cloud. Arthur looked down and saw a patchwork of treetops and land.

"Thank Ursa," he said, ready to stand on solid ground—if his sore legs could support him. If he'd learned anything on this journey, it was that riding a griffin for thousands of miles was not easy on one's thigh muscles.

He wouldn't think of complaining. The journey's end was fast approaching, and he had to devote all his mental energy to figuring out what he'd do when he reached the colony. What if the place was gated and secured? How would he find Gretchen's street and house, if there were streets and houses? Her world, he knew, was far different than the forests and fields of Faerie Britannia.

He dug his aching fingers deeper into the feathers of the griffin's neck as she made a sudden, swooping turn. Lights sparkled up at him from domed and rectangular buildings. The colony.

Gretchen's home.

Chapter Forty-Two

The aircraft hangar looked nothing like an aircraft hangar inside.

Through the efforts of Gretchen and a dozen assistants, it had been transformed into a Baroque period ballroom—with the incongruous addition, at Stepmother's insistence, of thousands of twentieth-century-A.D.-style twinkly lights. White and gold panels painted with arched windows and doorways covered three of the walls. The fourth wall had been painted with a hazy mural of a forest at twilight, and a small stage had been set up against it in anticipation of Stepmother's speech. Tall, ornate, golden candelabras stood near the walls, and two enormous crystal chandeliers hung from the ceiling. Urns of fresh flowers blossomed in the corners of the room, and vases of fragrant roses and ferns sat amid silver trays of cakes on long tables. Regal music wafted from unseen speakers. Everything looked perfect to Gretchen.

Toby squeezed her hand. "All this from someone who can't draw a pair of trousers?"

She squeezed back, hard. "Very funny. I did have help, I admit."

Stepmother, arrayed in a red and gold garment that looked like a sari had crash landed in Martha Washington's 1776 wardrobe, hurried to meet them. "It's almost six. Didn't you get my message? The caterers dropped the cake, the wine is warm, and—good gracious! What in the world are you wearing, Ruby? No, no. I don't want to hear about it. Just go deal with that idiot chef you hired. Toby, you come with me. We'll look good on the newsfeeds welcoming the guests. A man who knows how to dress is such a rarity these days." She whisked him away. He looked back over his shoulder as if to beg for rescue, but there was nothing she could do. Stepmother wouldn't let him go without a serious fight now that she'd made him her arm candy. Hopefully, he'd be able to sneak away from her eventually.

After a brief time in the kitchen, Gretchen returned to the ballroom. She stood beside an urn of chrysanthemums and ivy and surveyed the room. An announcer wearing a Baroque wig and knee-length satin breeches was announcing guests' names as they entered. A dozen well-dressed couples waltzed in the center of the room (Stepmother's anachronistic musical choice), and twenty or thirty more guests stood in line waiting to sample the canapés and drinks. She spotted poor Toby near the stage, Stepmother's arm looped through his like he was her date.

Gretchen threaded her way through the crowd, checking for anything out of place, enjoying the swish and sway of her skirts as she walked, and collecting compliments on her gown.

"Ruby Werner?" a female voice called after her. She spun to face a woman with a reporter's badge pinned to the chest of her curve-clinging black gown. "Yasmine Jones of the Colony Times News. Mind if I get a shot of you? That dress is totally scrumptious."

"My pleasure," Gretchen said with a Ruby-esque giggle. She smiled and posed like a film star. If the media named Ruby best-dressed instead of Stepmother, the woman would give birth to kittens. Well, she couldn't stop the news people from forming opinions, could she, and she might as well show off Toby's hard work. She made sure Miss Jones knew all about the up-and-coming designer Toby Alastair before continuing her lap of the room.

An hour passed before Toby slipped his arm around her shoulders. "Hey, stranger. Nice frock," he said. "Let's dance before your mom realizes I made a run for it."

They waltzed badly, laughing and tripping and bumping into other dancers. After two or three selections, they danced their way to the food tables.

"You feeling okay?" Toby asked. "You're looking a little …pinched."

"It's getting late, or at least part of me thinks so." She scratched her shoulder before realizing how unmannerly it was to do in public. Her thoughts were getting fuzzy, and most of her body itched faintly but constantly. "I'll have to leave before it's over and face the wrath of Ivory Werner tomorrow for it."

"That woman. Schmoozing around like a…something nasty and snakelike. Like I said before, you ought to ditch her and get a new life for yourself. Look what you did here. You can do anything you want to. I mean it."

"You're a good friend," Gretchen said. She picked up a gold plate and handed it to Toby.

Her wrist comm buzzed. She turned her arm to read the message. "It's Father's nurse, Lee. He was supposed to be sneaking Father out of the house about now, but Father's sick again—really sick. I need to go."

"Let's go, then." He set his plate down.

"No. You stay and enjoy the ball," Gretchen said as they tried to maneuver through the crowd. "You've been looking forward to it for ages."

"No way. It wouldn't be fun without you. Besides, I'm your best friend, right?"

"Right." Her knees buckled, and he caught her under the arm. The pelt was done whispering its request. The pain singed her veins like the worst possible fever. Her vision blurred.

"This is no time for drunken foolishness, Ruby," Stepmother said from behind her. "Stand up straight and get yourself together. It's time for my big announcement, and as my daughter, you have an obligation to stand by my side and show your support. No matter how tipsy you are."

Gretchen looked into Toby's face as he helped her follow Stepmother. She hoped he knew how grateful she was for his literal support. He must have had some kind of training in helping drunks cross rooms while looking stylish, because heck, he was good at it.

"Hey," he said into her ear. "If you need to bolt, just nod or something. I'll toss you over my shoulder and get you out of here quick, okay?"

"Thanks. I think I can hold on a bit longer. I hope."

The Baroque-costumed announcer took the stage and said grandly, "Presenting Ivory Werner, our candidate for prime minister of the North American Colonies!"

Ivory swept onto the stage and waved, her white teeth gleaming in the spotlight. "Thank you all for attending my nomination ball. I'm honored to be here in the company of my beautiful daughter, Ruby." She gestured, and the spotlight glared in Gretchen's face for a moment before returning its beam to her stepmother. "My one regret is that my beloved husband, Walter, is unable to join us this evening." She laid on hand on her heart and choked back a theatrical sob. "He is fighting for his life and might not see another sunrise, but the last words he spoke to me were, 'Darling, you must go to the ball. Your success means more to me than life itself.'" One fat tear rolled over her cheekbone.

"Liar," Gretchen muttered.

"As you know, I am no stranger to the pain of sacrifice. I lost my dear stepdaughter Gretchen to the treachery of the wicked faeries of Britannia mere months ago. If elected prime minister, I promise to implement plans for better rehabilitation of rebellious, troubled young girls, so that her tragedy is not repeated. I also promise to strengthen our defenses against the evil fae and develop strategies to subdue them so that humankind may once again rule the territory of the former British Isles."

Stepmother paused for applause. Gretchen trembled, held up only by the strength of Toby's arms.

As the crowd settled down, Stepmother said, "And so I dedicate this campaign to the memory of my darling child, Gretchen, and as a tribute to my ailing but faithful husband. They, and my precious daughter Ruby, have inspired me to become the leader you see here today: a woman challenged by life, pummeled by pain, familiar with grief, but ready to lead this new nation into a prosperous and victorious future." She reached for the glass of champagne the announcer held out on a tray. She raised the glass high in a toast. "To Gretchen and Walter, and to my victory in the next election!"

Gretchen trembled from head to toe, shaken by the pelt's demands but also by the fury Stepmother had sparked with her lies and manipulation. Poisoning her husband and using it for political gain was worse than any crime Gretchen had seen the faeries commit. And then to play the "dead stepdaughter" card on top of all that!

She wasn't going to allow it. It was time for the lies to end—including her own. The pelt's magic shot needles of pain through the marrow of every bone in her body, spurring her on.

"Toby," Gretchen said. "I'm going to change now."

"You can't do that here. Let me carry you out."

She shook her head and whispered to the magic, "Now."

Her body—Ruby's body—went limp in Toby's arms as the magic ripped skin from skin in the matter of a few fleeting seconds. She heard herself whimper, heard the gasp of the people around her, and felt the fur being wrapped around her body like a robe.

She opened her eyes and pushed away from Toby, standing on her own two Gretchen-sized feet. Ruby's dancing shoes and the torn ball gown lay on the floor.

"My name is Gretchen Werner, and that woman is a liar and a criminal!" Gretchen shouted, gesturing toward her stepmother. "She's been poisoning my father, and she sent Ruby to die in Britannia as part of a scheme to win votes."

"Impostor!" Stepmother said from the stage, pointing a scarlet fingernail. "Guards, arrest that intruder! She has a weapon!"

The guests gasped and scattered.

Gretchen ran toward the exit, clutching the bearskin around her body, weaving her way through the astonished partygoers. Passing a seating area, she grabbed an abandoned cloak to wear once she got outside. The pelt's weight was hard to bear when the magic left it, and she needed to get to her father as quickly as possible.

The automatic doors opened before her, and she fled into the night.

For two eternally long seconds, Arthur stood paralyzed as members of the panicked crowd swirled around him. Had he really just seen Gretchen change forms in the midst of a human party?

Just minutes ago, the griffin had delivered him directly to the site of the ball. After he'd slid off her back, she'd nudged him with her beak in the direction of the door. "In there?" he'd asked. "Gretchen's in there?"

The griffin had nodded, and then flown to perch in the top of a nearby oak tree.

The doors had swooshed open as if by magic, and he'd rushed into the biggest, most lavishly decorated building he'd ever beheld.

And then he'd seen her.

His eyes hadn't wasted one moment sweeping the room; they'd locked on her instantly. Something inside him recognized Gretchen even in the guise of Ruby. Perhaps his pelt's magic helped. Regardless, there she was, dressed in a sparkling gown and leaning heavily on a well-dressed young man.

The shift had happened quickly, almost unremarkably. She'd simply slumped into the man's arms and shuddered, emitting a slight glow—and then it had been over. The pelt had tumbled to her feet, entangled with her ruined dress. Quick as lightning, her companion had grabbed the fur and wrapped it around Gretchen's body.

She'd run for the door, stumbling like a newborn fawn, her face pale and etched with pain. The sight of her anguish made his already sick stomach churn all the more. The equinox magic had not given up meting out punishment just because he'd arrived on foreign shores. He was feverish and unsteady, but he had no time to indulge his illness.

He ran as fast as he could now, desperate to catch her. Hoping he could help her. Hoping she'd forgive him if his well-intentioned gift had caused her trouble. Hoping his aching legs could carry him until he reached her.

As he left the party behind, cool night air filled in his lungs. He saw Gretchen ahead in the moonlight, staggering up a small hill, dropping the pelt and wrapping a black garment around her body as she continued to move.

"Gretchen!" he called.

Trudging onward, she glanced over her shoulder at him. And then she stopped and turned, eyes wide with wonder.

"Arthur?"

Suddenly, his legs gained strength. He ran, his feet barely touching the ground, until he was close enough to pull her into his arms.

Chapter Forty-Three

Arthur was impossible.

His arms around her, his familiar piney, musky, wood-smoke scent, his heart pounding against her chest—all impossible.

She didn't decide to kiss him; she just kissed him. Or maybe he kissed her. Or they kissed each other. It didn't matter. For a moment, there was nothing wrong in the universe. They were together under the stars, alone on a patch of Earth.

"Whoa. Hey," Toby's voice said, breaking the spell. "You two know each other, I hope?"

Gretchen took a step back and felt her face flush. She clutched the dark cloak more tightly around her body.

"Oh my sainted grandma," Toby said. "You're him. The bear guy."

"Arthur, Toby," Gretchen said to introduce them. "We can't stand here and chat. Father's dying, and I have to hurry, or—"

Arthur whistled like he was calling a dog. "I can get us wherever you need to go, fast."

"And I brought your shoes and fur coat," Toby said, holding

up the pelt and one of the sparkly, glasslike shoes. "Dang. I must have dropped a shoe somewhere."

"I'm not a size six like Ruby now, so they wouldn't fit me anyway," said Gretchen. "And that fur's not mine anymore. I'm finished with all the pretending."

A blast of wind from above mussed her hair. She looked up at the circling, descending griffin, awestruck by the breadth of its feathered wings. "Um, Toby, don't freak out, but…"

Toby looked up. His jaw fell open. "Holy…"

"Enfys can only carry two of us," Arthur said. "I'm sorry." He took the pelt from Toby as the griffin's clawed feet met the grass a few yards from them.

"I'll meet you at the house," Toby said. "I'd rather take a hover cab than a mythical beast. Don't want to mess up the suit."

The griffin crouched low and Gretchen climbed onto its back. Clutching the pelt, Arthur climbed on in front of her. She wrapped her arms around his ribcage. He felt one hundred percent real. Warm and solid. But the night's events still seemed like a dream. She was having a hard time believing Arthur was actually with her, in the colony, minutes after she'd shown her true identity (and more skin than she cared to think about) to Stepmother and a ballroom full of witnesses.

"The house is on the western edge of the colony," she said. "Between the blue dome and the lake."

Enfys nodded. She walked, then galloped, then leapt into the air. Her huge wings flapped, and she carried Gretchen and Arthur over the hangar and the treetops. Gretchen tried hard to commit every detail to memory: the moonlit autumn leaves below her, the comfortable fit of her arms around Arthur's chest, the slow rhythm of the griffin's wing beats, the animal's feral scent. She wanted to be able to remember all of this in the future, when her father was safe and worry could no longer taint her enjoyment of the miraculous experience.

She rested her cheek against Arthur's shoulder. He reached back, his hand open, and she entwined her fingers with his. She had so many questions for him—but she shoved them out of her mind and focused on the sensation of his palm against hers.

Impossible, she thought. *Impossible and wonderful.*

Arthur spotted the pair of armed guards before Enfys landed, and so did Enfys.

Still carrying him and Gretchen, the griffin charged the men with her wings spread wide, bellowing a half-shriek, half-roar that rattled the windows of the house. The men fell flat on the ground, stunned unconscious by the enchantment of Enfys's battle cry.

Gretchen slid off the griffin's back. "This way," she said. Arthur followed her inside and up a flight of stairs. In the hallway, more guards lay face down and motionless.

"Your griffin's pretty amazing," she said.

"Grilsa's griffin," he replied in a scratchy voice. The equinox magic had launched another assault on him, punishing him with a pounding head and weakened limbs. He reached for the wall to support himself as a door slid open.

"Are you coming?" Gretchen said when he didn't rush after her.

The room spun and his legs gave out.

"You're sick," he heard her say. She sounded far, far away. "From not changing, right? Oh my word, I'm so sorry, Arthur."

He couldn't keep his eyes open, but he felt her hand on his shoulder.

"What can I do? Arthur? Should I get the bearskin?"

Unable to speak or move, he surrendered to the dark pull of unconsciousness.

Chapter Forty-Four

"Lee?" Gretchen called into her father's suite as she knelt next to Arthur's unconscious form. "Lee? I need help out here."

She glanced down at Arthur. He looked terrible. Dead. The slight rise and fall of his chest provided the only clue that he remained alive.

When Lee failed to respond, Gretchen stood and hurried into Father's bedroom. The newsfeed played on a screen across from the bed, reporting events that had occurred at the ball: the shape-shifting girl who'd been named best-dressed before her unbelievable transformation, the accused politician who vowed to track down the trespassing imposter who'd tried to smear her name.

Lee sat slumped in a chair, eyes shut. Not merely napping, but griffin-stricken.

"Darn it! Sorry about that, Lee," Gretchen said before turning her attention to her father. The monitor on the wall above his bed showed that his heart still beat slowly. "Hold on, Father," she said. "I'm going to get you out of here. Somehow."

"What is with all the passed out dudes?" Toby asked as he strode into the room. "Did the witch poison them, too?"

"The griffin knocked them out with her voice. Unfortunately, it worked on everyone in the house."

"So, what's the plan? Your dad doesn't exactly look ready to make a run for it, if that's what you were thinking."

"Nurse Lee was supposed to transport him to Kiki's uncle's research outpost to finish recovering. But he's out cold, and I don't have directions."

Sirens sounded in the distance. Toby mussed his perfect hair with his hands. "Think of another option. We need to get out of here, Gretch. Now."

"I'm trying!"

"Grilsa," Arthur said. Somehow, he'd crawled into the bedroom. "She can heal him if anyone can." He propped himself in the corner, breathing heavily.

Going back to Britannia seemed outrageous to Gretchen, but what other choice did they have? "We'll have to take my airskipper," she said. "Father's in no condition for a griffin ride, and besides, there are three of us."

"Four," Toby said. "You're not leaving me here to face the wrath of Ivory. She's going to assume I was in on this with you, and I despise the prison uniforms—even though I did help design them."

"Good," Arthur said. "You can help me stay on Enfys."

"Maybe the uniforms aren't so bad," Toby said. "Yeah. Kidding. Guess I'm going to co-pilot an eagle-headed lion in my best suit. And I thought tonight's biggest excitement was behind me."

Gretchen smirked. "Toby, help me get Father into that hover-chair. We'll go out the back way and get him into the airskipper, and then you can follow with Arthur on Enfys." She looked down at Arthur, whose face had gone from gray to pale—a slight improvement. "Can you get back to the griffin by yourself?"

"If Toby can help me outside, I'll call Enfys to meet us."

The wail of the sirens was growing louder by the second. Toby lifted Father into the chair and Gretchen commanded it to follow her. Then Toby picked up Arthur, slinging him over his shoulder like a fireman performing a rescue.

"Shizam, you're tall," Toby said.

"Come on," Gretchen said as the usually concealed servants' door opened in the wall. "I've summoned the airskipper to meet us at the edge of the garden. Let's go."

Sitting on a bench between rose bushes, Arthur watched Toby and Gretchen run across the garden with Gretchen's father's hover-chair at their heels. He whistled for Enfys, praying she'd hear him above the noise of the sirens and alarms.

A pair of black vehicles swooshed into the garden, lights flashing. Dark-clothed men jumped out, armed with black guns. Gretchen's stepmother emerged from one of the vehicles, her face a mask of rage.

"That way, you idiots," she said, pointing toward the path Gretchen had taken. "Get the girl!"

Enfys swooped down, talons bared. Stepmother stumbled backward and fell into a rose bush. She wriggled and kicked, making herself sink farther into the thorns.

"Shoot the monster!" she screamed. "Shoot it now!"

The men spun and aimed.

Enfys raised her head, opened her beak, and roared, knocking everyone in the vicinity to the ground and into a stunned state—except for Arthur.

"Thank you, Enfys," Arthur said. The griffin bowed to him and then flattened her body to the ground to allow him to mount. He used all the strength he had left to get astride the creature, settling onto the pelt she'd somehow arranged like a saddle. He touched the familiar fur and laid his throbbing head against the griffin's soft, feathered neck, taking what comfort they could give.

Soon, the equinox would end, and so would his suffering. Soon, he'd be with Gretchen again, and Papa, in the extraordinary land he knew and loved.

"Find Toby," he said, and Enfys must have done so, for when he next awoke, the blue-green ocean sparkled and splashed below him, and strong arms were firmly holding him in place from behind.

"Good morning," Toby said loudly over Arthur's shoulder. "I think we're almost to Britannia. At least I hope so. My thighs are killing me."

"Thank Ursa," Arthur said. He sat up straight and breathed deeply of the salty air. He felt strong again, as strong as he had before the equinox dawned.

Toby's grip around Arthur's ribcage relaxed now that Arthur could keep himself stuck to the creature's back. He shouted to be heard above the wind created by Enfys's wings. "So, what are my chances where you live? I mean, I've heard stories. Am I going to be kidnapped by ogres or fried by dragons or what?"

Arthur smiled. "You'll be fine if you follow a few rules, I think."

"Your certainty is very inspiring."

Arthur laughed, then said, "Few things are certain in Britannia. Magic is a fickle mistress, and magical beings are even more so."

"Not you, though, right? You're not going to be fickle about Gretchen. Because if you hurt her—"

"No," Arthur said. "Never." He remembered seeing her in

Toby's arms at the ball and wondered if it had meant something. Perhaps they'd been more than friends before he'd shown up to "rescue" her. He had to ask, or wondering would drive him mad. The sooner the better. He inhaled, exhaled, and forced out the words, "You care about her, don't you?"

"Yeah. She's pretty great."

"Were you…courting?" Saying it out loud made his stomach twist into a knot.

"Yeah—I mean, no. I was seeing Ruby, really. It was messed up, and I'm sorry about it. So, no. Gretchen and I weren't *together* together—just friends. No competition to worry about from me. Besides, she seemed way happier to see you last night than she's ever been to see me. Thought I'd have to pry her off your face, dude."

The memory of the kiss brought heat to Arthur's face. He'd imagined fifty different reunion scenes as he'd crossed the ocean to find Gretchen, but none of them had involved her kissing him before he had a chance to confess his feelings. And the way she'd kissed him—sweetly but with such fervor. As if she'd missed him as much as he'd missed her.

As if she loved him.

The shores of Britannia came into view, and Arthur threw back his head and shouted with joy. The quiet young man he'd been before the solstice would have celebrated silently, but *that boy* had not helped Gretchen survive a war, or given up his precious pelt, or ridden a griffin across the sea. *That boy* had not been kissed in the moonlight while enduring an unanswerable call to Change.

That boy was just a memory.

Chapter Forty-Five

23 September, 170 N.E.

Dressed in the simple, cream-colored linen shift and tan leggings Grilsa had provided, Gretchen was sitting at Grilsa's table eating a pink-iced cake when the moth flew through the open window and landed on the rim of her teacup.

"Millicent?" Gretchen ran a finger over the moth's furry back. "I've missed you."

"You know the moths here by name, Gretch? What the heck," Toby said with a crooked smile. He picked a yellow-iced petit four from the platter and held it up. "These cakes are enough to make me want to stay here forever, moth friends or no moth friends."

"Good thing Grilsa gave you the special marble so you don't have to stay because of the food. Unless you want to," Gretchen said. "You do remember what Professor Reynaud taught about faerie food being a trap, don't you?"

Arthur rushed into the room clutching a wilting bunch of green and white leaves. "Found it. The last thing Grilsa needed for your father's cure. Almost got mauled by an irate swamp pixie over this. They're even more territorial than bog trolls, it turns out."

"I'm glad you survived," Gretchen said, remembering her run-in with the hedge pixies. Arthur's eyes locked on hers for a second and her heart fluttered. "Go on," she said. "Grilsa's waiting."

"You must come with him, Gretchen," Grilsa said from the doorway of the next room. "Curatives work best when loved ones are near."

Gretchen followed Arthur, and Millicent followed Gretchen.

"Don't mind me. I'll just wait here with the cakes," Toby said.

In Grilsa's sitting room, Gretchen's father lay on a long, mustard-yellow, velvet couch. Grilsa had covered him from neck to feet with bright flowers and silvery leaves. Here and there, honeybees walked among the blossoms, buzzing softly in unison. Father's face was ashen, but his expression was serene.

Millicent settled onto the cushion that supported Father's head. She folded her wings and sat still as stone.

Arthur handed the bouquet of herbs to Grilsa. Grilsa turned to work at a high table strewn with leaves, twigs, and bottled powders.

"He's going to be fine," Arthur said, moving closer to Gretchen. He brushed a fingertip over her cheek, catching a tear she hadn't realized she'd shed.

"I know," she said. She took his hand. Maybe it was bad manners or even brazen behavior according to the Bearfolk. She wasn't going to ask. She needed his hand in hers. It made her feel safe and cherished, and somehow gave her hope.

"Ready at last," Grilsa said. Between her thumb and forefinger, she held a golden thimble full of fizzing liquid. "As his beloved daughter, it falls to you to administer this. A few drops in his mouth, and all should be well with him."

Gretchen's hand trembled. She feared she might spill every bit of the medicine before she got it to his mouth.

"Steady now," Arthur whispered encouragingly. "You're about to be his hero, you know."

"Are you trying to make me more nervous?" she asked with a shaky laugh.

Grilsa whispered a prayer as Gretchen pressed the thimble to Father's lips and poured the greenish-brown potion into his mouth. Thimble emptied, Gretchen stepped back. Her heart beat so hard it hurt. She squeezed Arthur's fingers, not daring to breathe as she waited for the medicine to take effect.

Father coughed three times. His eyes fluttered open, and he smiled. "Gretchen? I thought you were dead, my girl," he said.

"I thought the same of you," she replied, and she threw her arms around her father, laughing and crying at the same time.

After a few minutes, Gretchen straightened and wiped her tears with her sleeve. "Thank you, Grilsa," she said.

"Your joy has brought me joy," Grilsa replied. "Now, I must see to other matters. Please excuse me." She swept out of the room in her usual queenly manner.

"Who was that? And where am I?" Father asked. He shimmied into a sitting position on the couch. Arthur helped adjust the cushions behind him.

"Grilsa is a powerful faerie wise woman, and we are in her home." Gretchen said. "In Britannia. How we got here is a long story best saved for later. You should rest, Father."

"Nonsense. I feel twenty-five again. And how can I rest when you've just told me we're in Faerie Britannia?"

"You're safe here, sir," Arthur said. "Safer than you were in the colony."

"And you are?" Father asked.

"Arthur Woodley, sir. I've lived here in Britannia all my life."

"Well," Father began, but then Millicent landed on his forearm and distracted him.

"Hello there," Father said. "Aren't you lovely?" He brought his arm up so he could better inspect the moth, and then he said to Gretchen, "Your mother would have loved this pretty creature. She had a bit of an obsession with moths and butterflies. I don't suppose you remember."

"I had forgotten until now," Gretchen said. "That moth's been a good friend to me. I named her Millicent."

"Only that isn't her true name," Arthur said.

Gretchen looked at him curiously. "So, what is her name, then?"

"Grilsa told me your father would know. She said it was for him to speak."

Father stared into the black eyes of the moth, and the moth seemed to stare back at him. He drew a sharp breath and a look of wonderment came over his face. "Her name is Amara Siskin, and she was, and is, the love of my life."

The air in the room shimmered and hummed, and Gretchen found she could neither breathe nor move. She watched the moth hover, glow, break into a million pieces of rainbow-hued light, and reform into the shape of a woman.

A woman dressed in an expedition uniform style not used since Gretchen was a little girl. A woman with honey-gold hair streaked with silver like Gretchen's, and a smile Gretchen had almost forgotten.

"Mom?" Gretchen said, barely able to stand under the weight of her emotions.

The woman nodded and pulled her into her arms.

"They said you died in an orbiter repair accident," Gretchen said, too astonished to cry.

"That's what the authorities told us," her father said. He left the couch and joined Gretchen and her mother, wrapping his arms around them both. "They said you'd floated off into space, never to be recovered. I never thought to question it."

Amara said, "I was a covert member of a scientific expedition, on a top secret mission to collect data and biological samples from the fae and their island. When we were ambushed, I managed to escape, only to be enchanted by a yew tree sprite. She called herself merciful for changing me into a creature I loved, and as an extra, so-called kindness, she set the spell to expire if my true love ever found me, recognized me, and spoke my name. Of course, I never expected that to happen."

"Lately, a lot of things have happened I thought never would," Gretchen said. "But you're the best one of all, Mom. No offense, Arthur."

Arthur smiled timidly. He'd snuck into the corner of the room at some point, as if he felt out of place at the impromptu family reunion. "Come here," Gretchen said, reaching for his hand. "Mom, this is Arthur."

"I know Arthur well," Amara said. "We've been spending a lot of time together, although he did all the talking while I just flitted and fluttered." She pulled him close and embraced him. "Thank you for saving my daughter and my husband. I know what it cost you."

"I'd do it all again," Arthur said.

Arthur rejoiced with Gretchen at her reunion with her mother even as he missed his own mother's presence. As misguided as Lusela Woodley had been at the end of her life, she remained his mama. She'd loved him wholeheartedly, he knew, and she'd done her best to raise him to be a good member of the Bearfolk. Would she see him as a failure now, with his pelt's magic and his heart given away to a human? Perhaps it was better that he had no way of knowing.

Gretchen slipped her hand into his. "Let's go for a walk and let my parents catch up with each other. Have you seen Grilsa's gardens? They're beyond amazing. I haven't stopped thinking about them since the last time I was here," she babbled as she led him into the kitchen. He wondered if she had as many butterflies doing acrobatics in her stomach as he had at the prospect of being alone together.

She added in a whisper, "I'd say we should ask Toby to go along, but he looks rather uninterested."

Toby had fallen asleep in his chair at the dinner table, his chin resting on his chest.

"I agree," Arthur said.

One of Grilsa's brownie servants bustled about, clearing the table without making a sound. Arthur and Gretchen sidled past her, through the kitchen, and out into the section of the garden dedicated to culinary herbs.

The scent of thyme and sage hung heavy on the air, reminding Arthur of the Yuletide feasts of his childhood. He inhaled deeply, full of contentment even though he did not know whether he'd spend another holiday with his tribe. He'd been pardoned for giving his pelt to Gretchen; carrying on a relationship with her was another matter entirely.

"What are you thinking about?" Gretchen said. "Sorry. I know guys hate that question. You don't have to answer."

Arthur plucked a sage leaf and held it close to her nose so she could smell it. "Just this. It reminds me of the Bearfolk Yule celebrations. Those are the best feasts of the year: the pies, the roasted fowls, the puddings. And the dancing to the wedding songs—it goes on all night."

"I'm sorry I took that from you. I shouldn't have accepted

your pelt. It didn't occur to me that it was your actual magic bearskin until after I'd left Britannia, and then I—"

"Please don't regret my gift. I don't. We can make new traditions, can't we?"

"Of course we can. Let's start now." Gretchen pointed to a bush covered in gold-edged roses. "From now on, whenever we see a rose bush, we'll stop and remember this time in Grilsa's gardens. The smells, the colors of the leaves and flowers, those little green butterflies—and how I embarrassed myself by asking you to kiss me."

"Are you sure?" Arthur stopped and faced her. "We could be friends. A lot has happened. We don't need to rush into anything." Ursa above, he hoped she didn't want to be just friends—but neither did he want to take advantage of her when she'd been through so much in the last few months.

"We *are* friends," Gretchen said. "And also, I'm pretty sure I love you, Arthur Woodley."

"I'm pretty sure I love you, too," he replied, taking her into his arms and kissing her. All his sorrows and grief, every question he had about the future, and every care he had in the world floated off like a wisp of dandelion fluff chased away by a breath of wind.

CHAPTER FORTY-SIX

They walked together—Gretchen, her parents, Arthur, his father, and Toby—through a pine forest glazed in crystalline ice, eyes dazzled by the glint of needles in wintry sunlight. From time to time, one of them would slip, only to be saved from falling into the snow by the quick hand of another, and then they'd all laugh.

Three months had passed since Gretchen had brought her father to Britannia. For three months, she'd enjoyed the affection of a good and loving mother, and the devotion of a boy raised by bears.

Thorburn had given Gretchen, her parents, and Toby a long-abandoned cottage in the woods near his orchard, and Grilsa had granted them a magical hedge of protection that kept all fae of ill intent off the property. Almost daily, the two families shared suppers and walks, bonfires and times of storytelling.

On the day of the winter solstice, the call to Change had laid Arthur low, punishing him with fever and wracking his body with pain—and Gretchen sat at his bedside, holding his hand when he could endure her touch, and crying when he could not. She'd suffered with him from dusk until dawn, and when morning had broken the magic's grip, his fever lifted, and Thorburn returned from the Bearfolk celebrations as a man, weary but well.

Upon his return, Thorburn found a raven waiting on his doorstep. The bird carried a summons from the faerie high king, ruler over all faeriekind, calling Gretchen, Arthur, and Thorburn to appear before his Yuletide court at the Palace of Seven Silver Stars.

"Are you well enough to travel? You were almost dead a couple hours ago," Gretchen said to Arthur after Thorburn read the message aloud. He stood near the hearth drinking a mug of Christmas nog and looking as healthy as she'd ever seen him. Still… "Maybe we should ask for a springtime meeting." Truth was she was in no hurry to meet Prince Barrett's all-powerful father. What if he banished her from Britannia, or sentenced Arthur to death for mingling with humans? A shiver ran down her spine as she imagined some of the magical punishments a vengeful faerie king might mete out.

"The solstice is over. I'm as good as new," Arthur said.

"I just think it's a bad idea to go now. Or ever."

Arthur took her hand and met her gaze. "It's a worse idea to disobey a command from the high king, believe me. We'll be fine."

Thorburn nodded his agreement. "You'd best go. Try not to worry, lass. Why, if he wanted you dead, you'd be dead already."

Gretchen rolled her eyes heavenward. "Why does that not make me feel better?"

Neither Bear-man answered. Instead, they hurried to wrap

her in several woolen cloaks and scarves—as if to muffle any further argument. She submitted to being shod with fur boots and accepted a pair of colorful mittens from Arthur before Thorburn all but shoved her out the door.

Now, after walking two or three miles, the three travelers met two majestic Marendall stallions at the edge of a frosted meadow. Their elaborate leather saddles bore the seal of the king.

"Well now," Thorburn said. "You see? The king must be pleased with us if he's sent his finest horses."

Thorburn mounted a silver-gray as Arthur boosted Gretchen into the saddle of a midnight black horse. He climbed up behind her and wrapped his arms around her waist, setting the reins in her hands.

"But I'm really not good at driving a horse," she said. "I think I've proven that already."

Arthur laughed lightly, close to her ear, sending a pleasant chill through her body.

"Marendalls don't need to be driven. They know what to do. Just ask him nicely to go, and he will."

"Go, please," Gretchen said. The horse obeyed, leading the other horses slowly over the crunching meadow grass and then speeding up to a brisk canter through the woods. She gripped the reins hard, leaned back against Arthur's chest, and shut her eyes. Being strapped inside an airskipper felt so much safer than racing among dense trees and over unpredictable ground—yet she didn't wish she were anywhere else. What could be better than feeling the pure, bracing air of Faerie Britannia in her lungs, the strength of the Marendall stallion beneath her, and the warmth of Arthur's steady arms around her? It almost made her forget how much she dreaded meeting the king.

Side by side, Arthur and Gretchen passed through a pair

of glittering white doors twenty feet tall and into the throne room of the high king. Arthur cast one last, nervous glance back at his father, who'd been told to wait in the antechamber. Nausea roiled in his belly. Perhaps he should have listened to Gretchen and asked for a later appointment. It was all he could do to keep walking. If Gretchen had not been beside him, his partner in this daunting experience, he probably would have fainted dead away.

The courtiers fell silent as the king rose to his feet in front of his bejeweled silver throne. Arthur felt the weight of the royal stare as if it were a bag of lead set on his shoulders. He bowed low as Gretchen curtsied.

"Rise," the king said. He was tall and thin, with an avalanche of snow white locks cascading over the shoulders of his moonlight-colored robes. His eyes were the pure blue of a midsummer sky, but his voice was like a winter storm, full of power yet coolly beautiful. He spread his arms wide and continued, saying, "I have heard of the mighty deeds of the Silverhair who roused the Bearfolk to victory over my traitorous son and his armies. That selfsame maiden then dared to return to the land of men clad in Bearfolk magic, in order to rescue her father from the hands of a tyrant witch. And I have heard of the Bearfolk lad who treasured his tribe above all else, yet willingly gave up his sacred birthright for true love's sake. I have heard that the Silverhair was rewarded well by Fate, being granted reunion with her blood mother. And I have heard that the Bear-boy was forgiven for his sin of generosity, and allowed to dwell among his kind—until it became known that he'd given his heart to a human as well as his pelt. And then the Bearfolk elders spurned their son and his beloved, forgetting it was she who brought about the end of their long and terrible war."

Arthur nodded, gazing at his boots.

"The Bearfolk elders are hardhearted, and have laid aside love for the sake of their rules. But I hold sway over them, and I grant you this, Arthur Woodley of the Bearfolk and Gretchen Silverhair: you are Bearfolk full and for as long as you shall live—which shall be long indeed, as is the Bearfolk way. Although I cannot grant either of you the magic to Change, I declare that you shall dress in finery and celebrate every holiday with your tribe, sharing in their joy as if you wore the fur they hold so dear. This is my command, and it shall not be defied by any living creature, fae or otherwise. The king has spoken his will."

"Let the king's will be done," the faerie courtiers said in unison.

Arthur felt Gretchen shiver beside him as the king's magical gift of an increased lifespan swept over and into her.

"Go now, and observe the Yuletide with your kind," the king said. "I have sent my messenger raven ahead of you, and the elders will receive my edict before you arrive. Blessings and joy be upon you and your children."

Arthur fell to his knees in awe and gratitude. As musicians played a regal theme, Gretchen knelt beside him while the courtiers paraded out of the room in the wake of the trailing robes of the king.

"Did he say I'm Bearfolk?" Gretchen asked when the room quieted. Her cheeks were pink as the cherry blossoms that graced Papa's orchard behind their old cottage.

Arthur stood, pulled her to her feet, and kissed her. "Wait until you taste the Yule puddings. And the stargazy pie!"

"I can't believe I'm Bearfolk," Gretchen said.

"Full and for always. Which means we'll have hundreds of years together to discuss the wonders and privileges of Bear-folk-kind. Hundreds of years for you to document faerie plants and flowers, if you like. Now, however, I'm starving. Let's find my father and those horses and get to the feast before all the best pies are gone."

Gretchen's stomach growled loudly enough for Arthur to hear. She patted her belly and smiled. "I'd follow you nearly anywhere, Arthur Woodley, but especially toward pie."

Chapter Forty-Seven

Half an hour after leaving the palace, as they rode past a wooden cabin shaded by tall pines, an elderly Bear-woman stepped into the path of their Marendalls. Arthur recognized her unusual bright blue eyes and her voluminous apron. The stallions halted and nickered a greeting.
"Good day, travelers," she said. "I've been expecting you."

"Good day," Thorburn, Gretchen, and Arthur replied in unison.

"Do you remember me?" Arthur asked. "You directed me to the Cloverfields' house a few months ago."

The Bear-woman grinned. "Aye, of course. You're the lad with the scriptures etched upon his heart. And this girl who rides with you—her I've seen in my dreams. Come down, dear girl, for I've a message concerning you."

Arthur dismounted and offered Gretchen his hand. She slid off the stallion's back, smiling warmly, wonderingly at the stranger—and Arthur slid deeper into love. Now that he'd given up trying to stop himself from sinking in by inches, he plunged in by yards at a time. Miles.

The Bear-woman took both Gretchen's hands. "You've heard the Silverhair poem, I reckon."

Papa's dismissive grunt was low but plain enough.

The Bear-woman cocked her head and eyed Papa. "You care for it not, sir?"

"It's a tale that cost us dear," Papa said. "One I'd rather forget, mistress."

"Nevertheless, I must speak as Ursa compels me." She gazed into Gretchen's eyes as if they were alone in the forest. The birds and insects hushed. Not a limb or leaf quivered. "There are mysteries and wonders in ancient words. Truths and imaginings. Do you agree, young miss?"

Gretchen nodded.

"We are a forgetful lot, we Bearfolk, and more dedicated to feasting than scribing things we ought to remember. Truths become stories, stories become misshapen and tainted. Thus, the prophet's true words have been forgotten, all but the beginning verses of the Silverhair poem he gave our ancestors. Listen, girl, to what Ursa whispered into the ear of our forefather and the heart of this old spinster:

> *When war upon our sacred field is fought*
> *And Bearfolk fall before the axe and bow*
> *Then shall the human Silverhair arise*
> *And rally us to crush our many foes.*
>
> *She'll ride upon a charger black and white;*
> *Aloft she'll hold the standard of the brave.*
> *Her enemies shall tremble at the sight,*
> *Then yield to us or go down to their graves.*"

The Bear-woman paused. "That much you've heard, aye. But there is more:

The maiden shall take home a rare reward:
One steeped in pain and noble sacrifice—
Yet humbly tendered and without remorse
So Silverhair shall baffle mortal eyes.

The kindled flame of true love burns away
The dross of empty hopes and hopeless dreams.
Truth cannot shine when cloaked in thick deceit
But when unveiled, love's truth brings brighter days.

So Silverhair the savior shall be saved
The bright Yule moon shall light her pathway home
A heroine in wedding clothes arrayed
Bearkind shall henceforth claim her as their own."

Papa's sob rent the air. Gretchen's face blanched and then bloomed pink.

"As it was foreseen, so has it come to pass. May Ursa be praised forever," the Bear-woman whispered. "Go in peace."

Gretchen surprised Arthur by leaning in and kissing the Bear-woman's wrinkled cheek.

"Go on with you," the Bear-woman said, blushing and patting Gretchen's arm. "Your stallions are longing for their stable, by the look in their eyes."

"You're not coming to the Yuletide feast?" Arthur asked.

"I've seen well over two hundred years of them. I reckon I can sit this one out with my hedgehogs and my Cŵn Annwn pup. He'll wreck the place if left alone, the wee beast."

"Good bye, then," Arthur said.

The Bear-woman hobbled toward her cabin.

Arthur boosted Gretchen back onto the Marendall stallion. Her expression was unreadable. She said nothing. Of course she didn't, after hearing what she'd just heard. She'd been told the story of her life, of their lives, by someone she'd never met.

Gretchen had been adamant that she wasn't the Silverhair. But now, how could she deny it?

Gretchen lifted one hand in farewell as a parade of hedge-hogs followed the old woman into the cabin. Arthur mounted the Marendall, settling in front of her this time, and took the reins in hand. He turned his head and said, "Are you all right?"

She rested her cheek against his warm back. Wished she could burrow closer. "Stunned. Flabbergasted. But fine, I suppose." Hearing one's life narrated in centuries-old verse had been more than a little disturbing. She needed time to ponder it.

The stallion started to walk, navigating a narrow path between pines. With her body nestled close to Arthur's, she felt him inhale sharply as if preparing to speak, but he must have reconsidered before any words escaped his lips. She wrapped her arms tightly around his waist. He didn't have to speak to give her comfort.

The stallions splashed through a brook and trotted into a clearing. Ahead, peeking through the tangled branches of a grove of apple trees, a moon the color of old paper cast beams of pure, gentle light.

Over and over, the words of the poem repeated in Gretchen's mind. Like a song written with unfamiliar notes, or a mathematical equation far too advanced for her to solve. How could it be true?

But, oh. It was.

It had happened.

She, with her silver-streaked hair, had ridden into battle, accepted Arthur's "noble sacrifice," masqueraded as Ruby, found true love—and there was the Yuletide moon now, shining on her as the Marendall carried her to the Bearfolk wedding celebration.

A dozen emotions churned inside her, few of them pleasant. "What does it mean, Arthur?" she asked. "Does it mean we have no real choices in life? That we're cast in roles and end up wherever the overlords of the universe place us?"

"No," Arthur said. "I don't think that's it. What I want it to mean, what I *hope* it means is that everything works out in the end for those on the side of good. That love is our destiny and our reward. That the very stars believe we belong together."

She tightened her arms about his waist. "I can live with that. Although I still don't want to be the Silverhair. I just want to be Gretchen."

"We need never speak of it again. Not the poem, the other tales, or the Bear-woman's words."

Music and rowdy Bearfolk laughter came from beyond the next hill. The Marendalls had done their magical work, making a short journey from a long distance.

"I'll admit the end of the poem wasn't so bad," Gretchen said. "I did like the 'brighter days' part. I guess if I had to live the horrifying parts of the story, I might as well claim the happy ending."

Arthur reached down and took her hand. "My own love, brighter days are exactly what we'll have."

Chapter Forty-Eight

23 December, 170 N.E.

In a cavern lit by a hundred torches, Gretchen watched eight newly married Bearfolk couples dance their first dances together as spouses. On this, the third night of the Yuletide, the brides and grooms looked as human as any people Gretchen had ever met, wearing brightly colored dresses and suits embroidered with flowers and vines, their sacred furs draped over their shoulders and backs like thick capes. They turned and twirled, moving their young bodies with grace and purpose, reenacting the wedding dance Bearfolk had danced yearly in this very place since they'd arrived on the island from Germanic lands many hundreds of years ago, according to Arthur.

Gretchen adjusted the tight lace sash at the waist of her Bearfolk-made, green velvet dress. Three days of feasting on rich fare had its consequences. Not that she planned to avoid tonight's banquet tables. She'd be a fool to pass on sampling the jam-filled puffs and salmon toasts she'd spied when they arrived.

"I'd forgotten how complicated the wedding dances are,"

Arthur said, entwining his fingers with hers. "Every twelve-year-old Bear-child is forced to learn the steps. Which was torture, of course. My memories mostly consist of my partner, Lutta Frostcreek's, terrible breath and huge, toe-crushing clogs."

Gretchen laughed. "She sounds charming."

"Those wedding dresses are fab," Toby said from behind her. "But the short trousers with the ribbons are totally repulsive."

"Ruby would have agreed with you, but I kind of like them," Gretchen said. "I'd like to see Arthur in a pair. Now that would be a Christmas treat."

"They're only for weddings." Arthur nudged her with his elbow. "So you'll have to wait."

"I have a five-year plan," Gretchen said.

Toby slipped between them and draped his arms over their shoulders. "Did you guys just propose to each other? If so, that was the worst, laziest, most boring proposal I've heard of in my life. Way more revolting than the trousers."

"Maybe," Gretchen and Arthur said at the same time.

Toby rolled his eyes. A young Bear-woman with chestnut brown hair tapped Toby on the shoulder as the musicians began to play something livelier. He turned and assessed her outfit with an approving smile: a blue silk kirtle over a pearlescent satin chemise. "Care to dance?" she asked.

"Absolutely," Toby said. "Did you make that dress?"

Gretchen laughed. Arthur offered his hand to lead her into the dance, but she shook her head. "Plum cake first?"

"When you say such things, it makes me love you even more," Arthur said as they headed toward the food tables. "Are you sure you want to wait five years to marry?"

"It will take me that long to forgive you for locking me in your wardrobe."

"Look," Arthur said, pointing out her parents dancing and laughing like they, too, were newlyweds.

"They're flying back to the colony tomorrow," Gretchen said. "To get Father's marriage to Stepmother annulled and to file charges against her for poisoning him. She's going to be furious. And sent to prison. I almost wish I could see her face when she gets the news. Oh, and they're taking a letter to Kiki for me, explaining everything. She was a good friend, and I never got to tell her what really happened to Ruby. And that I wasn't who she thought I was."

"You could go tell her in person." He picked up a plate and handed it to her. "You're allowed to come and go as you please, you know."

"No. I'd miss you too much. Also, old Ayla Briarlea told me tomorrow night is apple pie night, so…"

"Well, thank Ursa for apple pie." Smiling wryly, he dumped a huge slice of plum cake onto her plate.

She kissed his cheek. She was crazy about him, but she wasn't going to say so in the middle of a cavern full of frolicking Bearfolk. She'd tell him later, when they were alone.

"Maybe four years will be long enough," she said.

Arthur lay on the ground under a starry sky, his pelt between his back and the cold earth. A family of luminescent dragonfly faeries flew over him, flashing blue and green. He closed his eyes.

It was not a day to Change, but if he concentrated, he could feel the old magic around him like another layer of air. It did not tug at his spirit, nor did it ask anything of him. It was simply there, as ancient and eternal as the rocks and the moon.

He loved it, as he loved the ways of the Bearfolk. As he always would—no matter how much pain it brought him on solstice and equinox nights.

He loved it as he loved his mother and his father, with all their faults and virtues.

He loved the magic as he loved Gretchen, with a willing heart, with courage, and with hope for the future.

The magic settled over him like a warm blanket, and whispered,

Someday.

Acknowledgements

The writer's life is a strange, solitary one—but at the same time, a life that depends on others. Writers need readers, editors, cover designers, and each other. Writers need supportive friends, understanding spouses, and tolerant children who indulge their weird flights of fancy, frequent neglect of the laundry, and thrown-together meals. I am blessed to have such people in my life.

Thank you to John, Spencer, Sarah, Ellen, Joel, Matthias, and Hudson—for being the unique and amazing family I adore. And you, too, Mary!

Thank you to my parents, Tim and Shelley, for helping me to turn out weird enough to do this job.

Thank you to my non-biological sisters, Jenny Brown and Lara Hughey. You're more precious to me than I can say.

Thank you to my darling Buffalo herd: Christine, Sunday, and Cindy. Here's to more adventures ahead!

Thanks to first readers Roberta Gore, Jenny Brown, and Hezekiah Brown. Your feedback was priceless and your enthusiasm for Gretchen and Arthur's tale made my heart happy.

Thanks to Amanda C. Davis for general writerly advice and encouragement (and fantastic macarons).

Thanks to artist Mike Corley for yet another breathtakingly beautiful cover, and for being a truly nice guy.

Thanks to my dear BSF sisters for love, prayers, and the friendship we'll share for eternity.

Thanks to Mike Parker, Kristen Ownby, the WordCrafts Press staff, and Joanne Brokaw—for helping this story make its way into the world.

Thanks to you, reader, for spending time with my imaginary friends.

Most of all, I thank God—for His love, saving grace, the gift of creativity, and the sure hope He's given the world in Jesus.

About Carrie Anne Noble

In the wake of her thrilling past as a theatre student, restaurant hostess, nurse aide, and newspaper writer, Carrie Anne Noble now crafts enchanting fiction for teens and adults. Her debut novel *The Mermaid's Sister* won the 2014 Amazon Breakthrough Novel Award for Young Adult Fiction and the 2016 Realm Award for Novel of the Year. Her second novel, *The Gold-Son,* follows the adventures of a teenage leprechaun. The audio book received Audiofile Magazine's Earphones Award and was included on its list of 2017's best audio books. Her short fiction has appeared in Deep Magic E-zine and Splickety Magazine.

Carrie lives in the mountains of Pennsylvania with her husband and kids, where she enjoys taking walks, letting her imagination run wild, and hosting the occasional tea party.

Connect with Carrie online at www.carrienoble.com